That Lass O' Lowrie's

Frances Hodgson Burnett

That Lass O' Lowrie's

The present edition is a reproduction of previous publication of this classic work. Minor typographical errors may have been corrected without note; however, for an authentic reading experience the spelling, punctuation, and capitalization have been retained from the original text.

ISBN: 978-1-64799-757-1

CONTENTS

CHAPTER I

A Difficult Case

They did not look like women, or at least a stranger new to the district might easily have been misled by their appearance, as they stood together in a group, by the pit's mouth. There were about a dozen of them there—all "pit-girls," as they were called; women who wore a dress more than half masculine, and who talked loudly and laughed discordantly, and some of whom, God knows, had faces as hard and brutal as the hardest of their collier brothers and husbands and sweethearts. They had lived among the coal-pits, and had worked early and late at the "mouth," ever since they had been old enough to take part in the heavy labor. It was not to be wondered at that they had lost all bloom of womanly modesty and gentleness. Their mothers had been "pit-girls" in their time, their grandmothers in theirs; they had been born in coarse homes; they had fared hardly, and worked hard; they had breathed in the dust and grime of coal, and, somehow or other, it seemed to stick to them and reveal itself in their natures as it did in their bold unwashed faces. At first one shrank from them, but one's shrinking could not fail to change to pity. There was no element of softness to rule or even influence them in their half savage existence.

On the particular evening of which I speak, the group at the pit's mouth were even more than usually noisy. They were laughing, gossiping and joking,—coarse enough jokes,—and now and then a listener might have heard an oath flung out as if all were well used to the sound. Most of them were young women, though there were a few older ones among them, and the principal figure in the group— the center figure, about whom the rest clustered—was a young woman. But she differed from the rest in two or three respects. The others seemed somewhat stunted in growth; she was tall enough to be imposing. She was as roughly clad as the poorest of them, but she wore her uncouth garb differently. The man's jacket of fustian, open at the neck, bared a handsome sunbrowned throat. The man's hat shaded a face with dark eyes that had a sort of animal beauty, and a well-molded chin. It was at this girl that all the rough jokes seemed to be directed.

"I'll tell thee, Joan," said one woman, "we'st ha' thee sweetheartin' wi' him afore th' month's out."

"Aye," laughed her fellows, "so we shall. Tha'st ha' to turn soft

1

after aw. Tha conna stond out again' th' Lunnon chap. We'st ha' thee sweetheartin', Joan, i' th' face o' aw tha'st said."

Joan Lowrie faced them defiantly:

"Tha'st noan ha' me sweetheartin' wi' siccan a foo'," she said, "I amna ower fond o' men folk at no time. I've had my fill on 'em; and I'm noan loike to tak' up wi' such loike as this un. An' he's no an a Lunnoner neither. He's on'y fro' th' South. An th' South is na Lunnon."

"He's getten' Lunnon ways tho'," put in another. "Choppin' his words up an' mincin' 'em sma'. He's noan Lancashire, ony gowk could tell."

"I dunnot see as he minces so," said Joan roughly. "He dunnot speak our loike, but he's well enow i' his way."

A boisterous peal of laughter interrupted her.

"I thowt tha' ca'ed him a foo' a minute sin'," cried two or three voices at once. "Eh, Joan, lass, tha'st goin' t' change thy moind, I see."

The girl's eyes flashed.

"Theer's others I could ca' foo's," she said; "I need na go far to foind foo's. Foo' huntin's th' best sport out, an' th' safest. Leave th' engineer alone an' leave me alone too. It 'll be th' best fur yo'."

She turned round and strode out of the group.

Another burst of derisive laughter followed her, but she took no notice of it She took no notice of anything—not even of the two men who at that very moment passed and turned to look at her as she went by.

"A fine creature!" said one of them.

"A fine creature!" echoed the other. "Yes, and you see that is precisely it, Derrick. 'A fine creature'—and nothing else."

They were the young engineer and his friend the Reverend Paul Grace, curate of the parish. There were never two men more unlike, physically and mentally, and yet it would have been a hard task to find two natures more harmonious and sympathetic. Still most people wondered at and failed to comprehend their friendship. The mild, nervous little Oxonian barely reached Derrick's shoulder; his finely cut face was singularly feminine and innocent; the mild eyes beaming from behind his small spectacles had an absent, dreamy look. One could not fail to see at the first glance, that this refined, restless, conscientious little gentleman was hardly the person to cope successfully with Riggan. Derrick strode by his side like a young son of Anak—brains and muscle evenly balanced and fully developed.

He turned his head over his shoulder to look at Joan Lowrie once again.

2

"That girl," said Grace, "has worked at the pit's mouth from her childhood; her mother was a pit girl until she died—of hard work, privation and ill treatment. Her father is a collier and lives as most of them do—drinking, rioting, fighting. Their home is such a home as you have seen dozens of since you came here; the girl could not better it if she tried, and would not know how to begin if she felt inclined. She has borne, they tell me, such treatment as would have killed most women. She has been beaten, bruised, felled to the earth by this father of hers, who is said to be a perfect fiend in his cups. And yet she holds to her place in their wretched hovel, and makes herself a slave to the fellow with a dogged, stubborn determination. What can I do with such a case as that, Derrick?"

"You have tried to make friends with the girl?" said Derrick.

Grace colored sensitively.

"There is not a man, woman or child in the parish," he answered, "with whom I have not conscientiously tried to make friends, and there is scarcely one, I think, with whom I have succeeded. Why can I not succeed? Why do I always fail? The fault must be with myself——"

"A mistake that at the outset," interposed Derrick. "There is no 'fault' in the matter; there is simply misfortune. Your parishioners are so unfortunate as not to be able to understand you, and on your part you are so unfortunate as to fail at first to place yourself on the right footing with them. I say 'at first' you observe. Give yourself time, Grace, and give them time too."

"Thank you," said the Reverend Paul. "But speaking of this girl—'That lass o' Lowrie's,' as she is always called—Joan I believe her name is. Joan Lowrie is, I can assure you, a weight upon me. I cannot help her and I cannot rid my mind of her. She stands apart from her fellows. She has most of the faults of her class, but none of their follies; and she has the reputation of being half feared, half revered. The man who dared to approach her with the coarse love-making which is the fashion among them, would rue it to the last day of his life. She seems to defy all the world."

"And it is impossible to win upon her?"

"More than impossible. The first time I went to her with sympathy, I felt myself a child in her hands. She never laughed nor jeered at me as the rest do. She stood before me like a rock, listening until I had finished speaking. 'Parson,' she said, 'if thal't leave me alone, I'll leave thee alone,' and then turned about and walked into the house. I am nothing but 'th' parson' to these people, and 'th' parson' is one for whom they have little respect and no sympathy."

He was not far wrong. The stolid heavy-natured colliers openly looked down upon 'th' parson.' A 'bit of a whipper snapper,'

3

even the best-natured called him in sovereign contempt for his insignificant physical proportions. Truly the sensitive little gentleman's lines had not fallen in pleasant places. And this was not all. There was another source of discouragement with which he had to battle in secret, though of this he would have felt it almost dishonor to complain. But Derrick's keen eyes had seen it long ago, and, understanding it well, he sympathized with his friend accordingly. Yet, despite the many rebuffs the curate had met with, he was not conquered by any means. His was not an easily subdued nature, after all. He was very warm on the subject of Joan Lowrie this evening—so warm, indeed, that the interest the mere sight of the girl had awakened in Derrick's mind was considerably heightened. They were still speaking of her when they stopped before the door of Grace's modest lodgings.

"You will come in, of course?" said Paul.

"Yes," Derrick answered, "for a short time. I am tired and shall feel all the better for a cup of Mrs. Burnie's tea," pushing the hair back from his forehead, as he had a habit of doing when a little excited.

He made the small parlor appear smaller than ever, when he entered it. He was obliged to bend his head when he passed through the door, and it was not until he had thrown himself into the largest easy chair, that the trim apartment seemed to regain its countenance.

Grace paused at the table, and with a sudden flush, took up a letter that lay there among two or three uninteresting-looking epistles.

"It is a note from Miss Anice," he said, coming to the hearth and applying his pen-knife in a gentle way to the small square envelope.

"Not a letter, Grace?" said Derrick with a smile.

"A letter! Oh dear, no! She has never written me a letter. They are always notes with some sort of business object. She has very decided views on the subject of miscellaneous letter-writing."

He read the note himself and then handed it to Derrick.

It was a compact, decided hand, free from the suspicion of an unnecessary curve.

"Dear Mr. Grace,—
"Many thanks for the book. You are very kind
indeed. Pray let us hear something more about
your people. I am afraid papa must find them
very discouraging, but I cannot help feeling
interested. Grandmamma wishes to be
remembered to you,

4

"With more thanks,

"Believe me your friend,

"Anice Barholm."

Derrick refolded the note and handed it back to his friend. To tell the truth, it did not impress him very favorably. A girl not yet twenty years old, who could write such a note as this to a man who loved her, must be rather too self-contained and well balanced.

"You have never told me much of this story, Grace," he said.

"There is not much to tell," answered the curate, flushing again. "She is the Rector's daughter. I have known her three years. You remember I wrote to you about meeting her while you were in India. As for the rest, I do not exactly understand myself how it is that I have gone so far, having so—so little encouragement—in fact having had no encouragement at all; but, however that is, it has grown upon me, Derrick,—my feeling for her has grown into my life. She has never cared for me. I am quite sure of that, you see. Indeed, I could hardly expect it. It is not her way to care for men as they are likely to care for her, though it will come some day, I suppose—with the coming man," half smiling. "She is simply what she signs herself here, my friend Anice Barholm, and I am thankful for that much. She would not write even that if she did not mean it."

"Bless my soul," broke in Derrick, tossing back his head impatiently; "and she is only nineteen yet, you say?"

"Only nineteen," said the curate, with simple trustfulness in his friend's sympathy, "but different, you know, from any other woman I have ever seen."

The tea and toast came in then, and they sat down together to partake of it Derrick knew Anice quite well before the meal was ended, and yet he had not asked many questions. He knew how Grace had met her at her father's house—an odd, self-reliant, very pretty and youthful-looking little creature, with the force and decision of half a dozen ordinary women hidden in her small frame; how she had seemed to like him; how their intimacy had grown; how his gentle, deep-rooted passion had grown with it; how he had learned to understand that he had nothing to hope for.

"I am a little fearful for the result of her first visit here," said Grace, pushing his cup aside and looking troubled. "I cannot bear to think of her being disappointed and disturbed by the half-savage state in which these people live. She knows nothing of the mining districts. She has never been in Lancashire, and they have always lived in the South. She is in Kent now, with Mrs. Barholm's mother. And though I have tried, in my short letters to her, to prepare her for the rough side of life she will be obliged to see, I am afraid it is impossible for her to realize it, and it may be a shock to her when she comes."

"She is coming to Riggan then?" said Derrick.

"In a few weeks. She has been visiting Mrs. Galloway since the Rector gave up his living at Ashley wolde, and Mrs. Barholm told me to-day that she spoke in her last letter of coming to them."

The moon was shining brightly when Derrick stepped out into the street later in the evening, and though the air was somewhat chill it was by no means unpleasant. He had rather a long walk before him. He disliked the smoke and dust of the murky little town, and chose to live on its outskirts; but he was fond of sharp exercise, and regarded the distance between his lodging and the field of his daily labor as an advantage.

"I work off a great deal of superfluous steam between the two places," he said to Grace at the door. "The wind coming across Boggart Brow has a way of scattering and cooling restless plans and feverish fancies, that is good for a man. Half a mile of the Knoll Road is often enough to blow all the morbidness out of a fellow."

To-night by the time he reached the corner that turned him upon the Knoll Road, his mind had wandered upon an old track, but it had been drawn there by a new object,—nothing other than Joan Lowrie, indeed. The impression made upon him by the story of Joan and her outcast life was one not easy to be effaced. The hardest miseries in the lot of a class in whom he could not fail to be interested, were grouped about that dramatic figure. He was struck, too, by a painful sense of incongruity.

"If she had been in this other girl's niche," he said, "if she had lived the life of this Anice——"

But he did not finish his sentence. Something, not many yards beyond him, caught his eye—a figure seated upon the road-side near a collier's cottage—evidently a pit girl in some trouble, for her head was bowed upon her hands, and there was a dogged sort of misery expressed in her very posture.

"A woman," he said aloud. "What woman, I wonder. This is not the time for any woman to be sitting here alone."

He crossed the road at once, and going to the girl, touched her lightly on the shoulder.

"My lass," he said good-naturedly, "what ails you?"

She raised her head slowly as if she were dizzy and bewildered. Her face was disfigured by a bruise, and on one temple was a cut from which the blood trickled down her cheek; but the moonlight showed him that it was Joan. He removed his hand from her shoulder and drew back a pace.

"You have been hurt!" he exclaimed.

"Aye," she answered deliberately, "I've had a hurt—a bad un."

He did not ask her how she had been hurt. He knew as well as if she had told him, that it had been done in one of her father's fits of drunken passion. He had seen this sort of thing before during his sojourn in the mining districts. But, shamefully repulsive as it had been to him, he had never felt the degradation of it as fiercely as he did now.

"You are Joan Lowrie?" he said.

"Aye, I'm Joan Lowrie, if it 'll do yo' ony good to know."

"You must have something done to that cut upon your temple."

She put up her hand and wiped the blood away, as if impatient at his persistence.

"It 'll do well enow as it is," she said.

"That is a mistake," he answered. "You are losing more blood than you imagine. Will you let me help you?"

She stirred uneasily.

Derrick took no notice of the objection. He drew his handkerchief from his pocket, and, after some little effort, managed to stanch the bleeding, and having done so, bound the wound up. Perhaps something in his sympathetic silence and the quiet consideration of his manner touched Joan. Her face, upturned almost submissively, for the moment seemed tremulous, and she set her lips together. She did not speak until he had finished, and then she rose and stood before him immovable as ever.

"Thank yo'," she said in a suppressed voice, "I canna say no more."

"Never mind that," he answered, "I could have done no less. If you could go home now——"

"I shall na go whoam to neet," she interrupted him.

"You cannot remain out of doors!" he exclaimed.

"If I do, it wunnot be th' first toime," meeting his startled glance with a pride which defied him to pity or question her. But his sympathy and interest must have stirred her, for the next minute her manner softened. "I've done it often," she added, "an' nowts nivver feared me. Yo' need na care, Mester, I'm used to it."

"But I cannot go away and leave you here," he said.

"You canna do no other," she answered.

"Have you no friends?" he ventured hesitatingly.

"No, I ha' not," she said, hardening again, and she turned away as if she meant to end the discussion. But he would not leave her. The spirit of determination was as strong in his character as in her own. He tore a leaf from his pocket-book, and, writing a few

7

lines upon it, handed it to her. "If you will take that to Thwates' wife," he said, "there will be no necessity for your remaining out of doors all night."

She took it from him mechanically; but when he finished speaking, her calmness left her. Her hand began to tremble, and then her whole frame, and the next instant the note fell to the ground, and she dropped into her old place again, sobbing passionately and hiding her face on her arms.

"I wunnot tak' it!" she cried. "I wunnot go no wheer an' tell as I'm turned loike a dog into th' street."

Her misery and shame shook her like a tempest. But she subdued herself at last.

"I dunnot see as yo' need care," she protested half resentfully. "Other folk dunnot. I'm left to mysen most o' toimes." Her head fell again and she trembled from head to foot.

"But I do care!" he returned. "I cannot leave you here and will not. If you will trust me and do as I tell you, the people you go to need know nothing you do not choose to tell them."

It was evident that his determination made her falter, and seeing this he followed up his advantage and so far improved it that at last, after a few more arguments, she rose slowly and picked up the fallen paper.

"If I mun go, I mun," she said, twisting it nervously in her fingers, and then there was a pause, in which she plainly lingered to say something, for she stood before him with a restrained air and downcast face. She broke the silence herself, however, suddenly looking up and fixing her large eyes full upon him.

"If I was a lady," she said, "happen I should know what to say to yo'; but bein' what I am, I dunnot. Happen as yo're a gentleman yo' know what I'd loike to say an' canna—happen yo' do."

Even as she spoke, the instinct of defiance in her nature struggled against that of gratitude; but the finer instinct conquered.

"We will not speak of thanks," he said. "I may need help some day, and come to you for it."

"If yo' ivver need help at th' pit will yo' come to me?" she demanded. "I've seen th' toime as I could ha' gi'en help to th' Mesters ef I'd had th' moind. If yo'll promise that——"

"I will promise it," he answered her.

"An' I'll promise to gi' it yo'," eagerly. "So that's settled. Now I'll go my ways. Good neet to yo'."

"Good night," he returned, and uncovering with as grave a courtesy as he might have shown to the finest lady in the land, or to his own mother or sister, he stood at the road-side and watched her until she was out of sight.

8

CHAPTER II

"Liz"

"Th' owd lad's been at his tricks again," was the rough comment made on Joan Lowrie's appearance when she came down to her work the next morning; but Joan looked neither right nor left, and went to her place without a word. Not one among them had ever heard her speak of her miseries and wrongs, or had known her to do otherwise than ignore the fact that their existence was well known among her fellow-workers.

When Derrick passed her on his way to his duties, she looked up from her task with a faint, quick color, and replied to his courteous gesture with a curt yet not ungracious nod. It was evident that not even her gratitude would lead her to encourage any advances. But, notwithstanding this, he did not feel repelled or disappointed. He had learned enough of Joan, in their brief interview, to prepare him to expect no other manner from her. He was none the less interested in the girl because he found himself forced to regard her curiously and critically, and at a distance.

He watched her as she went about her work, silent, self-contained and solitary.

"That lass o' Lowrie's!" said a superannuated old collier once, in answer to a remark of Derrick's. "Eh! hoo's a rare un, hoo is! Th' fellys is haaf feart on her. Tha' sees hoo's getten a bit o' skoolin'. Hoo con read a bit, if tha'll believe it, Mester," with a touch of pride.

"Not as th' owd chap ivver did owt fur her i' that road," the speaker went on, nothing loath to gossip with 'one o' th' Mesters.' "He nivver did nowt fur her but spend her wage i' drink. But theer wur a neet skoo' here a few years sen', an' th' lass went her ways wi' a few o' th' steady uns, an' they say as she getten ahead on 'em aw, so as it wur a wonder. Just let her set her mind to do owt an' she'll do it."

"Here," said Derrick to Paul that night, as the engineer leaned back in his easy chair, glowering at the grate and knitting his brows, "Here," he said, "is a creature with the majesty of a Juno—though really nothing but a girl in years—who rules a set of savages by the mere power of a superior will and mind, and yet a woman who works at the mouth of a coal-pit,—who cannot write her own name, and who is beaten by her fiend of a father as if she were a dog. Good Heaven! what is she doing here? What does it all mean?"

The Reverend Paul put up his delicate hand deprecatingly.

9

"My dear Fergus," he said, "if I dare—if my own life and the lives of others would let me—I think I should be tempted to give it up, as one gives up other puzzles, when one is beaten by them."

Derrick looked at him, forgetting himself in a sudden sympathetic comprehension.

"You have been more than ordinarily discouraged to-day," he said. "What is it, Grace?"

"Do you know Sammy Craddock?" was the reply.

"'Owd Sammy Craddock'?" said Derrick with a laugh. "Wasn't it 'Owd Sammy,' who was talking to me to-day about Joan Lowrie?"

"I dare say it was," sighing. "And if you know Sammy Craddock, you know one of the principal causes of my discouragement. I went to see him this afternoon, and I have not quite—quite got over it, in fact."

Derrick's interest in his friend's trials was stirred as usual at the first signal of distress. It was the part of his stronger and more evenly balanced nature to be constantly ready with generous sympathy and comfort.

"It has struck me," he said, "that Craddock is one of the institutions of Riggan. I should like to hear something definite concerning him. Why is he your principal cause of discouragement, in the first place?"

"Because he is the man of all others whom it is hard for me to deal with,—because he is the shrewdest, the most irreverent and the most disputatious old fellow in Riggan. And yet, in the face of all this, because he is so often right, I am forced into a sort of respect for him."

"Right!" repeated Derrick, raising his eyebrows. "That's bad."

Grace rose from the chair, flushing up to the roots of his hair,—

"Right!" he reiterated. "Yes, right I say. And how, I ask you, can a man battle against the faintest element of right and truth, even when it will and must arraign itself on the side of wrong? If I could shut my eyes to the right, and see only the wrong, I might leave myself at least a blind content, but I cannot—I cannot. If I could look upon these things as Barholm does——" But here he stopped, suddenly checking himself.

"Thank God you cannot," put in Derrick quietly.

For a few minutes the Reverend Paul paced the room in silence.

"Among the men who were once his fellow-workers, Craddock is an oracle," he went on. "His influence is not unlike Joan Lowrie's. It is the influence of a strong mind over weaker ones. His sharp sarcastic speeches are proverbs among the Rigganites; he amuses

10

them and can make them listen to him. When he holds up 'Th' owd parson' to their ridicule, he sweeps all before him. He can undo in an hour what I have struggled a year to accomplish. He was a collier himself until he became superannuated, and he knows their natures, you see."

"What has he to say about Barholm?" asked Derrick—without looking at his friend, however.

"Oh!" he protested, "that is the worst side of it—that is miserable—that is wretched! I may as well speak openly. Barholm is his strong card, and that is what baffles me. He scans Barholm with the eye of an eagle. He does not spare a single weakness. He studies him—he knows his favorite phrases and gestures by heart, and has used them until there is not a Riggan collier who does not recognize them when they are presented to him, and applaud them as an audience might applaud the staple jokes of a popular actor."

Explained even thus far, the case looked difficult enough; but Derrick felt no wonder at his friend's discouragement when he had heard his story to the end, and understood it fully.

The living at Riggan had never been happily managed. It had been presented to men who did not understand the people under their charge, and to men whom the people failed to understand; but possibly it had never before fallen into the hands of a man who was so little qualified to govern Rigganites, as was the present rector, the Reverend Harold Barholm. A man who has mistaken his vocation, and who has become ever so faintly conscious of his blunder, may be a stumbling-block in another's path; but restrained as he will be by his secret pangs of conscience, he can scarcely be an active obstructionist. But a man who, having mistaken the field of his life's labor, yet remains amiably self-satisfied, and unconscious of his unfitness, may do more harm in his serene ignorance than he might have done good if he had chosen his proper sphere. Such a man as the last was the Reverend Harold. A good-natured, broad-shouldered, tactless, self-sufficient person, he had taken up his work with a complacent feeling that no field of labor could fail to be benefited by his patronage; he was content now as always. He had been content with himself and his intellectual progress at Oxford; he had been content with his first parish at Ashley-wold; he had been content then with the gentle-natured, soft-spoken Kentish men and women; he had never feared finding himself unequal to the guidance of their souls, and he was not at all troubled by the prospect Riggan presented to him.

"It is a different sort of thing," he said to his curate, in the best of spirits, "and new to us—new of course; but we shall get over that—we shall get over that easily enough, Grace."

11

So with not a shadow of a doubt as to his speedy success, and with a comfortable confidence in ecclesiastical power, in whomsoever vested, he called upon his parishioners one after the other. He appeared at their cottages at all hours, and gave the same greeting to each of them. He was their new rector, and having come to Riggan with the intention of doing them good, and improving their moral condition, he intended to do them good, and improve them, in spite of themselves. They must come to church: it was their business to come to church, as it was his business to preach the gospel. All this implied, in half an hour's half-friendly, half-ecclesiastical conversation, garnished with a few favorite texts and religious platitudes, and the man felt that he had done his duty, and done it well.

Only one man nonplussed him, and even this man's effect upon him was temporary, only lasting as long as his call. He had been met with a dogged resentment in the majority of his visits, but when he encountered 'Owd Sammy Craddock' he encountered a different sort of opposition.

"Aye," said Owd Sammy, "an' so tha'rt th' new rector, art ta? I thowt as mich as another ud spring up as soon as th' owd un wur cut down. Tha parsens is a nettle as dunnot soon dee oot. Well, I'll leave thee to th' owd lass here. Hoo's a rare un fur gab when hoo' taks th' notion, an' I'm noan so mich i' th' humor t' argufy mysen today." And he took his pipe from the mantelpiece and strolled out with an imperturbable air. But this was not the last of the matter. The Rector went again and again, cheerfully persisting in bringing the old sinner to a proper sense of his iniquities. There would be some triumph in converting such a veteran as Sammy Craddock, and he was confident of winning this laurel for himself. But the result was scarcely what he expected. 'Owd Sammy' stood his ground like an old soldier. The fear of man was not before his eyes, and 'parsens' were his favorite game. He was as contumacious and profane as such men are apt to be, and he delighted in scattering his clerical antagonists as a task worthy of his mettle. He encountered the Reverend Harold with positive glee. He jeered at him in public, and sneered at him in private, and held him up to the mockery of the collier men and lads, with the dramatic mimicry which made him so popular a character. As Derrick had said, Sammy Craddock was a Riggan institution. In his youth, his fellows had feared his strength; in his old age they feared his wit. "Let Owd Sammy tackle him," they said, when a new-comer was disputatious, and hard to manage; "Owd Sammy's th' one to gi' him one fur his nob. Owd Sammy'll fettle him—graidely." And the fact was that Craddock's cantankerous sharpness of brain and tongue were usually efficacious. So he "tackled" Barholm, and so he "tackled" the curate. But, for some reason, he was never actually bitter against Grace. He spoke of him lightly, and rather sneered at his physical insignificance; but he did not hold him up to public ridicule.

"I hav' not quite settled i' my moind about th' little chap," he would say sententiously to his admirers. "He's noan siccan a foo' as th' owd un, for he's a graidely foo', he is, and no mistake. At any rate a little foo' is better nor a big un."

And there the matter stood. Against these tremendous odds Grace fought—against coarse and perverted natures,—worse than all, against the power that should have been ranged upon his side. And added to these discouragements, were the obstacles of physical delicacy, and an almost morbid conscientiousness. A man of coarser fibre might have borne the burden better—or at least with less pain to himself.

"A drop or so of Barholm's blood in Grace's veins," said Derrick, communing with himself on the Knoll Road after their interview—"a few drops of Barholm's rich, comfortable, stupid blood in Grace's veins would not harm him. And yet it would have to be but a few drops indeed," hastily. "On the whole I think it would be better if he had more blood of his own."

The following day Miss Barholm came. Business had taken Derrick to the station in the morning, and being delayed, he was standing upon the platform when one of the London trains came in. There were generally so few passengers on such trains who were likely to stop at Riggan, that the few who did so were of some interest to the bystanders. Accordingly he stood gazing, in rather a preoccupied fashion, at the carriages, when the door of a first-class compartment opened, and a girl stepped out upon the platform near him. Before seeing her face one might have imagined her to be a child of scarcely more than fourteen or fifteen. This was Derrick's first impression; but when she turned toward him he saw at once that it was not a child. And yet it was a small face, with delicate oval features, smooth, clear skin, and stray locks of hazel brown hair that fell over the low forehead. She had evidently made a journey of some length, for she was encumbered with travelling wraps, and in her hands she held a little flower-pot containing a cluster of early blue violets,—such violets as would not bloom so far north as Riggan for weeks to come. She stood upon the platform for a moment or so, glancing up and down as if in search of some one, and then, plainly deciding that the object of her quest had not arrived, she looked at Derrick in a business-like, questioning way. She was going to speak to him. The next minute she stepped forward without a shadow of girlish hesitation.

13

"May I trouble you to tell me where I can find a conveyance of some sort?" she said. "I want to go to the Rectory."

Derrick uncovered, recognizing his friend's picture at once.

"I think," he said with far more hesitancy than she had herself shown, "that this must be Miss Barholm."

"Yes," she answered, "Anice Barholm. I think," she said, "from what Mr. Grace has said to me, that you must be his friend."

"I am one of Grace's friends," he answered, "Fergus Derrick."

She managed to free one of her small hands, and held it out to him.

She had arrived earlier than had been expected, it turned out, and through some mysterious chance or other, her letters to her friends had not preceded her, so there was no carriage in waiting, and but for Derrick she would have been thrown entirely upon her own resources. But after their mutual introduction the two were friends at once, and before he had put her into the cab, Derrick had begun to understand what it was that led the Reverend Paul to think her an exceptional girl. She knew where her trunks were, and was quite definite upon the subject of what must be done with them. Though pretty and frail looking enough, there was no suggestion of helplessness about her. When she was safely seated in the cab, she spoke to Derrick through the open window.

"If you will come to the Rectory to-night, and let papa thank you," she said, "we shall all be very glad. Mr. Grace will be there, you know, and I have a great many questions to ask which I think you must be able to answer."

Derrick went back to his work, thinking about Miss Barholm, of course. She was different from other girls, he felt, not only in her fragile frame and delicate face, but with another more subtle and less easily defined difference. There was a suggestion of the development in a child of the soul of a woman.

Going down to the mine, Derrick found on approaching that there was some commotion among the workers at the pit's mouth, and before he turned in to his office, he paused upon the threshold for a few minutes to see what it meant. But it was not a disturbance with which it was easy for an outsider to interfere. A knot of women drawn away from their work by some prevailing excitement, were gathered together around a girl—a pretty but pale and haggard creature, with a helpless, despairing face—who stood at bay in the midst of them, clasping a child to her bosom—a target for all eyes. It was a wretched sight, and told its own story.

"Wheer ha' yo' been, Liz?" Derrick heard two or three voices exclaim at once. "What did you coom back for? This is what thy handsome face has browt thee to, is it?"

14

And then the girl, white, wild-eyed and breathless with excitement, turned on them, panting, bursting into passionate tears.

"Let me a-be:" she cried, sobbing. "There's none of yo' need to talk. Let me a-be! I didna coom back to ax nowt fro' none on you! Eh Joan! Joan Lowrie?"

Derrick turned to ascertain the meaning of this cry of appeal, but almost before he had time to do so, Joan herself had borne down upon the group; she had pushed her way through it, and was standing in the centre, confronting the girl's tormentors in a flame of wrath, and Liz was clinging to her.

"What ha' they been sayin' to yo', lass?" she demanded. "Eh! but yo're a brave lot, yo' are—women yo' ca' yo'rsens!—badgerin' a slip o' a wench loike this."

"I did na coom back to ax nowt fro' noan o' them," sobbed the girl. "I'd rayther dee ony day nor do it! I'd rayther starve i' th' ditch—an' it's comin' to that."

"Here," said Joan, "gi' me th' choild."

She bent down and took it from her, and then stood up before them all, holding it high in her strong arms—so superb, so statuesque, and yet so womanly a figure, that a thrill shot through the heart of the man watching her.

"Lasses," she cried, her voice fairly ringing, "do yo' see this? A bit o' a helpless thing as canna answer back yo're jeers! Aye! look at it well, aw' on yo'. Some on yo's getten th' loike at whoam. An' when yo've looked at th' choild, look at th' mother! Seventeen year owd, Liz is, an' th' world's gone wrong wi' her. I wunnot say as th' world's gone ower reet wi' ony on us; but them on us as has had th' strength to howd up agen it, need na set our foot on them as has gone down. Happen theer's na so much to choose betwixt us after aw. But I've gotten this to tell yo'—them as has owt to say o' Liz, mun say it to Joan Lowrie!"

Rough, and coarsely pitiless as the majority of them were, she had touched the right chord. Perhaps the bit of the dramatic in her championship of the girl had as much to do with the success of her half-commanding appeal as anything else. But at least, the most hardened of them faltered before her daring, scornful words, and the fire in her face. Liz would be safe enough from them henceforth, it was plain.

That evening while arranging his papers before going home, Derrick was called from his work by a summons at the office door, and going to open it, he found Joan Lowrie standing there, looking half abashed, half determined.

"I ha' summat to ax yo'," she said briefly, declining his invitation to enter and be seated.

15

"If there is anything I can do for—" began Derrick.

"It is na mysen," she interrupted him. "There is a poor lass as I'm fain to help, if I could do it, but I ha' not th' power. I dunnot know of any one as has, except yo'rsen and th' parson, an' I know more o' yo' than I do o' th' parson, so I thowt I'd ax yo' to speak to him about th' poor wench, an ax him if he could get her a bit o' work as ud help to keep her honest."

Derrick looked at her handsome face gravely, curiously.

"I saw you defend this girl against some of her old companions, a few hours ago, I believe," he said.

She colored, but did not return his glance.

"I dunnot believe in harryin' women down th' hill," she said.

Then, suddenly, she raised her eyes.

"Th' little un is a little lass," she said, "an' I canna bide th' thowt o' what moight fa' on her if her mother's life is na an honest un—I canna bide the thowt on it."

"I will see my friend to-night," said Derrick, "and I will speak to him. Where can he find the girl?"

"Wi' me," she answered. "I'm taken both on 'em whoam wi' me."

CHAPTER III

The Reverend Harold Barholm

When the Reverend Paul entered the parlor at the Rectory, he found that his friend had arrived before him. Mr. Barholm, his wife and Anice, with their guest, formed a group around the fire, and Grace saw at a glance that Derrick had unconsciously fallen into the place of the centre figure. He was talking and the others were listening—Mr. Barholm in his usual restless fashion, Mrs. Barholm with evident interest, Anice leaning forward on her ottoman, listening eagerly.

"Ah!" exclaimed Mr. Barholm, when the servant announced the visitor, "this is fortunate. Here is Grace. Glad to see you, Grace. Take a seat We are talking about an uncommonly interesting case. I dare say you know the young woman."

Anice looked up.

"We are talking about Joan Lowrie," she said. "Mr. Derrick is telling us about her."

"Most interesting affair—from beginning to end," continued the Rector, briskly. "Something must be done for the young woman. We must go and see her,—I will go and see her myself."

He had caught fire at once, in his usual inconsequent, self-secure style. Ecclesiastical patronage would certainly set this young woman right at once. There was no doubt of that. And who was so well qualified to bestow it as himself?

"Yes, yes! I will go myself," he said. "That kind of people is easily managed, when once one understands them. There really is some good in them, after all. You see, Grace, it is as I have told you—only understand them, and make them understand you, and the rest is easy."

Derrick glanced from father to daughter. The clear eyes of the girl rested on the man with a curious expression.

"Do you think," she said quickly, "that they like us to go and see them in that sort of way, papa? Do you think it is wise to remind them that we know more than they do, and that if they want to learn they must learn from us, just because we have been more fortunate? It really seems to me that the rebellious ones would ask themselves what right we had to be more fortunate."

"My dear," returned the Rector, somewhat testily—he was not partial to the interposition of obstacles even in suggestion—"My dear, if you had been brought into contact with these people as

17

closely as I have, or even as Grace has, you would learn that they are not prone to regard things from a metaphysical stand-point. Metaphysics are not in their line. They are more apt to look upon life as a matter of bread and bacon than as a problem."

A shadow fell upon Anice's face, and before the visit ended, Derrick had observed its presence more than once. It was always her father who summoned it, he noticed. And yet it was evident enough that she was fond of the man, and in no ordinary degree, and that the affection was mutual. As he was contented with himself, so Barholm was contented with his domestic relations. He was fond of his wife, and fond of his daughter, as much, perhaps, through his appreciation of his own good taste in wedding such a wife, and becoming the father of such a daughter, as through his appreciation of their peculiar charms. He was proud of them and indulgent to them. They reflected a credit on him of which he felt himself wholly deserving.

"They are very fond of him," remarked Grace afterward to his friend; "which shows that there must be a great deal of virtue in the man. Indeed there is a great deal of virtue in him. You yourself, Derrick, must have observed a certain kindliness and—and open generosity," with a wistful sound in his voice.

There was always this wistful appeal in the young man's tone when he spoke of his clerical master—a certain anxiety to make the best of him, and refrain from any suspicion of condemnation. Derrick was always reminded by it of the shadow on Anice's face.

"I want to tell you something," Miss Barholm said this evening to Grace at parting. "I do not think I am afraid of Riggan at all. I think I shall like it all the better because it is so new. Everything is so earnest and energetic, that it is a little bracing—like the atmosphere. Perhaps—when the time comes—I could do something to help you with that girl. I shall try at any rate." She held out her hand to him with a smile, and the Reverend Paul went home feeling not a little comforted and encouraged.

The Rector stood with his back to the fire, his portly person expressing intense satisfaction.

"You will remind me about that young woman in the morning, Anice," he said. "I should like to attend to the matter myself. Singular that Grace should not have mentioned her before. It really seems to me, you know, that now and then Grace is a little deficient in interest, or energy."

"Surely not interest, my dear," suggested Mrs. Barholm, gently.

"Well, well," conceded the Rector, "perhaps not interest, but energy or—or appreciation. I should have seen such a fine creature's

18

superiority, and mentioned it at once. She must be a fine creature. A young woman of that kind should be encouraged. I will go and see her in the morning—if it were not so late I would go now. Really, she ought to be told that she has exhibited a very excellent spirit, and that people approve of it. I wonder what sort of a household servant she would make if she were properly trained?"

"That would not do at all," put in Anice, decisively. "From the pit's mouth to the kitchen would not be a natural transition."

"Well, well, as usual, perhaps you are right. There is plenty of time to think of it, however. We can judge better when we have seen her."

He did not need reminding in the morning. He was as full of vague plans for Joan Lowrie when he arose as he had been when he went to bed. He came down to the charming breakfast-room in the most sanguine of moods. But then his moods usually were sanguine. It was scarcely to be wondered at. Fortune had treated him with great suavity from his earliest years. Wellborn, comfortably trained, healthy and easy-natured, the world had always turned its pleasant side to him. As a young man, he had been a strong, handsome fellow, whose convenient patrimony had placed him beyond the possibility of entire dependence upon his profession. When a curate he had been well enough paid and without private responsibilities; when he married he was lucky enough to win a woman who added to his comfort; in fact, life had gone smoothly with him for so long that he had no reason to suspect Fate of any intention to treat him ill-naturedly. It was far more likely that she would reserve her scurvy tricks for some one else.

Even Riggan had not perplexed him at all. Its difficulties were not such as would be likely to disturb him greatly. One found ignorance, and vice, and discomfort among the lower classes always; there was the same thing to contend against in the agricultural as in the mining districts. And the Rectory was substantial and comfortable, even picturesque. The house was roomy, the garden large and capable of improvement; there were trees in abundance, ivy on the walls, and Anice would do the rest. The breakfast-room looked specially encouraging this morning. Anice, in a pretty pale blue gown, and with a few crocuses at her throat, awaited his coming behind the handsomest of silver and porcelain, reading his favorite newspaper the while. Her little pot of emigrant violets exhaled a faint, spring-like odor from their sunny place at the window; there was a vase of crocuses, snow-drops and ivy leaves in the centre of the table; there was sunshine outside and comfort in. The Rector had a good appetite and an unimpaired digestion. Anice rose when he entered, and touched the bell.

19

"Mamma's headache will keep her upstairs for a while," she said. "She told me we were not to wait for her." And then she brought him his newspaper and kissed him dutifully.

"Very glad to see you home again, I am sure, my dear," remarked the Rector. "I have really missed you very much. What excellent coffee this is!—another cup, if you please." And, after a pause,

"I think really, you know," he proceeded, "that you will not find the place unpleasant, after all. For my part, I think it is well enough—for such a place; one cannot expect Belgravian polish in Lancashire miners, and certainly one does not meet with it; but it is well to make the best of things. I get along myself reasonably well with the people. I do not encounter the difficulties Grace complains of."

"Does he complain?" asked Anice; "I did not think he exactly complained."

"Grace is too easily discouraged," answered the Rector in off-handed explanation. "And he is apt to make blunders. He speaks of, and to, these people as if they were of the same fibre as himself. He does not take hold of things. He is deficient in courage. He means well, but he is not good at reading character. That other young fellow now—Derrick, the engineer—would do twice as well in his place. What do you think of that young fellow, by the way, my dear?"

"I like him," said Anice. "He will help Mr. Grace often."

"Grace needs a support of some kind," returned Mr. Barholm, frowning slightly, "and he does not seem to rely very much upon me—not so much as I would wish. I don't quite understand him at times; the fact is, it has struck me once or twice, that he preferred to take his own path, instead of following mine."

"Papa," commented Anice, "I scarcely think he is to blame for that. I am sure it is always best, that conscientious, thinking people—and Mr. Grace is a thinking man—should have paths of their own."

Mr. Barholm pushed his hair from his forehead. His own obstinacy confronted him sometimes through Anice in a finer, more baffling form.

"Grace is a young man, my dear," he said, "and—and not a very strong-minded one."

"I cannot believe that is true," said Anice. "I do not think we can blame his mind. It is his body that is not strong. Mr. Grace himself has more power than you and mamma and myself all put together."

One of Alice's peculiarities was a certain pretty sententiousness, which, but for its innate refinement, and its

20

sincerity, might have impressed people as being a fault. When she pushed her opposition in that steady, innocent way, Mr. Barholm always took refuge behind an inner consciousness which "knew better," and was fully satisfied on the point of its own knowledge.

When breakfast was over, he rose from the table with the air of a man who had business on hand. Anice rose too, and followed him to the hearth.

"You are going out, I suppose," she said.

"I am going to see Joan Lowrie," he said complacently. "And I have several calls to make besides. Shall I tell the young woman that you will call on her?"

Anice looked down at the foot she had placed on the shining rim of the steel fender.

"Joan Lowrie?" she said reflectively.

"Certainly, my dear. I should think it would please the girl to feel that we are interested in her."

"I should scarcely think—from what Mr. Grace and his friend say—that she is the kind of a girl to be reached in that way," said Anice.

The Rector shrugged his shoulders.

"My dear," he answered, "if we are always to depend upon what Grace says, we shall often find ourselves in a dilemma. If you are going to wait until these collier young women call on you after the manner of polite society, I am afraid you will have time to lose interest in them and their affairs."

He had no scruples of his own on the subject of his errand. He felt very comfortable as usual, as he wended his way through the village toward Lowrie's cottage, on the Knoll Road. He did not ask himself what he should say to the collier young woman, and her unhappy charge. Orthodox phrases with various distinct flavors— the flavor of encouragement, the flavor of reproof, the flavor of consolation,—were always ready with the man; he never found it necessary to prepare them beforehand. The flavor of approval was to be Joan's portion this morning; the flavor of rebuke her companion's. He passed down the street with ecclesiastical dignity, bestowing a curt, but not unamiable word of recognition here and there. Unkempt, dirty-faced children, playing hop-scotch or marbles on the flag pavement, looked up at him with a species of awe, not un-mingled with secret resentment; women lounging on door-steps, holding babies on their hips, stared in critical sullenness as he went by.

"Theer's th' owd parson," commented one sharp-tongued matron. "Hoo's goin' to teach some one summat, I warrant What th' owd lad dunnot know is na worth knowin'. Eh! hoo's a graidely foo',

21

that hoo is. Our Tommy, if tha dost na let Jane Ann be, tha'lt be gettin' a hidin'."

Unprepossessing as most of the colliers' homes were, Lowrie's cottage was a trifle less inviting than the majority. It stood upon the roadside, an ugly little bare place, with a look of stubborn desolation, its only redeeming feature a certain rough cleanliness. The same cleanliness reigned inside, Barholm observed when he entered; and yet on the whole there was a stamp upon it which made it a place scarcely to be approved of. Before the low fire sat a girl with a child on her knee, and this girl, hearing the visitor's footsteps, got up hurriedly, and met him with a half abashed, half frightened look on her pale face.

"Lowrie is na here, an' neyther is Joan," she said, without waiting for him to speak. "Both on 'em's at th' pit. Theer's no one here but me," and she held the baby over her shoulder, as if she would like to have hidden it.

Mr. Barholm walked in serenely, sure that he ought to be welcome, if he were not.

"At the pit, are they?" he answered. "Dear me! I might have remembered that they would be at this time. Well, well; I will take a seat, my girl, and talk to you a little. I suppose you know me, the minister at the church—Mr. Barholm?"

Liz, a slender slip of a creature, large-eyed, and woe-begone, stood up before him, staring at him irresolutely as he seated himself.

"I—I dunnot know nobody much now," she stammered. "I—I've been away fro' Riggan sin' afore yo' comn—if yo're th' new parson," and then she colored nervously and became fearfully conscious of her miserable little burden, "I've heerd Joan speak o' th' young parson," she faltered.

Her visitor looked at her gravely. What a helpless, childish creature she was, with her pretty face, and her baby, and her characterless, frightened way. She was only one of many—poor Liz, ignorant, emotional, weak, easily led, ready to err, unable to bear the consequences of error, not strong enough to be resolutely wicked, not strong enough to be anything in particular, but that which her surroundings made her. If she had been well-born and well brought up, she would have been a pretty, insipid girl, who needed to be taken care of; as it was, she had "gone wrong." The excellent Rector of St. Michael's felt that she must be awakened.

"You are the girl Elizabeth?" he said.

"I'm 'Lizabeth Barnes," she answered, pulling at the hem of her child's small gown, "but folks nivver calls me nowt but Liz."

Her visitor pointed to a chair considerately. "Sit down," he said, "I want to talk to you."

Liz obeyed him; but her pretty, weak face told its own story of distaste and hysterical shrinking. She let the baby lie upon her lap; her fingers were busy plaiting up folds of the little gown.

"I dunnot want to be talked to," she whimpered. "I dunnot know as talk can do folk as is i' trouble any good—an' th' trouble's bad enow wi'out talk."

"We must remember whence the trouble comes," answered the minister, "and if the root lies in ourselves, and springs from our own sin, we must bear our cross meekly, and carry our sorrows and iniquities to the fountain head. We must ask for grace, and—and sanctification of spirit."

"I dunnot know nowt about th' fountain head," sobbed Liz aggrieved. "I amna religious an' I canna see as such loike helps foak. No Methody nivver did nowt for me when I war i' trouble an' want Joan Lowrie is na a Methody."

"If you mean that the young woman is in an unawakened condition, I am sorry to hear it," with increased gravity of demeanor. "Without the redeeming blood how are we to find peace? If you had clung to the Cross you would have been spared all this sin and shame. You must know, my girl, that this," with a motion toward the frail creature on her knee, "is a very terrible thing."

Liz burst into piteous sobs—crying like an abused child:

"I know it's hard enow," she cried; "I canna get work neyther at th' pit nor at th' factories, as long as I mun drag it about, an' I ha' not got a place to lay my head, on'y this. If it wur na for Joan, I might starve, and the choild too. But I'm noan so bad as yo'd mak' out. I—I wur very fond o' him—I wur, an' I thowt he wur fond o' me, an' he wur a gentleman too. He were no laboring-man, an' he wur kind to me, until he got tired. Them sort allus gets tired o' yo' i' time, Joan says. I wish I'd ha' towd Joan at first, an' axed her what to do."

Barholm passed his hand through his hair uneasily. This shallow, inconsequent creature baffled him. Her shame, her grief, her misery, were all mere straws eddying on the pool of her discomfort. It was not her sin that crushed her, it was the consequence of it; hers was not a sorrow, it was a petulant unhappiness. If her lot had been prosperous outwardly, she would have felt no inward pang.

It became more evident to him than ever that something must be done, and he applied himself to his task of reform to the best of his ability. But he exhausted his repertory of sonorous phrases in vain. His grave exhortations only called forth fresh tears, and a new element of resentment; and, to crown all, his visit terminated with a discouragement of which his philosophy had never dreamed.

In the midst of his most eloquent reproof, a shadow darkened the threshold, and as Liz looked up with the explanation—"Joan!" a young woman, in pit girl guise, came in, her hat pushed off her forehead, her throat bare, her fustian jacket hanging over her arm. She glanced from one to the other questioningly, knitting her brows slightly at the sight of Liz's tears. In answer to her glance Liz spoke querulously.

"It's th' parson, Joan," she said. "He comn to talk like th' rest on 'em an' he maks me out too ill to burn."

Just at that moment the child set up a fretful cry and Joan crossed the room and took it up in her arms.

"Yo've feart th' choild betwixt yo'," she said, "if yo've managed to do nowt else."

"I felt it my duty as Rector of the parish," explained Barholm somewhat curtly, "I felt it my duty as Rector of the parish, to endeavor to bring your friend to a proper sense of her position."

Joan turned toward him.

"Has tha done it?" she asked.

The Reverend Harold felt his enthusiasm concerning the young woman dying out.

"I—I—" he stammered.

Joan interrupted him.

"Dost tha see as tha has done her any good?" she demanded. "I dunnot mysen."

"I have endeavored to the best of my ability to improve her mental condition," the minister replied.

"I thowt as much," said Joan; "I mak' no doubt tha'st done thy best, neyther. Happen tha'st gi'en her what comfort tha had to spare, but if yo'd been wiser than yo' are, yo'd ha' let her alone. I'll warrant theer is na a parson 'twixt here an' Lunnon, that could na ha' towd her that she's a sinner an' has shame to bear; but happen theer is na a parson 'twixt here an' Lunnon as she could na ha' towd that much to, hersen. Howivver, as tha has said thy say, happen it 'll do yo' fur this toime, an' yo' can let her be for a while."

Mr. Barholm was unusually silent during dinner that evening, and as he sat over his wine, his dissatisfaction rose to the surface, as it invariably did.

"I am rather disturbed this evening, Anice," he said.

Anice looked up questioningly.

"Why?" she asked.

"I went to see Joan Lowrie this morning," he answered hesitatingly, "and I am very much disappointed in her. I scarcely think, after all, that I would advise you to take her in hand. She is not an amiable young woman. In fact there is a positive touch of the vixen about her."

24

CHAPTER IV

"Love Me, Love My Dog"

Mr. Barholm had fallen into the habit of turning to Anice for it, when he required information concerning people and things. In her desultory pilgrimages, Anice saw all that he missed, and heard much that he was deaf to. The rough, hard-faced men and boisterous girls who passed to and from their work at the mine, drew her to the window whenever they made their appearance. She longed to know something definite of them—to get a little nearer to their unprepossessing life. Sometimes the men and women, passing, caught glimpses of her, and, asking each other who she was, decided upon her relationship to the family.

"Hoo's th' owd parson's lass," somebody said. "Hoo's noan so bad lookin' neyther, if hoo was na sich a bit o' a thing."

The people who had regarded Mr. Barholm with a spice of disfavor, still could not look with ill-nature upon this pretty girl. The slatternly women nudged each other as she passed, and the playing children stared after their usual fashion; but even the hardest-natured matron could find nothing more condemnatory to say than, "Hoo's noan Lancashire, that's plain as th' nose on a body's face;" or, "Theer is na much on her, at ony rate. Hoo's a bit of a weakly-like lass wi'out much blood i' her."

Now and then Anice caught the sound of their words, but she was used to being commented upon. She had learned that people whose lives have a great deal of hard, common discomfort and struggle, acquire a tendency to depreciation almost as a second nature. It is easier to bear one's own misfortunes, than to bear the good-fortune of better-used people. That is the insult added by Fate to injury.

Riggan was a crooked, rambling, cross-grained little place. From the one wide street with its jumble of old, tumble-down shops, and glaring new ones, branched out narrow, up-hill or down-hill thoroughfares, edged by colliers' houses, with an occasional tiny provision shop, where bread and bacon were ranged alongside potatoes and flabby cabbages; ornithological specimens made of pale sweet cake, and adorned with startling black currant eyes, rested unsteadily against the window-pane, a sore temptation to the juvenile populace.

It was in one of these side streets that Anice met with her first adventure.

25

Turning the corner, she heard the sharp yelp of a dog among a group of children, followed almost immediately by a ringing of loud, angry, boyish voices, a sound of blows and cries, and a violent scuffle. Anice paused for a few seconds, looking over the heads of the excited little crowd, and then made her way to it, and in a minute was in the heart of it. The two boys who were the principal figures, were fighting frantically, scuffling, kicking, biting, and laying on vigorous blows, with not unscientific fists. Now and then a fierce, red, boyish face was to be seen, and then the rough head ducked and the fight waxed fiercer and hotter, while the dog—a small, shrewd sharp-nosed terrier—barked at the combatants' heels, snapping at one pair, but not at the other, and plainly enjoying the excitement.

"Boys!" cried Anice. "What's the matter?"

"They're feighten," remarked a philosophical young by-stander, with placid interest,—"an' Jud Bates'll win."

It was so astonishing a thing that any outsider should think of interfering, and there was something so decided in the girlish voice addressing them, that almost at the moment the combatants fell back, panting heavily, breathing vengeance in true boy fashion, and evidently resenting the unexpected intrusion.

"What is it all about?" demanded the girl. "Tell me."

The crowd gathered close around her to stare, the terrier sat down breathless, his red tongue hanging out, his tail beating the ground. One of the boys was his master, it was plain at a glance, and, as a natural consequence, the dog had felt it his duty to assist to the full extent of his powers. But the other boy was the first to speak.

"Why could na he let me a-be then?" he asked irately. "I was na doin' owt t' him."

"Yea, tha was," retorted his opponent, a sturdy, ragged, ten-year-old.

"Nay, I was na."

"Yea, tha was."

"Well," said Anice, "what was he doing?"

"Aye," cried the first youngster, "tha tell her if tha con. Who hit th' first punse?" excitedly doubling his fist again. "I didna."

"Nay, tha didna, but tha did summat else. Tha punsed at Nib wi' thy clog, an' hit him aside o' th' yed, an' then I punsed thee, an' I'd do it agen fur—"

"Wait a minute," said Anice, holding up her little gloved hand. "Who is Nib?"

"Nib's my dog," surlily. "An' them as punses him, has getten to punse me."

26

Anice bent down and patted the small animal.

"He seems a very nice dog," she said. "What did you kick him for?"

Nib's master was somewhat mollified. A person who could appreciate the virtues of "th' best tarrier i' Riggan," could not be regarded wholly with contempt, or even indifference.

"He kicked him fur nowt," he answered. "He's allus at uther him or me. He bust my kite, an' he cribbed my marvels, didn't he?" appealing to the by-standers.

"Aye, he did. I seed him crib th' marvels mysen. He wur mad 'cos Jud wur winnen, and then he kicked Nib."

Jud bent down to pat Nib himself, not without a touch of pride in his manifold injuries, and the readiness with which they were attested.

"Aye," he said, "an' I did na set on him at first neyther. I nivver set on him till he punsed Nib. He may bust my kite, an' steal my marvels, an' he may ca' me ill names, but he shanna kick Nib. So theer!"

It was evident that Nib's enemy was the transgressor. He was grievously in the minority. Nobody seemed to side with him, and everybody seemed ready—when once the tongues were loosed—to say a word for Jud and "th' best tarrier i'Riggan." For a few minutes Anice could scarcely make herself heard.

"You are a good boy to take care of your dog," she said to Jud—"and though fighting is not a good thing, perhaps if I had been a boy," gravely deciding against moral suasion in one rapid glance at the enemy—"perhaps if I had been a boy, I would have fought myself. You are a coward," she added, with incisive scorn to the other lad, who slinked sulkily out of sight.

"Owd Sammy Craddock," lounging at his window, clay pipe in hand, watched Anice as she walked away, and gave vent to his feelings in a shrewd chuckle.

"Eh! eh!" he commented; "so that's th' owd parson's lass, is it? Wall, hoo may be o' th' same mate, but hoo is na o' th' same grain, I'll warrant. Hoo's a rare un, hoo is, fur a wench."

"Owd Sammy's" amused chuckles, and exclamations of "Eh! hoo's a rare un—that hoo is—fur a wench," at last drew his wife's attention. The good woman pounced upon him sharply.

"Tha'rt an owd yommer-head," she said. "What art tha ramblin' about now? Who is it as is siccan a rare un?"

Owd Sammy burst into a fresh chuckle, rubbing his knees with both hands.

"Why," said he, "I'll warrant tha could na guess i' tha tried, but

27

I'll gi'e thee a try. Who dost tha think wur out i' th' street just now i' th' thick of a foight among th' lads? I know thou'st nivver guess."

"Nay, happen I canna, an' I dunnot know as I care so much, neyther," testily.

"Why," slapping his knee, "th' owd parson's lass. A little wench not much higher nor thy waist, an' wi' a bit o' a face loike skim-milk, but steady and full o' pluck as an owd un."

"Nay now, tha dost na say so? What wor she doin' an' how did she come theer? Tha mun ha' been dreamin'!"

"Nowt o' th' soart. I seed her as plain as I see thee an' heerd ivvery word she said. Tha shouldst ha' seen her! Hoo med as if hoo'd lived wi' lads aw her days. Jud Bates and that young marplot o' Thorme's wur feightin about Nib—at it tooth and nail—an' th' lass sees 'em, an' marches into th' thick, an' sets 'em to reets. Yo' should ha' seen her! An' hoo tells Jud as he's a good lad to tak' care o' his dog, an' hoo does na know but what hoo'd fowt hersen i' his place, an' hoo ca's Jack Thorme a coward, an' turns her back on him, an' ends up wi' tellin' Jud to bring th' tarrier to th' Rectory to see her."

"Well," exclaimed Mrs. Craddock, "did yo' iwer hear th' loike!"

"I wish th' owd parson had seed her," chuckled her spouse irreverently. "That soart is na i' his loine. He'd a waved his stick as if he'd been king and council i' one, an' rated 'em fro' th' top round o' th' ladder. He canna get down fro' his perch. Th' owd lad'll stick theer till he gets a bit too heavy, an' then he'll coom down wi' a crash, ladder an' aw'—but th' lass is a different mak'."

Sammy being an oracle among his associates, new-comers usually passed through his hands, and were condemned, or approved, by him. His pipe, and his criticisms upon society in general, provided him with occupation. Too old to fight and work, he was too shrewd to be ignored. Where he could not make himself felt, he could make himself heard. Accordingly, when he condescended to inform a select and confidential audience that the "owd parson's lass was a rare un, lass as she was"—(the masculine opinion of Riggan on the subject of the weaker sex was a rather disparaging one)—the chances of the Rector's daughter began, so to speak, to "look up." If Sammy Craddock found virtue in the new-comer, it was possible such virtue might exist, at least in a negative form,—and open enmity was rendered unnecessary, and even impolitic. A faint interest began to be awakened. When Anice passed through the streets, the slatternly, baby-laden women looked at her curiously, and in a manner not absolutely unfriendly. She might not be so bad after all, if she did have "Lunnon ways," and was smiled upon by Fortune. At any rate, she differed from the parson himself, which was in her favor.

28

CHAPTER V

Outside the Hedge

Deeply as Anice was interested in Joan, she left her to herself. She did not go to see her, and still more wisely, she managed to hush in her father any awakening tendency toward parochial visits. But from Grace and Fergus Derrick she heard much of her, and through Grace she contrived to convey work and help to Liz, and encouragement to her protectress. From what source the assistance came, Joan did not know, and she was not prone to ask questions.

"If she asks, tell her it is from a girl like herself," Anice had said, and Joan had accepted the explanation.

In a very short time from the date of their first acquaintance, Fergus Derrick's position in the Barholm household had become established. He was the man to make friends and keep them. Mrs. Barholm grew fond of him; the Rector regarded him as an acquisition to their circle, and Anice was his firm friend. So, being free to come and go, he came and went, and found his unceremonious visits pleasant enough. On his arrival at Riggan, he had not anticipated meeting with any such opportunities of enjoyment. He had come to do hard work, and had expected a hard life, softened by few social graces. The work of opening the new mines was a heavy one, and was rendered additionally heavy and dangerous by unforeseen circumstances. A load of responsibility rested upon his shoulders, to which at times he felt himself barely equal, and which men of less tough fibre would have been glad to shift upon others. Naturally, his daily cares made his hours of relaxation all the more pleasant. Mrs. Barholm's influence upon him was a gentle and soothing one, and in Anice he found a subtle inspiration. She seemed to understand his trials by instinct, and even the minutiae of his work made themselves curiously clear to her. As to the people who were under his control, she was never tired of hearing of them, and of studying their quaint, rough ways. To please her he stored up many a characteristic incident, and it was through him that she heard most frequently of Joan. She did not even see Joan for fully two months after her arrival in Riggan, and then it was Joan who came to her.

As the weather became more spring-like she was oftener out in the garden. She found a great deal to do among the flower-beds and shrubbery, and as this had always been considered her department, she took the management of affairs wholly into her own hands. The old place, which had been rather neglected in the time of the previous inhabitant, began to bloom out into fragrant luxuriance, and passing Rigganites regarded it with admiring eyes. The colliers who had noticed her at the window in the colder weather, seeing her so frequently from a nearer point of view, felt themselves on more familiar terms. Some of them even took a sort of liking to her, and gave her an uncouth greeting as they went by; and, more than once, one or another of them had paused to ask for a flower or two, and had received them with a curious bashful awe, when they had been passed over the holly hedge.

Having gone out one evening after dinner to gather flowers for the house, Anice, standing before a high lilac bush, and pulling its pale purple tassels, became suddenly conscious that some one was watching her—some one standing upon the roadside behind the holly hedge. She did not know that as she stopped here and there to fill her basket, she had been singing to herself in a low tone. Her voice had attracted the passer-by.

This passer-by—a tall pit girl with a handsome, resolute face—stood behind the dark green hedge, and watched her. Perhaps to this girl, weary with her day's labor, grimed with coal-dust, it was not unlike standing outside paradise. Early in the year as it was, there were flowers enough in the beds, and among the shrubs, to make the spring air fresh with a faint, sweet odor. But here too was Anice in her soft white merino dress, with her basket of flowers, with the blue bells at her belt, and her half audible song. She struck Joan Lowrie with a new sense of beauty and purity. As she watched her she grew discontented—restless—sore at heart. She could not have told why, but she felt a certain anger against herself. She had had a hard day. Things had gone wrong at the pit's mouth; things had gone wrong at home. It was hard for her strong nature to bear with Liz's weakness. Her path was never smooth, but to-day it had been at its roughest. The little song fell upon her ear with strong pathos.

"She's inside o' th' hedge," she said to herself in a dull voice. "I'm outside, theer's th' difference. It a'most looks loike the hedge went aw' around an' she'd been born among th' flowers, and theer's no way out for her—no more than theer's a way in fur me."

Then it was that Anice turned round and saw her. Their eyes met, and, singularly enough, Anice's first thought was that this was Joan. Derrick's description made her sure. There were not two such women in Riggan. She made her decision in a moment. She stepped across the grass to the hedge with a ready smile.

"You were looking at my flowers," she said. "Will you have some?"

30

Joan hesitated.

"I often give them to people," said Anice, taking a handful from the basket and offering them to her across the holly. "When the men come home from the mines they often ask me for two or three, and I think they like them even better than I do—though that is saying a great deal."

Joan held out her hand, and took the flowers, holding them awkwardly, but with tenderness.

"Oh, thank yo'," she said. "It's kind o' yo' to gi' 'em away."

"It's a pleasure to me," said Anice, picking out a delicate pink hyacinth. "Here's a hyacinth." Then as Joan took it their eyes met. "Are you Joan Lowrie?" asked the girl.

Joan lifted her head.

"Aye," she answered, "I'm Joan Lowrie."

"Ah," said Anice, "then I am very glad."

They stood on the same level from that moment. Something as indescribable as all else in her manner, had done for Anice just what she had simply and seriously desired to do. Proud and stubborn as her nature was, Joan was subdued. The girl's air and speech were like her song. She stood inside the hedge still, in her white dress, among the flowers, looking just as much as if she had been born there as ever, but some fine part of her had crossed the boundary.

"Ah! then I am glad of that," she said.

"Yo' are very good to say as much," she answered, "but I dunnot know as I quite understand—"

Anice drew a little nearer.

"Mr. Grace has told me about you," she said. "And Mr. Derrick."

Joan's brown throat raised itself a trifle, and Anice thought color showed itself on her cheek.

"Both on 'em's been good to me," she said, "but I did na think as—"

Anice stopped her with a little gesture, "It was you who were so kind to Liz when she had no friend," she began.

Joan interrupted her with sudden eagerness.

"It wur yo' as sent th' work an' th' things fur th' choild," she said.

"Yes, it was I," answered Anice. "But I hardly knew what to send. I hope I sent the right things, did I?"

"Yes, miss; thank yo'." And then in a lower voice, "They wur a power o' help to Liz an' me. Liz wur hard beset then, an' she's only a young thing as canna bear sore trouble. Seemed loike that th' thowt as some un had helped her wur a comfort to her."

31

Anice took courage.

"Perhaps if I might come and see her," she said. "May I come? I should like to see the baby. I am very fond of little children."

There was a moment's pause, and then Joan spoke awkwardly.

"Do yo' know—happen yo' dunnot—what Liz's trouble is? Bein' as yo're so young yorsen, happen they did na tell yo' all. Most o' toimes folk is na apt to be fond o' such loike as this little un o' hers."

"I heard all the story."

"Then come if yo' loike,—an' if they'll let yo', some ud think there wur harm i' th' choild's touch. I'm glad yo' dunna."

She did not linger much longer. Anice watched her till she was out of sight. An imposing figure she was—moving down the road in her rough masculine garb—the massive perfection of her form clearly outlined against the light. It seemed impossible that such a flower as this could blossom, and decay, and die out in such a life, without any higher fruition.

"I have seen Joan Lowrie," said Anice to Derrick, when next they met.

"Did she come to you, or did you go to her?" Fergus asked.

"She came to me, but without knowing that she was coming."

"That was best," was his comment.

Joan Lowrie was as much a puzzle to him as she was to other people. Despite the fact that he saw her every day of his life, he had never found it possible to advance a step with her. She held herself aloof from him, just as she held herself aloof from the rest. A common greeting, and oftener than not, a silent one, was all that passed between them. Try as he would, he could get no farther;— and he certainly did make some effort. Now and then he found the chance to do her a good turn, and such opportunities he never let slip, though his way of doing such things was always so quiet as to be unlikely to attract any observation. Usually he made his way with people easily, but this girl held him at a distance, almost ungraciously. And he did not like to be beaten. Who does? So he persevered with a shade of stubbornness, hidden under a net-work of other motives. Once, when he had exerted himself to lighten her labor somewhat, she set aside his assistance openly.

"Theer's others as needs help more nor me," she said. "Help them, an' I'll thank yo'."

In course of time, however, he accidentally discovered that there had been occasions when, notwithstanding her apparent ungraciousness, she had exerted her influence in his behalf.

The older colliers resented his youth, the younger ones his

authority. The fact that he was "noan Lancashire" worked against him too, though even if he had been a Lancashire man, he would not have been likely to find over-much favor. It was enough that he was "one o' th' mesters." To have been weak of will, or vacillating of purpose, would have been death to every vestige of the authority vested in him; but he was as strong mentally as physically—strong-willed to the verge of stubbornness. But if they could not frighten or subdue him, they could still oppose and irritate him, and the contention was obstinate. This feeling even influenced the girls and women at the "mouth." They, too, organized in petty rebellion, annoying if not powerful.

"I think yo' will find as yo' may as well leave th' engineer be," Joan would say dryly. "Yo' will na fear him much, an' yo'll tire yo'rsens wi' yo're clatter. I donna see the good o' barkin' so much when yo' canna bite."

"Aye," jeered one of the boldest, once, "leave th' engineer be. Joan sets a power o' store by th' engineer."

There was a shout of laughter, but it died out when Joan confronted the speaker with dangerous steadiness of gaze.

"Save thy breath to cool thy porridge," she said. "It will be better for thee."

But it was neither the first nor the last time that her companions flung out a jeer at her "sweetheartin'." The shrewdest among them had observed Derrick's interest in her. They concluded, of course, that Joan's handsome face had won her a sweetheart. They could not accuse her of encouraging him; but they could profess to believe that she was softening, and they could use the insinuation as a sharp weapon against her, when such a course was not too hazardous.

Of this, Derrick knew nothing. He could only see that Joan set her face persistently against his attempts to make friends with her, and the recognition of this fact almost exasperated him at times. It was quite natural that, seeing so much of this handsome creature, and hearing so much of her, his admiration should not die out, and that opposition should rather invite him to stronger efforts to reach her.

So it was that hearing Miss Barholm's story he fell into unconscious reverie. Of course this did not last long. He was roused from it by the fact that Anice was looking at him. When he looked up, it seemed as if she awakened also, though she did not start.

"How are you getting on at the mines?" she asked.

"Badly. Or, at least, by no means well. The men are growing harder to deal with every day." "And your plans about the fans?" The substitution of the mechanical fan for the old furnace at the

33

base of the shaft, was one of the projects to which Derrick clung most tenaciously. During a two years' sojourn among the Belgian mines, he had studied the system earnestly. He had worked hard to introduce it at Riggan, and meant to work still harder. But the miners were bitterly opposed to anything "newfangled," and the owners were careless. So that the mines were worked, and their profits made, it did not matter for the rest. They were used to casualties, so well used to them in fact, that unless a fearful loss of life occurred, they were not alarmed or even roused. As to the injuries done to a man's health, and so on—they had not time to inquire into such things. There was danger in all trades, for the matter of that. Fergus Derrick was a young man, and young men were fond of novelties.

Opposition was bad enough, but indifference was far more baffling. The colliers opposed Derrick to the utmost, the Company was rather inclined to ignore him—some members good-naturedly, others with an air of superiority, not unmixed with contempt. The colliers talked with rough ill-nature; the Company did not want to talk at all.

"Oh," answered Derrick, "I do not see that I have made one step forward; but it will go hard with me before I am beaten. Some of the men I have to deal with are as bat-blind as they are cantankerous. One would think that experience might have taught them wisdom. Would you believe that some of those working in the most dangerous parts of the mine have false keys to their Davys, and use the flame to light their pipes? I have heard of the thing being done before, but I only discovered the other day that we had such madmen in the pits here. If I could only be sure of them I would settle the matter at once, but they are crafty enough to keep their secret, and it only drifts to the master as a rumor."

"Have you no suspicion as to who they are?" asked Anice.

"I suspect one man," he answered, "but only suspect him because he is a bad fellow, reckless in all things, and always ready to break the rules. I suspect Dan Lowrie."

"Joan's father?" exclaimed Anice in distress.

Derrick made a gesture of assent.

"He is the worst man in the mines," he said, "The man with the worst influence, the man who can work best if he will, the man whose feeling against any authority is the strongest, and whose feeling against me amounts to bitter enmity."

"Against you? But why?"

"I suppose because I have no liking for him myself, and because I will have orders obeyed, whether they are my orders or

34

the orders of the owners. I will have work done as it should be done, and I will not be frightened by bullies."

"But if he is a dangerous man—"

"He would knock me down from behind, or spoil my beauty with vitriol as coolly as he would toss off a pint of beer, if he had the opportunity, and chanced to feel vicious enough at the time," said Derrick, "But his mood has not quite come to that yet. Just now he feels that he would like to have a row,—and really, if we could have a row, it would be the best thing for us both. If one of us could thrash the other at the outset, it might never come to the vitriol."

He was cool enough himself, and spoke in quite a matter-of-fact way, but Anice suddenly lost her color. When, later, she bade him goodnight—

"I am afraid of that man," she said, as he held her hand for the moment. "Don't let him harm you."

"What man?" asked Derrick. "Is it possible you are thinking about what I said of Lowrie?"

"Yes. It is so horrible. I cannot bear the thought of it. I am not used to hear of such things. I am afraid for you."

"You are very good," he said, his strong hand returning her grasp with warm gratitude. "But I am sorry I said so much, if I have frightened you. I ought to have remembered how new such things were to you. It is nothing, I assure you." And bidding her good-night again, he went away quite warmed at heart by her innocent interest in him, but blaming himself not a little for his indiscretion.

CHAPTER VI

Joan and the Child

To the young curate's great wonder, on his first visit to her after the advent of Liz and her child, Joan changed her manner towards him. She did not attempt to repel him, she even bade him welcome in a way of her own. Deep in Joan's heart was hidden a fancy that perhaps the work of this young fellow who was "good enow fur a parson," lay with such as Liz, and those who like Liz bore a heavy burden.

"If yo' can do her any good," she said, "come and welcome. Come every day. I dunnot know much about such like mysen, but happen yo' ha' a way o' helpin' folk as canna help theirsens i' trouble—an' Liz is one on 'em."

Truly Liz was one of these. She clung to Joan in a hopeless, childish way, as her only comfort. She could do nothing for herself, she could only obey Joan's dictates, and this she did in listless misery. When she had work to do, she made weak efforts at doing it, and when she had none she sat and held the child upon her knee, her eyes following her friend with a vague appeal. The discomfort of her lot, the wretchedness of coming back to shame and tears, after a brief season of pleasure and luxury, was what crushed her. So long as her lover had cared for her, and she had felt no fear of hunger or cold, or desertion, she had been happy—happy because she could be idle and take no thought for the morrow, and was almost a lady. But now all that was over. She had come to the bitter dregs of the cup. She was thrown on her own resources, nobody cared for her, nobody helped her but Joan, nobody called her pretty and praised her ways. She was not to be a lady after all, she must work for her living and it must be a poor one too. There would be no fine clothes, no nice rooms, no flattery and sugar-plums. Everything would be even far harder, and more unpleasant than it had been before. And then, the baby? What could she do with it?—a creature more helpless than herself, always to be clothed and taken care of, when she could not take care of herself, always in the way, always crying and wailing and troubling day and night. She almost blamed the baby for everything. Perhaps she would not have lost her lover if it had not been for the baby. Perhaps he knew what a trouble it would be, and wanted to be rid of her before it came, and that was why he had gone away. The night Joan had brought her home she had taken care of the child, and told Liz to sit down and rest, and had sat down

36

herself with the small creature in her arms, and after watching her for a while, Liz had broken out into sobs, and slipped down upon the floor at her feet, hiding her wretched, pretty face upon her friend's knee.

"I canna abide the sight o' it," she cried. "I canna see what it wur born fur, mysen. I wish I'd deed when I wur i' Lunnon—when he cared fur me. He wor fond enow o' me at th' first. He could na abide me to be out o' his sight. I nivver wur so happy i' my life as I wur then. Aye! I did na think then, as th' toime ud come when he'd cast me out i' th' road. He had no reet to do it," her voice rising hysterically. "He had no reet to do it, if he wur a gentleman; but it seems gentlefolk can do owt they please. If he did na mean to stick to me, why could na he ha' let me a-be."

"That is na gentlefolks' way," said Joan bitterly, "but if I wur i' yo're place, Liz, I would na hate th' choild. It has na done yo' as much harm as yo' ha' done it."

After a while, when the girl was quieter, Joan asked her a question.

"You nivver told me who yo' went away wi', Liz," she said. "I ha' a reason fur wantin' to know, or I would na ax, but fur a' that if yo' dunnot want to tell me, yo' need na do it against yo're will."

Liz was silent a moment.

"I would na tell ivverybody," she said. "I would na tell nobody but yo'. It would na do no good, an' I dunnot care to do harm. You'll keep it to yo'rsen, if I tell yo', Joan?"

"Aye," Joan answered, "as long as it needs be kept to mysen. I am na one to clatter."

"Well," said Liz with a sob, "it wur Mester Landsell I went wi'—young Mester Landsell—Mester Ralph."

"I thout as much," said Joan, her face darkening.

She had had her suspicions from the first, when Mr. Ralph Landsell had come to Riggan with his father, who was one of the mining company. He was a graceful, fair-faced young fellow, with an open hand and the air of a potentate, and his grandeur had pleased Liz. She was not used to flattery and "fine London ways," and her vanity made her an easy victim.

"He wur allus after me," she said, with fresh tears. "He nivver let me be till I promised to go. He said he would make a lady o' me an' he wur allus givin' me things. He wur fond o' me at first,—that he wur,—an' I wur fond o' him. I nivver seed no one loike him afore. Oh! it's hard, it is.—Oh! it's bitter hard an' cruel, as it should come to this."

And she wailed and sobbed until she wore herself out, and wearied Joan to the very soul.

37

But Joan bore with her and never showed impatience by word or deed. Childish petulances and plaints fell upon her like water upon a rock—but now and then the strong nature was rasped beyond endurance by the weak one. She had taken no small task upon herself when she gave Liz her word that she would shield her. Only after a while, in a few weeks, a new influence began to work upon Liz's protectress. The child for whom there seemed no place in the world, or in any pitying heart—the child for whom Liz felt nothing but vague dislike and resentment—the child laid its light but powerful hand upon Joan. Once or twice she noticed as she moved about the room that the little creature's eyes would follow her in a way something like its mother's, as if with appeal to her superior strength. She fell gradually into the habit of giving it more attention. It was so little and light, so easily taken from Liz's careless hold when it was restless, so easily carried to and fro, as she went about her household tasks. She had never known much about babies until chance had thrown this one in her path; it was a great novelty. It liked her strong arms, and Liz was always ready to give it up to her, feeling only a weak bewilderment at her fancy for it. When she was at home it was rarely out of her arms. It was no source of weariness to her perfect strength. She carried it here and there, she cradled it upon her knees, when she sat down by the fire to rest; she learned in time a hundred gentle woman's ways through its presence. Her step became lighter, her voice softer—a heavy tread, or a harsh tone might waken the child. For the child's sake she doffed her uncouth working-dress when she entered the house; for the child's sake she made an effort to brighten the dulness, and soften the roughness of their surroundings.

The Reverend Paul, in his visits to the house, observed with tremor, the subtle changes wrought in her. Catching at the straw of her negative welcome, he went to see Liz whenever he could find a tangible excuse. He had a sensitive dread of intruding even upon the poor privacy of the "lower orders," and he could rarely bring himself to the point of taking them by storm as a mere matter of ecclesiastical routine. But the oftener he saw Joan Lowrie, the more heavily she lay upon his mind. Every day his conscience smote him more sorely for his want of success with her. And yet how could he make way against her indifference. He even felt himself a trifle spell-bound in her presence. He often found himself watching her as she moved to and fro,—watching her as Liz and the child did.

But "th' parson" was "th' parson" to her still. A good-natured, simple little fellow, who might be a trifle better than other folks, but who certainly seemed weaker; a frail little gentleman in spectacles, who was afraid of her, or was at least easily confounded; who might be of use to Liz, but who was not in her line,—better in his way than his master in his; but still a person to be regarded with just a touch of contempt.

The confidence established between Grace and his friend Fergus Derrick, leading to the discussion of all matters connected with the parish and parishioners, led naturally to the frequent discussion of Joan Lowrie among the rest. Over tea and toast in the small parlor the two men often drew comfort from each other. When Derrick strode into the little place and threw himself into his favorite chair, with knit brows and weary irritation in his air, Grace was always ready to detect his mood, and wait for him to reveal himself; or when Grace looked up at his friend's entrance with a heavy, pained look on his face, Derrick was equally quick to comprehend. There was one trouble in which Derrick specially sympathized with his friend. This was in his feeling for Anice.

Duty called Paul frequently to the house, and his position with regard to its inhabitants was necessarily familiar. Mr. Barholm did not spare his curate; he was ready to delegate to him all labor in which he was not specially interested himself, or which he regarded as scarcely worthy of his mettle.

"Grace makes himself very useful in some cases," he would say; "a certain kind of work suits him, and he is able to do himself justice in it. He is a worthy enough young fellow in a certain groove, but it is always best to confine him to that groove."

So, when there was an ordinary sermon to be preached, or a commonplace piece of work to be done, it was handed over to Grace, with a few tolerant words of advice or comment, and as commonplace work was rather the rule than the exception, the Reverend Paul's life was not idle. Anice's manner toward her father's curate was so gentle and earnest, so frank and full of trust in him, that it was not to be wondered at that each day only fixed her more firmly in his heart. Nothing of his conscientious labor was lost upon her; nothing of his self-sacrifice and trial was passed by indifferently in her thoughts of him; his pain and his effort went to her very heart. Her belief in him was so strong that she never hesitated to carry any little bewilderment to him or to speak to him openly upon any subject. Small marvel, that he found it delicious pain to go to the house day after day, feeling himself so near to her, yet knowing himself so far from any hope of reaching the sealed chamber of her heart.

Notwithstanding her knowledge of her inability to alter his position, Anice still managed to exert some slight influence over her friend's fate.

39

"Do you not think, papa, that Mr. Grace has a great deal to do?" she suggested once, when he was specially overburdened.

"A great deal to do?" he said. "Well, he has enough to do, of course, my dear, but then it is work of a kind that suits him. I never leave anything very important to Grace. You do not mean, my dear, that you fancy he has too much to do?"

"Rather too much of a dull kind," answered Anice. "Dull work is tiring, and he has a great deal of it on his hands. All that school work, you know, papa—if you could share it with him, I should think it would make it easier for him."

"My dear Anice," the rector protested; "if Grace had my responsibilities to carry on his shoulders,—but I do not leave my responsibilities to him. In my opinion he is hardly fitted to bear them—they are not in his line;" but seeing a dubious look on the delicate face opposite him—"but if you think the young fellow has really too much to do, I will try to take some of these minor matters upon myself. I am equal to a good deal of hard work,"—evidently feeling himself somewhat aggrieved.

But Anice made no further comment; having dropped a seed of suggestion, she left it to fructify, experience teaching her that this was her best plan. It was one of the good rector's weaknesses, to dislike to find his course disapproved even by a wholly uninfluential critic, and his daughter was by no means an uninfluential critic. He was never exactly comfortable when her views did not strictly accord with his own. To find that Anice was regarding a favorite whim with questioning, was for him to begin to falter a trifle inwardly, however testily rebellious he might feel. He was a man who thrived under encouragement, and sank at once before failure; failure was unpleasant, and he rarely contended long against unpleasantness; it was not a "fair wind and no favor" with him, he wanted both the fair wind and the favor, and if either failed him he felt himself rather badly used. So it was, through this discreetly exerted influence of Anice's, that Grace, to his surprise, found some irksome tasks taken from his shoulders at this time. He did not know that it was Anice he had to thank for the temporary relief.

CHAPTER VII

Anice at the Cottage

ANICE went to see Liz. Perhaps if the truth were told, she went to see Joan more than to visit Joan's protégée though her interest extended from the one to the other. But she did not see Joan, she only heard of her. Liz met her visitor without any manifestations of enthusiasm. She was grateful, but gratitude was not often a powerful emotion with her. But Anice began to attract her somewhat before she had been in the house ten minutes. Liz found, first, that she was not one of the enemy, and did not come to read a homily to her concerning her sins and transgressions; having her mind set at ease thus far, she found time to be interested in her. Her visitor's beauty, her prettiness of toilet, a certain delicate grace of presence, were all virtues in Liz's eyes. She was so fond of pretty things herself, she had been wont to feel such pleasure and pride in her own beauty, that such outward charms were the strongest of charms to her. She forgot to be abashed and miserable, when, after talking a few minutes, Anice came to her and bent over the child as it lay on her knee. She even had the courage to regard the material of her dress with some degree of interest.

"Yo'n getten that theer i' Lunnon," she ventured, wistfully touching the pretty silk with her finger. "Theer's noan sich i' Riggan."

"Yes," answered Anice, letting the baby's hand cling to her fingers. "I bought it in London."

Liz touched it again, and this time the wistfulness in her touch crept up to her eyes, mingled with a little fretfulness.

"Ivverything's fine as comes fro' Lunnon," she said. "It's the grandest place i' th' world. I dunnot wonder as th' queen lives theer. I wur happy aw th' toime I wur theer. I nivver were so happy i' my life. I—I canna hardly bear to think on it—it gi'es me such a wearyin' an' long-in'; I wish I could go back, I do"—ending with a sob.

"Don't think about it any more than you can help," said Anice gently. "It is very hard I know; don't cry, Liz."

"I canna help it," sobbed Liz; "an' I can no more help thinkin' on it, than th' choild theer can help thinkin' on its milk. I'm hungerin' aw th' toime—an' I dunnot care to live; I wakken up i' th' noight hungerin' an' cryin' fur—fur what I ha' not got, an' nivver shall ha' agen."

The tears ran down her cheeks and she whimpered like a

41

child. The sight of the silk dress had brought back to her mind her lost bit of paradise as nothing else would have done—her own small store of finery, the gayety and novelty of London sounds and sights.

Anice knelt down upon the flagged floor, still holding the child's hand.

"Don't cry," she said again. "Look at the baby, Liz. It is a pretty baby. Perhaps if it lives, it may be a comfort to you some day."

"Nay! it wunnot;" said Liz, regarding it resentfully. "I nivver could tak' no comfort in it. It's nowt but a trouble. I dunnot loike it. I canna. It would be better if it would na live. I canna tell wheer Joan Lowrie gets her patience fro'. I ha' no patience with the little marred thing mysen—allus whimperin' an' cryin'; I dunnot know what to do wi' it half th' toime."

Anice took it from her lap, and sitting down upon a low wooden stool, held it gently, looking at its small round face. It was a pretty little creature, pretty with Liz's own beauty, or at least, with the baby promise of it. Anice stooped and kissed it, her heart stirred by the feebly-strong clasp of the tiny fingers.

During the remainder of her visit, she sat holding the child on her knee, and talking to it as well as to its mother. But she made no attempt to bring Liz to what Mr. Barholm had called, "a fitting sense of her condition." She was not fully settled in her opinion as to what Liz's "fitting sense" would be. So she simply made an effort to please her, and awaken her to interest, and she succeeded very well. When she went away, the girl was evidently sorry to see her go.

"I dunnot often want to see folk twice," she said, looking at her shyly, "but I'd loike to see yo'. Yo're not loike th' rest. Yo' dunnot harry me wi' talk. Joan said yo' would na."

"I will come again," said Anice.

During her visit, Liz had told her much of Joan. She seemed to like to talk of her, and certainly Anice had been quite ready to listen.

"She is na easy to mak' out," said Liz, "an' p'r'aps that's th' reason why folks puts theirsens to so much trouble to mak' her out."

When he passed the cottage on the Knoll Road in going home at night, Fergus could not help looking out for Joan. Sometimes he saw her, and sometimes he did not. During the warm weather, he saw her often at the door, or near the gate; almost always with the child in her arms. There was no awkward shrinking in her manner at such times, no vestige of the clumsy consciousness usually exhibited by girls of her class. She met his glance with a grave quietude, scarcely touched with interest, he thought; he never observed that she smiled, though he was uncomfortably conscious now and then that she stood and calmly watched him out of sight.

42

CHAPTER VIII

The Wager of Battle

"Owd Sammy Craddock" rose from his chair, and going to the mantel-piece, took down a tobacco jar of red and yellow delft, and proceeded to fill his pipe with solemn ceremony. It was a large, deep clay pipe, and held a great deal of tobacco—particularly when filled from the store of an acquaintance. "It's a good enow pipe to borrow wi'," Sammy was wont to remark. In the second place, Mr. Craddock drew forth a goodly portion of the weed, and pressed it down with ease and precision into the top of the foreign gentleman's turban which constituted the bowl. Then he lighted it with a piece of paper, remarking to his wife between long indrawn puffs, "I'm goin'—to th' Public."

The good woman did not receive the intelligence as amicably as it had been given.

"Aye," she said, "I'll warrant tha art. When tha art no fillin' thy belly tha art generally either goin' to th' Public, or comin' whoam. Aw Riggan ud go to ruin if tha wert na at th' Public fro' morn till neet looking after other folkses business. It's well for th' toun as tha'st getten nowt else to do."

Sammy puffed away at his pipe, without any appearance of disturbance.

"Aye," he consented dryly, "it is, that. It ud be a bad thing to ha' th' pits stop workin' aw because I had na attended to 'em, an' gi'en th' mesters a bit o' encouragement. Tha sees mine's what th' gentlefolk ca' a responsible position i' society. Th' biggest trouble I ha', is settlin' i' my moind what th' world 'ill do when I turn up my toes to th' daisies, an' how the government'll mak' up their moinds who shall ha' th' honor o' payin' for th' moniment."

In Mr. Craddock's opinion, his skill in the solution of political and social problems was only equalled by his aptitude in managing the weaker sex. He never lost his temper with a woman. He might be sarcastic, he was sometimes even severe in his retorts, but he was never violent. In any one else but Mr. Craddock, such conduct might have been considered weak by the male population of Riggan, who not unfrequently settled their trifling domestic difficulties with the poker and tongs, chairs, or flat-irons, or indeed with any portable piece of household furniture. But Mr. Craddock's way of disposing of feminine antagonists was tolerated. It was pretty well known that Mrs. Craddock had a temper, and since he could manage her, it was not worth while to criticise the method.

"Tha'rt an owd yommer-head," said Mrs. Craddock, as oracularly as if she had never made the observation before. "Tha deserves what tha has na getten."

"Aye, that I do," with an air of amiable regret "Tha'rt reet theer fur once i' thy loife. Th' country has na done its duty by me. If I'd had aw I deserved I'd been th' Lord Mayor o' Lunnon by this toime, an' tha'd a been th' Lady Mayoress, settin' up i' thy parlor wi' a goold crown atop o' thy owd head, sortin' out thy cloathes fur th' wesh woman i'stead o' dollyin' out thy bits o' duds fur thysen. Tha'rt reet, owd lass—tha'rt reet enow."

"Go thy ways to th' Public," retorted the old dame driven to desperation. "I'm tired o' hearkenin' to thee. Get thee gone to th' Public, or we'st ha' th' world standin' still; an' moind tha do'st na set th' horse-ponds afire as tha goes by em.

"I'll be keerful, owd lass," chuckled Sammy, taking his stick. "I'll be keerful for th' sake o' th' town."

He made his way toward the village ale-house in the best of humors. Arriving at The Crown, he found a discussion in progress. Discussions were always being carried on there in fact, but this time it was not Craddock's particular friends who were busy. There were grades even among the visitors at The Crown, and there were several grades below Sammy's. The lowest was composed of the most disreputable of the colliers—men who with Lowrie at their head were generally in some mischief. It was these men who were talking together loudly this evening, and as usual, Lowrie was the loudest in the party. They did not seem to be quarrelling. Three or four sat round a table listening to Lowrie with black looks, and toward them Sammy glanced as he came in.

"What's up in them fellys?" he asked of a friend.

"Summat's wrong at th' pit," was the answer. "I canna mak' out what mysen. Summat about one o' th' mesters as they're out wi'. What'll tha tak', owd lad?"

"A pint o' sixpenny." And then with another sidelong glance at the debaters:

"They're an ill set, that lot, an' up to summat ill too, I'll warrant. He's not the reet soart, that Lowrie."

Lowrie was a burly fellow with a surly, sometimes ferocious, expression. Drink made a madman of him, and among his companions he ruled supreme through sheer physical superiority. The man who quarrelled with him might be sure of broken bones, if not of something worse. He leaned over the table now, scowling as he spoke.

"I'll ha' no lads meddlin' an' settin' th' mesters agen me," Craddock heard him say. "Them on yo' as loikes to tak' cheek mun

44

tak' it, I'm too owd a bird fur that soart o' feed. It sticks i' my crop. Look thee out o' that theer window, Jock, and watch who passes. I'll punse that lad into th' middle o' next week, as sure as he goes by."

"Well," commented one of his companions, "aw I've gotten to say is, as tha'll be loike to ha' a punse on it, fur he's a strappin' youngster, an' noan so easy feart."

"Da'st ta mean to say as I conna do it?" demanded Lowrie fiercely.

"Nay—nay, mon," was the pacific and rather hasty reply. "Nowt o' th' soart. I on'y meant as it was na ivvery mon as could."

"Aye, to be sure!" said Sammy testily to his friend. "That's th' game is it? Theer's a feight on hond. That's reet, my lads, lay in thy beer, an' mak' dom'd fools o' thysens, an' tha'lt get a chance to sleep on th' soft side o' a paving-stone i' th' lock-ups."

He had been a fighting man himself in his young days, and had prided himself particularly upon "showing his muscle," in Riggan parlance, but he had never been such a man as Lowrie. His comparatively gentlemanly encounters with personal friends had always been fair and square, and in many cases had laid the foundation for future toleration, even amiability. He had never hesitated to "tak' a punse" at an offending individual, but he had always been equally ready to shake hands when all was over, and in some cases, when having temporarily closed a companion's eyes in the heat of an argument, he had been known to lead him to the counter of "th' Public," and bestow nectar upon him in the form of "sixpenny." But of Lowrie, even the fighting community, which was the community predominating in Riggan, could not speak so well. He was "ill-farrant," and revengeful,—ready to fight, but not ready to forgive. He had been known to bear a grudge, and remember it, when it had been forgotten by other people. His record was not a clean one, and accordingly he was not a favorite of Sammy Craddock's.

A short time afterward somebody passed the window facing the street, and Lowrie started up with an oath.

"Theer he is!" he exclaimed. "Now fur it. I thowt he'd go this road. I'll see what tha's getten to say fur thysen, my lad."

He was out in the street almost before Craddock and his companion had time to reach the open window, and he had stopped the passer-by, who paused to confront him haughtily.

"Why!" cried Sammy, slapping his knee, "I'm dom'd if it is na th' Lunnon engineer chap."

Fergus Derrick stood before his enemy with anything but a propitiatory air. That this brutal fellow who had caused him trouble enough already, should interfere with his very progress in the street, was too much for his high spirit to bear.

"I comn out here," said Lowrie, "to see if tha had owt to say to me."

"Then," replied Fergus, "you may go in again, for I have nothing."

Lowrie drew a step nearer to him.

"Art tha sure o' that?" he demanded. "Tha wert so ready wi' thy gab about th' Davys this mornin' I thowt happen tha'd loike to say summat more if a mon ud gi' yo' a chance. But happen agen yo're one o' th' soart as sticks to gab an' goes no further."

Derrick's eyes blazed, he flung out his open hand in a contemptuous gesture.

"Out of the way," he said, in a suppressed voice, "and let me pass."

But Lowrie only came nearer.

"Nay, but I wunnot," he said, "until I've said my say. Tha wert goin' to mak' me obey th' rules or let th' mesters hear on it, wert tha? Tha wert goin' to keep thy eye on me, an' report when th' toime come, wert tha? Well, th' toime has na come yet, and now I'm goin' to gi' thee a thrashin'."

He sprang upon him with a ferocity which would have flung to the earth any man who had not possessed the thews and sinews of a lion. Derrick managed to preserve his equilibrium. After the first blow, he could not control himself. Naturally, he had longed to thrash this fellow soundly often enough, and now that he had been attacked by him, he felt forbearance to be no virtue. Brute force could best conquer brute nature. He felt that he would rather die a thousand deaths than be conquered himself. He put forth all his strength in an effort that awakened the crowd—which had speedily surrounded them, Owd Sammy among the number—to wild admiration.

"Get thee unto it, lad," cried the old sinner in an ecstasy of approbation, "Get thee unto it! Tha'rt shapin' reet I see. Why, I'm dom'd," slapping his knee as usual—"I'm dom'd if he is na goin' to mill Dan Lowrie!"

To the amazement of the by-standers, it became evident in a very short time, that Lowrie had met his match. Finding it necessary to defend himself, Derrick was going to do something more. The result was that the breathless struggle for the mastery ended in a crash, and Lowrie lay upon the pavement, Fergus Derrick standing above him pale, fierce and panting.

"Look to him," he said to the men about him, in a white heat, "and remember that the fellow provoked me to it. If he tries it again, I will try again too." And he turned on his heel and walked away.

He had been far more tolerant, even in his wrath, than most men would have been, but he had disposed of his enemy effectually. The fellow lay stunned upon the ground. In his fall, he had cut his head upon the curbstone, and the blood streamed from the wound when his companions crowded near, and raised him. Owd Sammy Craddock offered no assistance; he leaned upon his stick, and looked on with grim satisfaction.

"Tha's getten what tha deserved, owd lad," he said in an undertone. "An' tha'st getten no more. I'st owe th' Lunnon chap one fro' this on. He's done a bit o' work as I'd ha' takken i' hond mysen long ago, if I'd ha' been thirty years younger, an' a bit less stiff i' th' hinges."

Fergus had not escaped without hurt himself, and the first angry excitement over, he began to feel so sharp an ache in his wrist, that he made up his mind to rest for a few minutes at Grace's lodgings before going home. It would be wise to know the extent of his injury.

Accordingly, he made his appearance in the parlor, somewhat startling his friend, who was at supper.

"My dear Fergus!" exclaimed Paul. "How excited you look!"

Derrick flung himself into a chair, feeling rather dubious about his strength, all at once.

"Do I?" he said, with a faint smile. "Don't be alarmed, Grace, I have no doubt I look as I feel. I have been having a brush with that scoundrel Lowrie, and I believe something has happened to my wrist."

He made an effort to raise his left hand and failed, succumbing to a pain so intense that it forced an exclamation from him.

"I thought it was a sprain," he said, when he recovered himself, "but it is a job for a surgeon. It is broken."

And so it proved under the examination of the nearest practitioner, and then Derrick remembered a wrench and shock which he had felt in Lowrie's last desperate effort to recover himself. Some of the small bones had broken.

Grace called in the surgeon himself, and stood by during the strapping and bandaging with an anxious face, really suffering as much as Derrick, perhaps a trifle more. He would not hear of his going home that night, but insisted that he should remain where he was.

"I can sleep on the lounge myself," he protested. "And though

47

I shall be obliged to leave you for half an hour, I assure you I shall not be away a longer time."

"Where are you going?" asked Derrick.

"To the Rectory. Mr. Barholm sent a message an hour ago, that he wished to see me upon business."

Fergus agreed to remain. When Grace was on the point of leaving the room, he turned his head.

"You are going to the Rectory, you say?" he remarked.

"Yes."

"Do you think you shall see Anice?"

"It is very probable," confusedly.

"I merely thought I would ask you not to mention this affair to her," said Derrick. The Curate's face assumed an expression at that moment, which it was well that his friend did not see. A shadow of bewilderment and anxiety fell upon it and the color faded away.

"You think—" faltered he.

"Well, I thought that perhaps it would shock or alarm her," answered Derrick. "She might fancy it to have been a more serious matter than it was."

"Very well. I think you are right, perhaps."

CHAPTER IX

The News at the Rectory

If she did not hear of the incident from Grace, Anice heard of it from another quarter.

The day following, the village was ringing with the particulars of "th' feight betwix' th' Lunnon chap an' Dan Lowrie."

Having occasion to go out in the morning, Mr. Barholm returned to luncheon in a state of great excitement.

"Dear me!" he began, almost as soon as he entered the room. "Bless my life! what ill-conditioned animals these colliers are!"

Anice and her mother regarded him questionably.

"What do you suppose I have just heard?" he went on. "Mr. Derrick has had a very unpleasant affair with one of the men who work under him—no other than that Lowrie—the young woman's father. They are a bad lot it seems, and Lowrie had a spite against Derrick, and attacked him openly, and in the most brutal manner, as he was going through the village yesterday evening."

"Are you sure?" cried Anice. "Oh! papa," and she put her hand upon the table as if she needed support.

"There is not the slightest doubt," was the answer, "everybody is talking about it. It appears that it is one of the strictest rules of the mine that the men shall keep their Davy lamps locked while they are in the pit—indeed they are directed to deliver up their keys before going down, and Derrick having strong suspicions that Lowrie had procured a false key, gave him a rather severe rating about it, and threatened to report him, and the end of the matter was the trouble of yesterday. The wonder is, that Derrick came off conqueror. They say he gave the fellow a sound thrashing. There is a good deal of force in that young man," he said, rubbing his hands. "There is a good deal of—of pluck in him—as we used to say at Oxford."

Anice shrank from her father's evident enjoyment, feeling a mixture of discomfort and dread. Suppose the tables had turned the other way. Suppose it had been Lowrie who had conquered. She had heard of horrible things done by such men in their blind rage. Lowrie would not have paused where Derrick did. The newspapers told direful tales of such struggles ending in the conquered being stamped upon, maimed, beaten out of life.

"It is very strange," she said, almost impatiently. "Mr. Grace must have known, and yet he said nothing. I wish he would come."

As chance had it, the door opened just at that moment, and

the Curate was announced. He was obliged to drop in at all sorts of unceremonious hours, and to-day some school business had brought him. The Rector turned to greet him with unwonted warmth. "The very man we want," he exclaimed. "Anice was just wishing for you. We have been talking of this difficulty between Derrick and Lowrie, and we are anxious to hear what you know about it."

Grace glanced at Anice uneasily.

"We wanted to know if Mr. Derrick was quite uninjured," she said. "Papa did not hear that he was hurt at all, but you will be able to tell us."

There was an expression in her upraised eyes the Curate had never seen there.

"He met with an injury," he answered, "but it was not a severe one. He came to my rooms last night and remained with me. His wrist is fractured."

He was not desirous of discussing the subject very freely, it was evident, even to Mr. Barholm, who was making an effort to draw him out. He seemed rather to avoid it, after he had made a brief statement of what he knew. In his secret heart, he shrank from it with a dread far more nervous than Anice's. He had doubts of his own concerning Lowrie's action in the future. Thus the Rector's excellent spirits grated on him, and he said but little.

Anice was silent too. After luncheon, however, she went into a small conservatory adjoining the room, and before Grace took his departure, she called him to her.

"It is very strange that you did not tell us last night," she said; "why did you not?"

"It was Derrick's forethought for you," he answered. "He was afraid that the story would alarm you, and as I agreed with him that it might, I remained silent. I might as well have spoken, it appears."

"He thought it would frighten me?" she said.

"Yes."

"Has this accident made him ill?"

"No, not ill, though the fracture is a very painful and inconvenient one."

"I am very sorry; please tell him so. And, Mr. Grace, when he feels able to come here, I have something to say to him."

Derrick marched into the Barholm parlor that very night with his arm in splints and bandages.

It was a specially pleasant and homelike evening to him; Mrs. Barholm's gentle heart went out to the handsome invalid. She had never had a son of her own, though it must be confessed she had yearned for one, strong and deep as was her affection for her girl.

But it was not till Derrick bade Anice good-night, that he heard what she intended to say to him. When he was going, just as he stepped across the threshold of the entrance door, she stopped him.

"Wait a minute, if you will be so good," she said, "I have something to ask of you."

He paused, half smiling.

"I thought you had forgotten," he returned.

"Oh! no, I had not forgotten," she answered. "But it will only seem a very slight thing to you perhaps." Then she began again, after a pause. "If you please, do not think I am a coward," she said.

"A coward!" he repeated.

"You were afraid to let Mr. Grace tell me about your accident last night and though it was very kind of you, I did not like it. You must not think that because these things are new and shock me, I am not strong enough to trust in. I am stronger than I look."

"My dear Miss Barholm," he protested, "I am sure of that. I ought to have known better. Forgive me if—"

"Oh," she interposed, "you must not blame yourself. But I wanted to ask you to be so kind as to think better of me than that. I want to be sure that if ever I can be of use to anybody, you will not stop to think of the danger or annoyance. Such a time may never come, but if it does—"

"I shall certainly remember what you have said," Fergus ended for her.

CHAPTER X

On the Knoll Road

The moon was shining brightly when he stepped into the open road—so brightly that he could see every object far before him unless where the trees cast their black shadows, which seemed all the blacker for the light. "What a grave little creature she is!" he was saying to himself. But he stopped suddenly; under one of the trees by the roadside some one was standing motionless; as he approached, the figure stepped boldly out into the moonlight before him. It was a woman.

"Dunnot be afeard," she said, in a low, hurried voice. "It's me, mester—it's Joan Lowrie."

"Joan Lowrie!" he said with surprise. "What has brought you out at this hour, and whom are you waiting for?"

"I'm waiting for yo'rsen," she answered.

"For me?"

"Aye; I ha' summat to say to you."

She looked about her hurriedly.

"Yo'd better come into th' shade o' them trees," she said, "I dunnot want to gi' any one a chance to see me nor yo' either."

It was impossible that he should not hesitate a moment. If she had been forced into entrapping him!

She made a sharp gesture.

"I am na goin' to do no harm," she said. "Yo' may trust me. It's th' other way about."

"I ask pardon," he said, feeling heartily ashamed of himself the next instant, "but you know—"

"Aye," impatiently, as they passed into the shadow, "I know, or I should na be here now."

A moonbeam, finding its way through a rift in the boughs and falling on her face, showed him that she was very pale.

"Yo' wonder as I'm here at aw," she said, not meeting his eyes as she spoke, "but yo' did me a good turn onct, an' I ha' na had so many done me i' my loife as I can forget one on 'em. I'm come here—fur I may as well mak' as few words on't as I con—I come here to tell yo' to tak' heed o' Dan Lowrie."

"What?" said Fergus. "He bears me a grudge, does he?"

"Aye, he bears thee grudge enow," she said. "He bears thee that much grudge that if he could lay his hond on thee, while th' heat's on him, he'd kill thee or dee. He will na be so bitter after a

52

while, happen, but he'd do it now, and that's why I warn thee. Tha has no reet to be goin' out loike this," glancing at his bandaged arm. "How could tha help thysen if he were to set on thee? Tha had better tak' heed, I tell thee."

"I am very much indebted to you," began Fergus.

She stopped him.

"Tha did me a good turn," she said. And then her voice changed. "Dan Lowrie's my feyther, an' I've stuck to him, I dunnot know why—happen cause I never had nowt else to hold to and do for; but feyther or no feyther I know he's a bad un when th' fit's on an' he has a spite agen a mon. So tak' care, I tell thee agen. Theer now, I've done. Will tha walk on first an' let me follow thee?"

Something in her mode of making this suggestion impressed him singularly.

"I do not quite understand—" he said.

She turned and looked at him, her face white and resolute.

"I dunnot want harm done," she answered. "I will na ha' harm done if I con help it, an' if I mun speak th' truth I know theer's harm afoot toneet. If I'm behind thee, theer is na a mon i' Riggan as dare lay hond on thee to my face, if I am nowt but a lass. That's why I ax thee to let me keep i' soight."

"You are a brave woman," he said, "and I will do as you tell me, but I feel like a coward."

"Theer is no need as you should," she answered in a softened voice, "Yo' dunnot seem loike one to me."

Derrick bent suddenly, and taking her hand, raised it to his lips. At this involuntary act of homage—for it was nothing less—Joan Lowrie looked up at him with startled eyes.

"I am na a lady," she said, and drew her hand away.

They went out into the road together, he first, she following at a short distance, so that nobody seeing the one could avoid seeing the other. It was an awkward and trying position for a man of Derrick's temperament, and under some circumstances he would have rebelled against it; as it was, he could not feel humiliated.

At a certain dark bend in the road not far from Lowrie's cottage, Joan halted suddenly and spoke.

"Feyther," she said, in a clear steady voice, "is na that yo' standin' theer? I thowt yo'd happen to be comin' whoam this way. Wheer has tha been?" And as he passed on, Derrick caught the sound of a muttered oath, and gained a side glimpse of a heavy, slouching figure coming stealthily out of the shadow.

53

CHAPTER XI

Nib and His Master Make a Call

"Hoo's a queer little wench," said one of the roughest Rigganite matrons, after Anice's first visit, "I wur i' th' middle o' my weshin when she coom,—up to th' neck i' th' suds,—and I wur vexed enow when I seed her standin' i' th' door, lookin' at me wi' them big eyes o' hers—most loike a babby's wonderin' at summat. 'We dunnot want none,' I says, soart o' sharp loike, th' minute I clapped my eyes on her. 'Theer's no one here as can read, an' none on us has no toime to spare if we could, so we dunnot want none.' 'Dunnot want no what?' she says. 'No tracks,' says I. And what do yo' think she does, lasses? Why, she begins to soart o' dimple up about th' corners o' her mouth as if I'd said summat reight down queer, an' she gi'es a bit o' a laff. 'Well,' she says, 'I'm glad o' that. It's a good thing, fur I hav'n't got none.' An' then it turns out that she just stopped fur nowt but to leave some owd linen an' salve for to dress that sore hond Jack crushed i' th' pit. He'd towd her about it as he went to his work, and she promised to bring him some. An' what's more, she wouldna coom in, but just gi' it me, an' went her ways, as if she had na been th' Parson's lass at aw, but just one o' th' common koind, as knowd how to moind her own business an' leave other folkses a-be."

The Rigganites became quite accustomed to the sight of Anice's small low phaeton, with its comfortable fat gray pony. She was a pleasant sight herself as she sat in it, her little whip in her small gloved hand, and no one was ever sorry to see her check the gray pony before the door.

"Anice!" said Mr. Barholm to his curate, "well! you see Anice understands these people, and they understand her. She has the faculty of understanding them. There is nothing, you may be assured, Grace, like understanding the lower orders, and entering into their feelings."

There was one member of Riggan society who had ranged himself among Miss Barholm's disciples from the date of his first acquaintance with her, who was her staunch friend and adviser from that time forward—the young master of "th' best tarrier i' Riggan." Neither Jud Bates nor Nib faltered in their joint devotions from the hour of their first introduction to "th' Parson's daughter." When they presented themselves at the Rectory together, the cordiality of Nib's reception had lessened his master's awkwardness. Nib was neither awkward nor one whit abashed upon his entrée into

54

a sphere so entirely new to him as a well-ordered, handsomely furnished house. Once inside the parlor, Jud had lost courage and stood fumbling his ragged cap, but Nib had bounced forward, in the best of good spirits, barking in friendly recognition of Miss Barholm's greeting caress, and licking her hand. Through Nib, Anice contrived to inveigle Jud into conversation and make him forget his overwhelming confusion. Catching her first glimpse of the lad as he stood upon the threshold with his dubious garments and his abashed air, she was not quite decided what she was to do with him. But Nib came to her assistance. He forced himself upon her attention and gave her something to say, and her manner of receiving him was such, that in a few minutes she found Jud sidling toward her, as she half knelt on the hearth patting his favorite's rough back. Jud looked down at her, and she looked up at Jud.

"Have you taught him to do anything?" she asked. "Does he know any tricks?"

"He'll kill more rats i' ten minutes than ony dog i' Riggan. He's th' best tarrier fur rats as tha ivver seed. He's th' best tarrier for owt as tha ivver seed. Theer is nowt as he canna do. He con feight ony dog as theer is fro' heer to Marfort." And he glowed in all the pride of possession, and stooped down to pat Nib himself.

He was quite communicative after this. He was a shrewd little fellow and had not spent his ten years in the mining districts for nothing. He was thoroughly conversant with the ways of the people his young hostess wished to hear about. He had worked in the pits a little, and he had tramped about the country with Nib at his heels a great deal. He was supposed to live with his father and grandmother, but he was left entirely to himself, unless when he was put to a chance job. He knew Joan Lowrie and pronounced her a "brave un;" he knew and reverenced "Owd Sammy Craddock;" he knew Joan's father and evidently regarded him with distrust; in fact there was not a man, woman or child in the place of whom he did not know something.

Mr. Barholm happening to enter the room during the interview, found his daughter seated on a low seat with Nib's head on her knee, and Jud a few feet from her. She was so intent on the task of entertaining her guest that she did not hear her father's entrance, and the Reverend Harold left the three together, himself in rather a bewildered frame of mind.

"Do you know?" he asked of his wife when he found her, "do you know who it is Anice is amusing in the parlor? What singular fancies the girl has, with all her good sense!"

CHAPTER XII

On Guard

Though they saw comparatively little of each other, the friendly feeling established between Anice and Joan, in their first interview, gained strength gradually as time went on. Coming home from her work at noon or at night, Joan would see traces of Anice's presence, and listen to Liz's praises of her. Liz was fond of her and found comfort in her. The days when the gray pony came to a stop in his jog-trot on the roadside before the gate had a kind of pleasurable excitement in them. They were the sole spice of her life. She understood Anice as little as she understood Joan, but she liked her. She had a vague fancy that in some way Anice was like Joan; that there was the same strength in her,—a strength upon which she herself might depend. And then she found even a stronger attraction in her visitor's personal adornments, in her graceful dress, in any elegant trifle she wore. She liked to look at her clothes and ask questions about them, and wonder how she would look if she were the possessor of such beautiful things.

"She wur loike a pictur," she would say mournfully to Joan. "She had a blue gown on, an' a hat wi' blue-bells in it, an' summat white an' soft frilled up round her neck. Eh! it wur pretty. I wish I wur a lady. I dunnot see why ivverybody canna be a lady an' have such loike."

Later Joan got up and went to the child, who lay upon the bed in a corner of the room.

There were thoughts at work within her of which Liz knew nothing. Liz only looked at her wondering as she took the sleeping baby in her arms, and began to pace the floor, walking to and fro with a slow step.

"Have I said owt to vex yo'?" said Liz.

"No, lass," was the answer, "it is na thee as worrits me. I con scarce tell what it is mysen, but it is na thee, nivver fear."

But there was a shadow upon her all the rest of the night. She did not lay the child down again, but carried it in her arms until they went to bed, and even there it lay upon her breast.

"It's queer to me as yo' should be so fond o' that choild, Joan," said Liz, standing by the side of the bed.

Joan raised her head from the pillow and looked down at the small face resting upon her bosom, and she touched the baby's cheek lightly with her finger, flushing curiously.

56

"It's queer to me too," she answered, "Get thee into bed, Liz."

Many a battle was fought upon that homely couch when Liz was slumbering quietly, and the child's soft regular breathing was the only sound to be heard in the darkened room. Amid the sordid cares and humiliations of Joan's rough life, there had arisen new ones. She had secret struggles—secret yearnings,—and added to these, a secret terror. When she lay awake thinking, she was listening for her father's step. There was not a night in which she did not long for, and dread to hear it. If he stayed out all night, she went down to her work under a load of foreboding. She feared to look into the faces of her work-fellows, lest they should have some evil story to tell, she feared the road over which she had to pass, lest at some point, its very dust should cry out to her in a dark stain. She knew her father better than the oldest of his companions, and she watched him closely.

"He's what yo' wenches ud ca' a handsum chap, that theer," said Lowrie to her, the night of his encounter with Derrick. "He's a tall chap an' a strappin' chap an' he's getten a good-lookin' mug o' his own, but," clenching his fist slowly and speaking, "I've not done wi' him yet—I has not quite done wi' him. Wait till I ha', an' then see what yo'll say about his beauty. Look yo' here, lass,"—more slowly and heavily still,—"he'll noan be so tall then nor yet so straight an' strappin'. I'll smash his good-lookin' mug if I'm dom'd to hell fur it. Heed tha that?"

Instead of taking lodgings nearer the town or avoiding the Knoll Road, as Grace advised him to do when he heard of Joan's warning, Derrick provided himself with a heavy stick, stuck a pistol into his belt every night when he left his office, and walked home as usual, keeping a sharp lookout, however.

"If I avoid the fellow," he said to Grace, "he will suspect at once that I feel I have cause to fear him; and if I give him grounds for such a belief as that I might as well have given way at first."

Strange to say he was not molested. The excitement seemed to die a natural death in the course of a few days. Lowrie came back to his work looking sullen and hard, but he made no open threats, and he even seemed easier to manage. Certainly Derrick found his companions more respectful and submissive. There was less grumbling among them and more passive obedience. The rules were not broken, openly, at least, and he himself was not defied. It was not pleasant to feel that what reason and civility could not do, a tussle had accomplished, but this really seemed to be the truth of the matter, and the result was one which made his responsibilities easier to bear.

But during his lonely walks homeward on these summer

57

nights, Derrick made a curious discovery. On one or two occasions he became conscious that he had a companion who seemed to act as his escort. It was usually upon dark or unpleasant nights that he observed this, and the first time he caught sight of the figure which always walked on the opposite side of the road, either some distance before or behind him, he put his hand to his belt, not perceiving for some moments that it was not a man but a woman. It was a woman's figure, and the knowledge sent the blood to his heart with a rush that quickened its beatings. It might have been chance, he argued, that took her home that night at this particular time; but when time after time, the same thing occurred, he saw that his argument had lost its plausibility. It was no accident, there was purpose in it; and though they never spoke to each other or in any manner acknowledged each other's presence, and though often he fancied that she convinced herself that he was not aware of her motive, he knew that Joan's desire to protect him had brought her there.

He did not speak of this even to Grace.

One afternoon in making her visit at the cottage, Anice left a message for Joan. She had brought a little plant-pot holding a tiny rose-bush in full bloom, and when she went away she left her message with Liz.

"I never see your friend when I am here," she said, "will you ask her to come and see me some night when she is not too tired?"

When Joan came home from her work, the first thing that caught her eye was a lovely bit of color,—the little rose-bush blooming on the window-sill where Anice herself had placed it.

She went and stood before it, and when Liz, who had been temporarily absent, came into the room, she was standing before it still.

"She browt it," explained Liz, "she wur here this afternoon."

"Aye," she answered, "wur she?"

"Aye," said Liz. "An', Joan, what do yo' think she towd me to tell yo'?"

Joan shook her head.

"Why, she said I were to tell yo' to go and see her some neet when yo' wur na tired,—just th' same as if yo' wur a lady. Shanna yo' go?"

"I dunnot know," said Joan awakening, "I canna tell. What does she want o' me?"

"She wants to see thee an' talk to thee, that's what,"— answered Liz,—"just th' same as if tha was a lady, I tell thee. That's her way o' doin' things. She is na a bit loike the rest o' gentlefolk. Why, she'll sit theer on that three-legged stool wi' the choild on her

58

knee an' laff an' talk to me an' it, as if she wur nowt but a common lass an' noan a lady at aw. She's ta'en a great fancy to thee, Joan. She's allus axin me about thee. If I wur thee I'd go. Happen she'd gi' thee some o' her owd cloas as she's ta'en to thee so."

"I dunnot want no owd cloas," said Joan brusquely, "an' she's noan so daft as to offer 'em to me."

"Well, I nivver did!" exclaimed Liz. "Would na tha tak' 'em? Tha nivver means to say, tha would na tak' 'em, Joan? Eh! tha art a queer wench! Why, I'd be set up for th' rest o' my days, if she'd offer 'em to me."

"Thy ways an' mine is na loike," said Joan. "I want no gentlefolks' finery. An' I tell you she would na offer 'em to me."

"I nivver con mak' thee out," Liz said, in a fret. "Tha'rt as grand as if tha wur a lady thy-sen. Tha'lt tak' nowt fro' nobody."

"Wheer's th' choild?" asked Joan.

"She's laid on th' bed," said Liz. "She wur so heavy she tired me an' I gave her a rose-bud to play wi' an' left her. She has na cried sin'. Eh! but these is a noice color," bending her pretty, large-eyed face over the flowers, and inhaling their perfume; "I wish I had a bit o' ribbon loike 'em."

CHAPTER XIII
Joan and the Picture

Notwithstanding Anice's interference in his behalf, Paul did not find his labors become very much lighter. And then after all his labor, the prospect before him was not promising. Instead of appearing easier to cope with as he learned more of it and its inhabitants, Riggan seemed still more baffling. His "district" lay in the lower end of the town among ugly back streets, and alleys; among dirt and ignorance and obstinacy. He spent his days in laboring among people upon whom he sometimes fancied he had obtained no hold. It really seemed that they did not want him— these people; and occasionally a more distressing view of the case presented itself to his troubled mind,—namely, that to those who might chance to want him he had little to offer.

He had his temporal thorn too. He found it difficult to read, hard to fix his mind on his modest sermons; occasionally he even accused himself of forgetting his duty. This had come since the night when he stood at the door and listened to his friend's warning concerning the Rector's daughter. Derrick's words were simple enough in themselves, but they had fallen upon the young Curate's ears with startling significance. He had given this significance to them himself,—in spite of himself,—and then all at once he had fallen to wondering why it was that he had never thought of such a possible denouement before. It was so very possible, so very probable; nay, when he came to think of it seriously, it was only impossible that it should not be. He had often told himself, that some day a lover would come who would be worthy of the woman he had not even hoped to win. And who was more worthy than Fergus Derrick—who was more like the hero to whom such women surrender their hearts and lives. If he himself had been such a man, he thought with the simplicity of affection, he would not have felt that there was need for fear. And the two had been thrown so much together and would be thrown together so frequently in the future. He remembered how Fergus had been taken into the family circle, and calling to mind a hundred trifling incidents, smiled at his own blindness. When the next day he received Anice's message, he received it as an almost positive confirmation. It was not like her to bestow favors from an idle impulse.

It was not so easy now to meet the girl in his visits to the Rectory: it was not easy to listen to Mr. Barholm while Anice and

60

Fergus Derrick sat apart and talked. Sometimes he wondered if the time could ever come, when his friend would be less his friend because he had rivalled him. The idea of such a possibility only brought him fresh pain. His gentle chivalric nature shrank within itself at the thought of the bereavement that double loss would be. There was little room in his mind for the envies of stronger men. Certainly Fergus had no suspicion of the existence of his secret pain. He found no alteration in his gentle friend.

Among the Reverend Paul's private ventures was a small night school which he had managed to establish by slow degrees. He had picked up a reluctant scholar here, and one there,—two or three pit lads, two or three girls, and two or three men for whose attendance he had worked so hard and waited so long that he was quite surprised at his success in the end. He scarcely knew how he had managed it, but the pupils were there in the dingy room of the National School, waiting for him on two nights in the week, upon which nights he gave them instruction on a plan of his own. He had thought the matter so little likely to succeed at first, that he had engaged in it as a private work, and did not even mention it until his friends discovered it by chance.

Said Jud Bates to Miss Barholm, during one of their confidential interviews:

"Did tha ivver go to a neet skoo?"

"No," said Anice.

Jud fondled Nib's ears patronizingly.

"I ha', an' I'm goin' again. So is Nib. He's getten one."

"Who?" for Jud had signified by a gesture that he was not the dog, but some indefinite person in the village.

"Th' little Parson."

"Say, Mr. Grace," suggested Anice. "It sounds better."

"Aye—Mester Grace—but ivverybody ca's him th' little Parson. He's getten a neet skoo i' th' town, an' he axed me to go, an' I went I took Nib an' we larned our letters; leastways I larned mine, an' Nib he listened wi' his ears up, an' th' Par—Mester Grace laffed. He wur na vext at Nib comin'. He said 'let him coom, as he wur so owdfashioned.'"

So Mr. Grace found himself informed upon, and was rather abashed at being confronted with his enterprise a few days after by Miss Barholm.

"I like it," said Anice. "Joan Lowrie learned to read and write in a night school. Mr. Derrick told me so."

A new idea seemed to have been suggested to her.

"Mr. Grace," she said, "why could not I help you? Might I?"

His delight revealed itself in his face. His first thought was a selfish, unclerical one, and sudden consciousness sent the color to his forehead as he answered her, though he spoke quite calmly.

"There is no reason why you should not—if you choose," he said, "unless Mr. Barholm should object. I need not tell you how grateful I should be."

"Papa will not object," she said, quietly.

The next time the pupils met, she presented herself in the school-room.

Ten minutes after Grace had given her work to her she was as much at home with it as if she had been there from the first.

"Hoo's a little un," said one of the boys, "but hoo does na seem to be easy feart. Hoo does not look a bit tuk back."

She had never been so near to Paul Grace during their friendship as when she walked home with him. A stronger respect for him was growing in her,—a new reverence for his faithfulness. She had always liked and trusted him, but of late she had learned to do more. She recognized more fully the purity and singleness of his life. She accused herself of having underrated him.

"Please let me help you when I can, Mr. Grace," she said; "I am not blaming anybody—there is no real blame, even if I had the right to attach it to any one; but there are mistakes now and then, and you must promise me that I may use my influence to prevent them."

She had stopped at the gate to say this, and she held out her hand. It was a strange thing that she could be so utterly oblivious of the pain she inflicted. But even Derrick would have taken her hand with less self-control. He was so fearful of wounding or disturbing her, that he was continually on his guard in her presence, and especially when she was thus warm and unguarded herself.

He had fancied before, sometimes, that she had seen his difficulties, and sympathized with him, but he had never hoped that she would be thus unreserved. His thanks came from the depths of his heart; he felt that she had lightened his burden.

After this, Miss Barholm was rarely absent from her place at the school. The two evenings always found her at work among her young women, and she made very steady progress among them.

By degrees the enterprise was patronized more freely. New pupils dropped in, and were usually so well satisfied that they did not drop out again. Grace gave all the credit to Anice, but Anice knew better than to accept it. She had been his "novelty" she said; time only would prove whether her usefulness was equal to her power of attraction.

She had been teaching in the school about three weeks, when

a servant came to her one night as she sat reading, with the information that a young woman wished to see her.

"A fine-looking young woman, Miss," added the girl. "I put her into your own room, as you give orders."

The room was a quiet place, away from the sounds of the house, which had gradually come to be regarded as Miss Barholm's. It was not a large room but it was a pretty one, with wide windows and a good view, and as Anice liked it, her possessions drifted into it until they filled it,—her books, her pictures,—and as she spent a good deal of her time there, it was invariably spoken of as her room, and she had given orders to the servants that her village visitors should be taken to it when they came.

Carrying her book in her hand, she went upstairs. She had been very much interested in what she was reading, and had hardly time to change the channel of her thought. But when she opened the door, she was brought back to earth at once.

Against the end wall was suspended a picture of Christ in the last agony, and beneath it was written, "It is finished." Before it, as Anice opened the door, stood Joan Lowrie, with Liz's sleeping child on her bosom. She had come upon the picture suddenly, and it had seized on some deep, reluctant emotion. She had heard some vague history of the Man; but it was different to find herself in this silent room, confronting the upturned face, the crown, the cross, the anguish and the mystery. She turned toward Anice, forgetting all else but her emotion. She even looked at her for a few seconds in questioning silence, as if waiting for an answer to words she had not spoken.

When she found her voice, it was of the picture she spoke, not of the real object of her visit.

"Tha knows," she said, "I dunnot, though I've heerd on it afore. What is it as is finished? I dunnot quite see. What is it?"

"It means," said Anice, "that God's Son has finished his work."

Joan did not speak.

"I have no words of my own, to explain," continued Anice. "I can tell you better in the words of the men who loved him and saw him die."

Joan turned to her.

"Saw him dee!" she repeated.

"There were men who saw him when he died you know," said Anice. "The New Testament tells us how. It is as real as the picture, I think. Did you never read it?"

The girl's face took an expression of distrust and sullenness.

"Th' Bible has na been i' my line," she answered;

63

"I've left that to th' parsons an' th' loike; but th' pictur' tuk my eye. It seemt different."

"Let us sit down," said Anice, "you will be tired of standing."

When they sat down, Anice began to talk about the child, who was sleeping, lowering her voice for fear of disturbing it. Joan regarded the little thing with a look of half-subdued pride.

"I browt it because I knowed it ud be easier wi' me than wi' Liz," she said. "It worrits Liz an' it neer worrits me. I'm so strong, yo' see, I con carry it, an' scarce feel its weight, but it wears Liz out, an' it seems to me as it knows it too, fur th' minute she begins to fret it frets too."

There was a certain shamefacedness in her manner, when at last she began to explain the object of her errand. Anice could not help fancying that she was impelled on her course by some motive whose influence she reluctantly submitted to. She had come to speak about the night school.

"Theer wur a neet skoo here once afore as I went to," she said; "I larnt to reed theer an' write a bit, but—but theer's other things I'd loike to know. Tha canst understand," she added a little abruptly, "I need na tell yo'. Little Jud Bates said as yo' had a class o' yore own, an' it come into my moind as I would ax yo' about it. If I go to th' skoo I—I'd loike to be wi' ye."

"You can come to me," said Anice. "And do you know, I think you can help me." This thought had occurred to her suddenly. "I am sure you can help me," she repeated.

When Joan at last started to go away, she paused before the picture, hesitating for a moment, and then she turned to Anice again.

"Yo' say as th' book maks it seem real as th' pictur," she said.

"It seems so to me," Anice answered.

"Will yof lend me th' book?" she asked abruptly.

Anice's own Bible lay upon a side-table. She took it up and handed it to the girl, saying simply, "I will give you this one if you will take it. It was mine."

And Joan carried the book away with her.

CHAPTER XIV

The Open "Davy"

Mester Derik

*Th' rools is ben broak agen on th' quiet bi them as broak em
afore, i naim no naimes an wudnt say nowt but our loifes is
in danger And more than one, i Only ax yo' tu Wach out. i am*

Respekfully

A honest man wi a famly tu fede

The engineer found this letter near his plate one morning on
coming down to breakfast. His landlady explained that her daughter
had picked it up inside the garden gate, where it had been thrown
upon the gravel-walk, evidently from the road.

Derrick read it twice or three times before putting it in his
pocket. Upon the whole, he was not unprepared for the intelligence.
He knew enough of human nature—such human nature as Lowrie
represented—to feel sure that the calm could not continue. If for the
present the man did not defy him openly, he would disobey him in
secret, while biding his time for other means of retaliation.

Derrick had been on the lookout for some effort at revenge;
but so far since the night Joan had met him upon the road, Lowrie
outwardly had been perfectly quiet and submissive.

After reading the letter, Derrick made up his mind to prompt
and decisive measures, and set about considering what these
measures should be, There was only one certain means of redress
and safety,—Lowrie must be got rid of at once. It would not be a
difficult matter either. There was to be a meeting of the owners that
very week, and Derrick had reports to make, and the mere mention
of the violation of the rules would be enough.

"Bah!" he said aloud. "It is not pleasant; but it must be done."

The affair had several aspects, rendering it unpleasant, but
Derrick shut his eyes to them resolutely. It seemed, too, that it was
not destined that he should have reason to remain undecided. That
very day he was confronted with positive proof that the writer of the
anonymous warning was an honest man, with an honest motive.

During the morning, necessity called him away from his men
to a side gallery, and entering this gallery, he found himself behind
a man who stood at one side close to the wall, his Davy lamp open,

his pipe applied to the flame. It was Dan Lowrie, and his stealthy glance over his shoulder revealing to him that he was discovered, he turned with an oath.

"Shut that lamp," said Derrick, "and give me your false key."

Lowrie hesitated.

"Give me that key," Derrick repeated, "or I will call the gang in the next gallery and see what they have to say about the matter."

"Dom yore eyes! does tha think as my toime 'll nivver coom?"

But he gave up the key.

"When it comes," he said, "I hope I shall be ready to help myself. Now I've got only one thing to do. I gave you fair warning and asked you to act the man toward your fellows. You have played the scoundrel instead, and I have done with you. I shall report you. That's the end of it."

He went on his way, and left the man uttering curses under his breath. If there had not been workers near at hand, Derrick might not have gotten away so easily. Among the men in the next gallery there were some who were no friends to Lowrie, and who would have given him rough handling if they had caught him just at that moment, and the fellow knew it.

Toward the end of the week, the owners came, and Derrick made his report. The result was just what he had known it would be. Explosions had been caused before by transgressions of the rules, and explosions were expensive and disastrous affairs. Lowrie received his discharge, and his fellow-workmen a severe warning, to the secret consternation of some among them.

That the engineer of the new mines was a zealous and really amiable young man, if rather prone to innovations, became evident to his employers. But his innovations were not encouraged. So, notwithstanding his arguments, the blast-furnaces held their own, and "for the present," as the easy-natured manager put it, other matters, even more important, were set aside.

"There is much to be done, Derrick," he said; "really so much that requires time and money, that we must wait a little. 'Rome, etc'."

"Ah, Rome!" returned Derrick. "I am sometimes of the opinion that Rome had better never been built at all. You will not discharge your imperfect apparatus for the same reason that you will discharge a collier,—which is hardly fair to the collier. Your blast-furnaces expose the miners to as great danger as Lowrie's pipe. The presence of either may bring about an explosion when it is least expected."

"Well, well," was the good-natured response; "we have not exploded yet; and we have done away with Lowrie's pipe."

Derrick carried the history of his ill-success to Anice, somewhat dejectedly.

"All this is discouraging to a man," said Derrick, and then he added meditatively, "As to the rest, I wonder what Joan Lowrie will think of it."

A faint sense of discomfort fell upon Anice—not exactly easy to understand. The color fluttered to her cheek and her smile died away. But she did not speak,—merely waited to hear what Derrick had to say.

He had nothing more to say about Joan Lowrie:—when he recovered himself, as he did almost immediately, he went back to the discussion of his pet plans, and was very eloquent on the subject.

Going home one evening, Derrick found himself at a turn of the road only a few paces behind Joan. He had thought much of her of late, and wondered whether she was able to take an utterly unselfish view of his action. She had a basket upon her arm and looked tired. He strode up to her side and spoke to her without ceremony.

"Let me carry that," he said. "It is too heavy for you."

The sun was setting redly, so perhaps it was the sunset that flung its color upon her face as she turned to look at him.

"Thank yo'," she answered. "I'm used to carryin' such-loike loads."

But he took her burden from her, and even if she had wished to be left to herself she had no redress, and accordingly submitted. Influences long at work upon her had rendered her less defiant than she had been in the past. There was an element of quiet in her expression, such as Derrick had not seen when her beauty first caught his attention.

They walked together silently for a while.

"I should like to hear you say that you do not blame me," said Derrick, at last, abruptly.

She knew what he meant, it was evident.

"I conna blame yo' fur doin' what were reet," she answered.

"Right,—you thought it right?"

"Why should na I? Yo' couldna ha' done no other."

"Thank you for saying that," he returned. "I have thought once or twice that you might have blamed me."

"I did na know," was her answer. "I did na know as I had done owt to mak' yo' think so ill of me."

He did not find further comment easy. He felt, as he had felt before, that Joan had placed him at a disadvantage. He so often made irritating mistakes in his efforts to read her, and in the end he seldom found that he had made any advance. Anice Barholm, with her problems and her moods, was far less difficult to comprehend than Joan Lowrie.

Liz was at the cottage door when they parted, and Liz's eyes had curiosity and wonder in them when she met her friend.

"Joan," she said, peering over the door-sill at Derrick's retreating figure, "is na that one o' th' mesters? Is na it the Lunnon engineer, Joan?"

"Yes," Joan answered briefly.

The pretty, silly creature's eyes grew larger, with a shade of awe.

"Is na it th' one as yore feyther's so bitter agen?"

"Yes."

"An' is na he a gentleman? He dunnot look loike a workin' mon. His cloas dunnot fit him loike common foakes. He mun be a gentleman."

"I've heerd foak ca' him one; an' if his cloas fit him reet, he mun be one, I suppose."

Liz looked after him again.

"Aye," she sighed, "he's a gentleman sure enow. I've seed gentlemen enow to know th' look on 'em. Did——" hesitating fearfully, but letting her curiosity get the better of her discretion nevertheless,—"did he court thee, Joan?"

The next moment she was frightened into wishing she had not asked the question. Joan turned round and faced her suddenly, pale and wrathful.

"Nay, he did na," she said. "I am na a lady, an' he is what tha ca's him—a gentleman."

68

CHAPTER XV

A Discovery

The first time that Joan appeared at the night school, the men and girls looked up from their tasks to stare at her, and whisper among themselves; but she was, to all appearances, oblivious of their scrutiny, and the flurry of curiosity and excitement soon died out. After the first visit her place was never vacant. On the nights appointed for the classes to meet, she came, did the work allotted to her, and went her way again, pretty much as she did at the mines. When in due time Anice began to work out her plan of co-operation with her, she was not disappointed in the fulfilment of her hopes. Gradually it became a natural thing for a slow and timid girl to turn to Joan Lowrie for help.

As for Joan's own progress, it was not long before Miss Barholm began to regard the girl with a new wonder. She was absolutely amazed to find out how much she was learning, and how much she had learned, working on silently and by herself. She applied herself to her tasks with a determination which seemed at times almost feverish.

"I mun learn," she said to Anice once. "I will," and she closed her hand with a sudden nervous strength.

Then again there were times when her courage seemed to fail her, though she never slackened her efforts.

"Dost tha think," she said, "dost tha think as I could ivver learn as much as tha knows thysen? Does tha think a workin' lass ivver did learn as much as a lady?"

"I think," said Anice, "that you can do anything you try to do."

By very slow degrees she had arrived at a discovery which a less close observer might have missed altogether, or at least only arrived at much later in the day of experience. Anice's thoughts were moved in this direction the night that Derrick slipped into that half soliloquy about Joan. She might well be startled. This man and woman could scarcely have been placed at a greater distance from each other, and yet those half dozen words of Fergus Derrick's had suggested to his hearer that each, through some undefined attraction, was veering toward the other. Neither might be aware of this; but it was surely true. Little as social creeds influenced Anice, she could not close her eyes to the incongruous—the unpleasant features of this strange situation. And, besides, there was a more intimate and personal consideration. Her own feeling toward

Fergus Derrick was friendship at first, and then she had suddenly awakened and found it something more. That had startled her, too, but it had not alarmed her till her eyes were opened by that accidental speech of Derrick's. After that, she saw what both Derrick and Joan were themselves blind to.

Setting her own pain aside, she stood apart, and pitied both. As for herself, she was glad that she had made the discovery before it was too late. She knew that there might have been a time when it would have been too late. As it was, she drew back,—with a pang, to be sure; but still she could draw back.

"I have made a mistake," she said to herself in secret; but it did not occur to her to visit the consequences of the mistake upon any other than herself.

The bond of sympathy between herself and Joan Lowrie only seemed to increase in strength. Meeting oftener, they were knit more closely, and drawn into deeper faith and friendship. With Joan, emotion was invariably an undercurrent. She had trained herself to a stubborn stoicism so long, and with such determination, that the habit of complete self-control had become a second nature, and led her to hold the world aloof. It was with something of secret wonder that she awoke to the consciousness of the fact that she was not holding Anice Barholm aloof, and that there was no necessity for doing so. She even found that she was being attracted toward her, and was submitting to her influence as to a spell. She did not understand at first, and wondered if it would last; but the nearer she was drawn to the girl, the less doubting and reluctant she became. There was no occasion for doubt, and her proud suspiciousness melted like a cloud in the spring sunshine. Having armed herself against patronage and curiosity, she encountered earnest friendship and good faith. She was not patronized, she was not asked questions, she was left to reveal as much of herself as she chose, and allowed to retain her own secrets as if they were her own property. So she went and came to and from the Rectory; and from spending a few minutes in Anice's room, at last fell into the habit of spending hours there. In this little room the books, and pictures, and other refinements appealed to senses unmoved before. She drew in some fresh experience with almost every breath.

One evening, after a specially discouraging day, it occurred to Grace that he would go and see Joan; and dropping in upon her on his way back to town, after a visit to a parishioner who lived upon the high-road, he found the girl sitting alone—sitting as she often did, with the child asleep upon her knee; but this time with a book lying close to its hand and her own. It was Anice's Bible.

"Will yo' set down?" she said in a voice whose sound was new to him. "Theer's a chair as yo' con tak'. I conna move fur fear o' wakenin' th' choild. I'm fain to see yo' toneet."

He took the chair and thanked her, and waited for her next words. Only a few moments she was silent, and then she looked up at him.

"I ha' been readin' th' Bible," she said, as if in desperation. "I dunnot know why, unless happen some un stronger nor me set me at it. Happen it coom out o' settin here wi' th' choild. An'—well, queer enow, I coom reet on summat about childer,—that little un as he tuk and set i' th' midst o' them, an' then that theer when he said 'Suffer th' little childer to coom unto me.' Do yo' say aw that's true? I nivver thowt on it afore,—but somehow I should na loike to think it wur na. Nay, I should na!" Then, after a moment's pause—"I nivver troubled mysen wi' readin' th' Bible afore," she went on, "I ha' na lived wi' th' Bible soart; but now—well that theer has stirred me up. If he said that—if he said it hissen—Ah! mester,"—and the words breaking from her were an actual cry,—"Aye, mester, look at th' little un here! I munnot go wrong—I munnot, if he said it hissen!"

He felt his heart beat quick, and his pulses throb. Here was the birth of a soul; here in his hands perhaps lay the rescue of two immortal beings. God help him! he cried inwardly. God help him to deal rightly with this woman. He found words to utter, and uttered them with courage and with faith. What words it matters not,—but he did not fail. Joan listened wondering, and in a passion of fear and belief.

She clasped her arms about the child almost as if seeking help from it, and wept.

"I munnot go wrong," she said over and over again. "How could I hold th' little un back, if he said hissen as she mun coom? If it's true as he said that, I'll believe aw th' rest an' listen to yo'. 'Forbid them not—'. Nay, but I wunnot—I could na ha' th' heart."

71

CHAPTER XVI

"Owd Sammy" in Trouble

"Craddock is in serious trouble," said Mr. Barholm to his wife and daughter.

"'Owd Sammy' in trouble," said Anice. "How is that, papa?"

The Reverend Harold looked at once concerned and annoyed. In truth he had cause for irritation. The laurels he had intended to win through Sammy Craddock were farther from being won to-day than they had ever been. He was beginning to feel a dim, scarcely developed, but sore conviction, that they were not laurels for his particular wearing.

"It is that bank failure at Illsbery," he answered. "You have heard of it, I dare say. There has been a complete crash, and Craddock's small savings being deposited there, he has lost everything he depended upon to support him in his old age. It is a hard business."

"Have you been to see Craddock?" Mrs. Barholm asked.

"Oh! yes," was the answer, and the irritation became even more apparent than before. "I went as soon as I heard it, last night indeed; but it was of no use. I had better have stayed away. I don't seem to make much progress with Craddock, somehow or other. He is such a cross-grained, contradictory old fellow, I hardly know what to make of him. And to add to his difficulties, his wife is so prostrated by the blow that she is confined to her bed. I talked to them and advised them to have patience, and look for comfort to the Fountain-head; but Craddock almost seemed to take it ill, and was even more disrespectful in manner than usual."

It was indeed a heavy blow that had fallen upon "Owd Sammy." For a man to lose his all at his time of life would have been hard enough anywhere; but it was trebly hard to meet with such a trial in Riggan. To have money, however small a sum, "laid by i' th' bank," was in Riggan to be illustrious. The man who had an income of ten shillings a week was a member of society whose opinion bore weight; the man with twenty was regarded with private awe and public respect. He was deferred to as a man of property; his presence was considered to confer something like honor upon an assembly, or at least to make it respectable. The Government was supposed to be not entirely oblivious of his existence, and his remarks upon the affairs of the nation, and the conduct of the Prime Minister and Cabinet, were regarded as having something more than local interest. Sammy Craddock had been the man with twenty shillings income. He had worked hard in his youth and had been too shrewd and far-sighted to spend hard. His wife had helped him, and a lucky windfall upon the decease of a parsimonious relative had done the rest. The weekly deposit in the old stocking hidden under the mattress had become a bank deposit, and by the time he was incapacitated from active labor, a decent little income was ready. When the Illsbery Bank stopped payment, not only his daily bread but his dearly valued importance was swept away from him at one fell blow. Instead of being a man of property, with a voice in the affairs of the nation, he was a beggar. He saw himself set aside among the frequenters of The Crown, his political opinions ignored, his sarcasms shorn of their point. Knowing his poverty and misfortune; the men who had stood in awe of him would begin to suspect him of needing their assistance and would avoid him accordingly.

"It's human natur'," he said. "No one loikes a dog wi' th' mange, whether th' dog's to blame or no. Th' dog may ha' getten it honest. Tis na th' dog, it's the mange as foakes want to get rid on."

"Providence?" said he to the Rector, when that portly consoler called on him. "It's Providence, is it? Well, aw I say is, that if that's th' ways o' Providence, th' less notice Providence takes o' us, th' better."

His remarks upon his first appearance at The Crown among his associates, after the occurrence of the misfortune, were even more caustic and irreverent. He was an irreverent old sinner at his best, and now Sammy was at his worst. Seeing his crabbed, wrinkled old face drawn into an expression signifying defiance at once of his ill luck and worldly comment, his acquaintances shook their heads discreetly. Their reverence for him as a man of property could not easily die out. The next thing to being a man of property, was to have possessed worldly goods which had been "made away wi'," it scarcely mattered how. Indeed even to have "made away wi' a mort o' money" one's self, was to be regarded a man of parts and of no inconsiderable spirit.

"Yo're in a mort o' trouble, Sammy, I mak' no doubt," remarked one oracle, puffing at his long clay.

"Trouble enow," returned Sammy, shortly, "if you ca' it trouble to be on th' road to th' poor-house."

"Aye, indeed!" with a sigh. "I should think so. But trouble's th' lot o' mon. Riches is deceitful an' beauty is vain—not as tha wur ivver much o' a beauty, Sammy; I canna mean that."

"Dunnot hurt thysen explaining I nivver set up fur one. I left that to thee. Thy mug wus allus thy fortune."

73

"Tha'rt fretted now, Sammy," he said. "Tha'rt fretted, an' it maks thee sharp-tongued."

"Loike as not," answered Sammy. "Frettin' works different wi' some foak to what it does wi' others. I nivver seed thee fretted, mysen. Does it ha' th' same effect on thee? If it happens to, I should think it would na harm thee,—or other foak either. A bit o' sharpness is na so hard to stand wheer it's a variety."

"Sithee, Sammy," called out a boisterous young fellow from the other side of the room. "What did th' Parson ha' to say to thee? Thwaite wur tellin' me as he carried th' prayer-book to thee, as soon as he heerd th' news. Did he read thee th' Christenin' service, or th' Burial, to gi' thee a bit o' comfort?"

"Happen he gi' him both, and throwed in th' Litany," shouted another. "How wur it, Sammy? Let's hear."

Sammy's face began to relax. A few of the knots and wrinkles showed signs of dispersing. A slow twisting of the features took place, which might have been looked upon as promising a smile in due course of time. These young fellows wanted to hear him talk, and "tak' off th' Parson." His occupation was not entirely gone, after all. It was specially soothing to his vanity to feel that his greatest importance lay in his own powers, and not altogether in more corruptible and uncertain attractions. He condescended to help himself to a pipe-full of a friend's tobacco.

"Let's hear," cried a third member of the company. "Gi' us th' tale owt an' owt, owd lad. Tha'rt th' one to do it graidely."

Sammy applied a lucifer to the fragrant weed, and sucked at his pipe deliberately.

"It's noan so much of a tale," he said, with an air of disparagement and indifference. "Yo' chaps mak' so much out o' nowt. Th' Parson's well enow i' his way, but," in naïve self-satisfaction, "I mun say he's a foo', an' th' biggest foo' fur his size I ivver had th' pleasure o' seein'."

They knew the right chord was touched. A laugh went round, but there was no other interruption and Sammy proceeded.

"Whatten yo' lads think as th' first thing he says to me wur?" puffing vigorously. "Why, he cooms in an' sets hissen down, an' he swells hissen out loike a frog i' trouble, an' ses he, 'My friend, I hope you cling to th' rock o' ages.' An' ses I, 'No I dunnot nowt o' th' soart, an' be dom'd to yo'. 'It wur na hospitible,'" with a momentary touch of deprecation,—"An' I dunnot say as it wur hospitible, but I wor na i' th' mood to be hospitible just at th' toime. It tuk him back too, but he gettin round after a bit, an' he tacklet me agen, an' we had it back'ard and for'ard betwixt us for a good haaf hour. He said it wur Providence, an' I said, happen it wur, an' happen it wurn't. I wur na

74

so friendly and familiar wi' th' Lord as he seemed to be, so I could na tell foak aw he meant, and aw he did na mean. Sithee here, lads," making a fist of his knotty old hand and laying it upon the table, "that theer's what stirs me up wi' th' parson kind. They're allus settin down to explain what th' Lordamoigty's up to, as if he wur a confidential friend o' theirs as they wur bound to back up i' some road; an' they mun drag him in endways or sideways i' their talk whether or not, an' they wun-not be content to leave him to work fur hissen. Seems to me if I wur a disciple as they ca' it, I should be ashamed i' a manner to be allus apologizin' fur him as I believed in. I dunnot say for 'em to say nowt, but I do say for 'em not to be so dom'd free an' easy about it. Now theer's th' owd Parson, he's getten a lot o' Bible words as he uses, an' he brings 'em in by the scruft o' th' neck, if he canna do no better,—fur bring 'em in he mun,—an' it looks loike he's aw i' a fever till he's said 'em an' getten 'em off his moind. An' it seems to me loike, when he has said 'em, he soart o' straightens hissen out, an' feels comfortable, loike a mon as has done a masterly job as conna be mended. As fur me, yo' know, I'm noan the Methody soart mysen, but I am na a foo', an' I know a foine loike principle when I see it, an' this matter o' religion is a foine enow thing if yo' could get it straightforward an' plain wi'out so much trimmins. But——" feeling perhaps that this was a large admission, "I am noan o' th' Methody breed mysen."

"An' so tha tellt Parson, I'll warrant," suggested one of his listeners, who was desirous of hearing further particulars of the combat.

"Well, well," admitted Craddock with the self-satisfaction of a man who feels that he has acquitted himself creditably. "Happen I did. He wur fur havin' me thank th' A'moighty fur aw ut had happent me, but I towd him as I did na quoite see th' road clear. I dunnot thank a chap as gi'es me a crack at th' soide o' th' yed. I may stand it if so be as I conna gi' him a crack back, but I dunnot know as I should thank him fur th' favor, an' not bein' one o' th' regenerate, as he ca's 'em, I dunnot feel loike singin' hymns just yet; happen it's 'cause I'm onregenerate, or happen it's human natur'. I should na wonder if it's 'pull devil, pull baker,' wi' th' best o' foak,— foak as is na prize foo's, loike th' owd Parson. Ses I to him, 'Not bein' regenerate, I dunnot believe i' so much grace afore meat. I say, lets ha' th' meat first, an' th' grace arterward.'"

These remarks upon matters theological were applauded enthusiastically by Craddock's audience. "Owd Sammy" had finished his say, however, and believing that having temporarily exhausted his views upon any subject, it was well to let the field lie fallow, he did not begin again. He turned his attention from his audience to his pipe, and the intimate friends who sat near.

"What art tha goin' to do, owd lad?" asked one.

"Try fur a seat i' Parlyment," was the answer, "or pack my bits o' duds i' a wheelbarrow, an' set th' owd lass on 'era an' tak' th' nighest road to th' Union. I mun do summat fur a bein'.'"

"That's true enow. We're main sorry fur thee, Sammy. Tak' another mug o' sixpenny to keep up thy sperrets. Theer's nowt as cheers a mon loike a sup o' th' reet soart."

"I shanna get much on it if I go to th' poor-house," remarked Sammy, filling his beer mug. "Skilly an' water-gruel dunnot fly to a raon's head, I'll warrant. Aye! I wonder how th' owd lass'll do wi'out her drop o' tea, an' how she'll stand bein' buried by th' parish? That'll be worse than owt else. She'd set her moind on ridin' to th' grave-yard i' th' shiniest hearse as could be getten, an' wi' aw th' black feathers i' th' undertaker's shop wavin' on th' roof. Th' owd wench wur quoite set i' her notion o' bein' a bit fashynable at th' last. I believe hoo'd ha' enjoyed th' ride in a quiet way. Eh, dear! I'm feart she'll nivver be able to stand th' thowt o' bein' put under i' a common style. I wish we'd kept a bit o' brass i' th' owd stockin'.'"

"It's a bad enow lookout," granted another, "but I would na gi' up aw at onct, Sammy. Happen tha could find a bit o' leet work, as ud keep thee owt o' th' Union. If tha could get a word or two spoke to Mester Hoviland, now. He's jest lost his lodge-keeper an' he is na close about payin' a mon fur what he does. How would tha loike to keep the lodge?"

"It ud be aw I'd ax," said Sammy. "I'd be main well satisfied, yo' mebbe sure; but yo' know theer's so mony lookin' out for a job o' that koind, an' I ha' na mony friends among th' quality. I nivver wur smooth-tongued enow."

True enough that. Among the country gentry, Sammy Craddock was regarded as a disrespectful, if not a dangerous, old fellow. A man who made satirical observations upon the ways and manners of his social superiors, could not be much better than a heretic. And since his associates made an oracle of him, he was all the more dangerous. He revered neither Lords nor Commons, and was not to be awed by the most imposing institutions. He did not take his hat off when the gentry rode by, and it was well known that he had jeered at several of the most important individuals in county office. Consequently, discreet persons who did not believe in the morals of "the masses" shook their heads at him, figuratively speaking, and predicted that the end of his career would be unfortunate. So it was not very likely that he would receive much patronage in the hour of his downfall.

Sammy Craddock was in an uncomfortable frame of mind when he left his companions and turned homeward. It was a bad lookout for himself, and a bad one for "th' owd lass." His sympathy for the good woman was not of a sentimental order, but it was sympathy nevertheless. He had been a good husband, if not an effusive one. "Th' owd lass" had known her only rival in The Crown and his boon companions; and upon the whole, neither had interfered with her comfort, though it was her habit and her pleasure to be loud in her condemnation and disparagement of both. She would not have felt her connubial life complete without a grievance, and Sammy's tendency to talk politics over his pipe and beer was her standard resource.

When he went out, he had left her lying down in the depths of despair, but when he entered the house, he found her up and dressed, seated by the window in the sun, a bunch of bright flowers before her.

"Well now!" he exclaimed. "Tha niwer says! What's takken thee? I thowt tha wur bedrid fur th' rest o' thy days."

"Howd thy tongue," she answered with a proper touch of wifely irritation at his levity. "I've had a bit o' company an' it's chirked me up summat. That little lass o' th' owd Parson has been settin wi' me."

"That's it, is it?"

"Aye, an' I tell yo' Sammy, she's a noice little wench. Why, she's getten th' ways o' a woman, stead o' a lass,—she's that theer quoiet an' steady, an' she's getten a face as pretty as her ways, too."

Sammy scratched his head and reflected.

"I mak' no doubt on it," he answered. "I mak' no doubt on it. It wur her, tha knows, as settlet th' foight betwixt th' lads an' th' dog. I'm wonderin' why she has na been here afore."

"Well now!" taking up a stitch in her knitting, "that's th' queer part o' it. Whatten yo' think th'little thing said, when I axt her why? She says, 'It did na seem loike I was needed exactly, an' I did na know as yo'd care to ha' a stranger coom wi'out bein' axt.' Just as if she had been nowt but a neebor's lass, and would na tak' th' liberty."

"That's noan th' owd Parson's way," said Sammy.

"Th' owd Parson!" testily; "I ha' no patience wi' him. Th' little lass is as different fro' him as chalk is fro' cheese."

77

CHAPTER XVII

The Member of Parliament

The morning following, Anice's father being called away by business left Riggan for a few days' absence, and it was not until after he had gone, that the story of Mr. Haviland's lodge-keeper came to her ears. Mr. Haviland was a Member of Parliament, a rich man with a large estate, and his lodge-keeper had just left him to join a fortunate son in America. Miss Barholm heard this from one of her village friends when she was out with the phaeton and the gray pony, and she at once thought of Sammy Craddock. The place was the very thing for him. The duties were light, the lodge was a pretty and comfortable cottage, and Mr. Haviland was known to be a generous master. If Sammy could gain the situation, he was provided for. But of course there were other applicants, and who was to speak for him? She touched up the gray pony with her whip, and drove away from the woman who had told her the news, in a perplexed frame of mind. She herself knew Mr. Haviland only by sight, his estate was three miles from the village, her father was away, and there was really no time to be lost. She drove to the corner of the road and paused there for a moment.

"Oh indeed, I must go myself," she said at last. "It is unconventional, but there is no other way." And she bent over and touched the pony again and turned the corner without any further delay.

She drove her three miles at a pretty steady trot, and at the end of the third,—at the very gates of the Haviland Park, in fact,— fortune came to her rescue. A good-humored middle-aged gentleman on a brown horse came cantering down the avenue and, passing through the gates, approached her. Seeing her, he raised his hat courteously; seeing him, she stopped her pony, for she recognized Mr. Haviland.

She bent forward a little eagerly, feeling the color rise to her face.

It was somewhat trying to find herself obliged by conscience to stop a gentleman on the highway and ask a favor of him.

"Mr. Haviland," she said. "If you have a moment to spare——"

He drew rein by her phaeton, removing his hat again. He had heard a great deal of Miss Barholm from his acquaintance among the county families. He had heard her spoken of as a rather singular young lady who had the appearance of a child, and the views of a feminine reconstructor of society. He had heard of her little phaeton too, and her gray pony, and so, though he had never seen her before, he recognized her at once.

"Miss Barholm?" he said with deference.

"Yes," answered Anice. "And indeed I am glad to have been fortunate enough to meet you here. Papa is away from home, and I could not wait for his return, because I was afraid I should be too late. I wanted to speak to you about the lodge-keeper's place, Mr. Haviland."

He had been rather of the opinion that Miss Barholm must be a terrible young woman, with a tendency to model cottages and night schools.

Young ladies who go out of the ordinary groove are not apt to be attractive to the average English mind. There are conventional charities in which they may indulge,—there are Sunday-schools, and rheumatic old women, and flannel night-caps, and Dorcas societies, and such things to which people are used and which are likely to alarm nobody. Among a class of discreet persons these are held to afford sufficient charitable exercise for any well regulated young woman; and girls whose plans branch out in other directions are looked upon with some coldness. So the country gentry, hearing of Miss Barholm and her novel fancies,—her teaching in a night school with a young curate, her friendship for the daughter of a dissipated collier, her intimate acquaintance with ragged boys and fighting terriers, her interest in the unhappy mothers of nameless babies,— hearing of these things, I say, the excellent nonenthusiasts shook their heads as the very mildest possible expression of dissent. They suspected strong-mindedness and "reform"—perhaps even politics and a tendency to advance irregular notions concerning the ballot. "At any rate," said they, "it does not look well, and it is very much better for young persons to leave these matters alone and do as others do who are guided wholly by their elders."

It was an agreeable surprise to Mr. Haviland to see sitting in her modest phaeton, a quiet girl who looked up at him with a pair of the largest and clearest eyes he had ever seen, while she told him about Sammy Craddock.

"I want the place very much for him, you see," she ended. "But of course I do not wish to be unfair to any one who may want it, and deserve it more. If there is any one who really is in greater need of it, I suppose I must give it up."

"But I am glad to tell you, there is nobody," answered Mr. Haviland quite eagerly. "I can assure you, Miss Barholm, that the half dozen men who have applied to me are without a solitary exception, unmitigated scamps—great strong burly fellows, who would, ten to one, spend their days in the public house, and their nights in my preserves, and leave their wives and children to attend to my gates. This Craddock is evidently the very man for me; I am not a model landowner, but I like to combine charity with subservience to my own interest occasionally. I have heard of the old fellow. Something of a demagogue, isn't he? But that will not frighten me. I will allow him to get the better of me in political discussion, if he will leave my pheasants alone."

"I will answer for the pheasants," said Anice, "if you will let me send him to you."

"I will see him to-morrow morning with pleasure," said Mr. Haviland. "And if there is anything else I can do, Miss Barholm——"

"Thank you, there is nothing else at present. Indeed, you do not know how grateful I feel."

Before an hour had passed, Sammy Craddock heard the good news. Anice drove back to his house and told him, without delay.

"If you will go to-morrow morning, Mr. Haviland will see you," she ended; "and I think you will be good friends, Mr. Craddock."

"Owd Sammy" pushed his spectacles up on his forehead, and looked at her.

"An' tha went at th' business o' thy own accord an' managt it i' haaf an hour!" he said. "Well, I'm dom'd,—axin your pardin fur takkin th' liberty; it's a habit I've getten—but I be, an' no mistake."

He had not time to get over his grateful amazement and recover his natural balance before she had said all she had come to say, and was gone, leaving him with "th' owd lass" and his admiration.

"Well," said Sammy, "I mun say I nivver seed nowt loike it i' my loife. To think o' th' little wench ha'in' so mich gumption, an' to think o' her takkin th' matter i' hond th' minnit she struck it! Why! hoo's getten as mich sense as a mon. Eh! but hoo's a rare un—I said it when I seed her amongst th' lads theer, an' I say it again. An' hoo is na mich bigger nor six penn'orth o' copper neyther. An' I warrant hoo nivver thowt o' fillin her pocket wi' tracks by way o' comfort. Well, tha'st noan ha' to dee i' th' Union after aw, owd lass, an' happen we con save a bit to gi' thee a graidely funeral if tha'lt mak' up thy moind to stay to th' top a bit longer."

CHAPTER XVIII

A Confession of Faith

The Sunday following the Curate's visit to Lowrie's cottage, just before the opening of the morning service at St, Michael's, Joan Lowrie entered, and walking up the side aisle, took her place among the free seats. The church members turned to look at her as she passed their pews. On her part, she seemed to see nobody and to hear nothing of the rustlings of the genteel garments stirred by the momentary excitement caused by her appearance.

The Curate, taking his stand in the pulpit that morning, saw after the first moment only two faces among his congregation. One, from among the old men and women in the free seats, looked up at him with questioning in its deep eyes, as if its owner had brought to him a solemn problem to be solved this very hour, or forever left at rest; the other, turned toward him from the Barholm pew, alight with appeal and trust. He stood in sore need of the aid for which he asked in his silent opening prayer.

Some of his flock who were somewhat prone to underrate the young Parson's talents, were moved to a novel comprehension of them this morning. The more appreciative went home saying among themselves that the young man had power after all, and for once at least he had preached with uncommon fire and pathos. His text was a brief one,—but three words,—the three words Joan had read beneath the picture of the dead Christ: "It is finished!"

If it was chance that led him to them to-day, it was a strange and fortunate chance, and surely he had never preached as he preached then.

After the service, Anice looked for Joan in vain; she had gone before the rest of the congregation.

But in the evening, being out in the garden near the holly hedge, she heard her name spoken, and glancing over the leafy barrier, saw Joan standing on the side path, just as she had seen her the first time they had spoken to each other.

"I ha' na a minnit to stay," she said without any prelude, "but I ha' summat to say to yo'."

Her manner was quiet, and her face wore a softened pallor. Even her physical power for a time appeared subdued. And yet she looked steady and resolved.

"I wur at church this mornin'." she began again almost immediately.

81

"I saw you," Anice answered.

"I wur nivver theer before. I went to see fur mysen. I ha' read the book yo' g' me, an' theer's things in it as I nivver heerd on. Mester Grace too,—he coom to see me an' I axt him questions. Theer wur things as I wanted to know, an' now it seems loike it looks clearer. What wi' th' pickur',—it begun wi' th' pictur',—an' th' book, an' what he said to-day i' church, I've made up my moind."

She paused an instant, her lips trembled.

"I dunnot want to say much about it now," she said, "I ha' not getten th' words. But I thowt as yo'd loike to know. I believe i' th' Book; I believe i' th' Cross; I believe i' Him as deed on it! That's what I coom to say."

The woman turned without another word and went away.

Anice did not remain in the garden. The spirit of Joan Lowrie's intense mood communicated itself to her. She, too, trembled and her pulse beat rapidly. She thought of Paul Grace and wished for his presence. She felt herself drawn near to him again. She wanted to tell him that his harvest had come, that his faithfulness had not been without its reward. Her own labor she only counted as chance-work.

She found Fergus Derrick in the parlor, talking to her mother.

He was sitting in his favorite position, leaning back in a chair before a window, his hands clasped behind his head. His friendly intercourse with the family had extended beyond the ceremonious epoch, when a man's attitudes are studied and unnatural. In these days Derrick was as much at ease at the Rectory as an only son might have been.

"I thought some one spoke to you across the hedge, Anice?" her mother said.

"Yes," Anice answered. "It was Joan Lowrie."

She sat down opposite Fergus, and told him what had occurred. Her voice was not quite steady, and she made the relation as brief as possible. Derrick sat looking out of the window without moving.

"Mr. Derrick," said Anice at last, after a few minutes had elapsed, "What now is to be done with Joan Lowrie?"

Derrick roused himself with a start to meet her eyes and find them almost sad.

"What now?" he said. "God knows! For one, I cannot see the end."

CHAPTER XIX

Ribbons

The light in the cottage upon the Knoll Road burned late in these days, and when Derrick was delayed in the little town, he used to see it twinkle afar off, before he turned the bend of the road on his way home. He liked to see it. It became a sort of beacon light, and as such he began to watch for it. He used to wonder what Joan was doing, and he glanced in through the curtainless windows as he passed by. Then he discovered that when the light shone she was at work. Sometimes she was sitting at the wooden table with a book, sometimes she was laboring at some task with pen and ink, sometimes she was trying to use her needle.

She had applied to Anice for instruction in this last effort. It was not long before Anice found that she was intent upon acquiring the womanly arts her life had put it out of her power to learn.

"I'd loike to learn to sew a bit," she had said, and the confession seemed awkward and reluctant "I want to learn to do a bit o' woman's work. I'm tired o' bein' neyther th' one thing nor th' other. Seems loike I've allus been doin' men's ways, an' I am na content."

Two or three times Derrick saw her passing to and fro before the window, hushing the child in her arms, and once he even heard her singing to it in a low, and evidently rarely used voice. Up to the time that Joan first sang to the child, she had never sung in her life. She caught herself one day half chanting a lullaby she had heard Anice sing. The sound of her own voice was so novel to her, that she paused all at once in her walk across the room, prompted by a queer impulse to listen.

"It moight ha' been somebody else," she said. "I wonder what made me do it. It wur a queer thing."

Sometimes Derrick met Joan entering the Rectory (at which both were frequent visitors); sometimes, passing through the hall on her way home; but however often he met her, he never felt that he advanced at all in her friendship.

On one occasion, having bidden Anice goodnight and gone out on the staircase, Joan stepped hurriedly back into the room and stood at the door as if waiting.

"What is it?" Anice asked.

Joan started. She had looked flushed and downcast, and when

83

Anice addressed her, an expression of conscious self-betrayal fell upon her.

"It is Mester Derrick," she answered, and in a moment she went out.

Anice remained seated at the table, her hands clasped before her.

"Perhaps," at last she said aloud, "perhaps this is what is to be done with her. And then—" her lips tremulous,—"it will be a work for me to do."

Derrick's friendship and affection for herself held no germ of warmer feeling. If she had had the slightest doubt of this, she would have relinquished nothing. She had no exaggerated notions of self-immolation. She would not have given up to another woman what Heaven had given to herself, any more than she would have striven to win from another woman what had been Heaven's gift to her. If she felt pain, it was not the pain of a small envy, but of a great tenderness. She was capable of making any effort for the ultimate good of the man she could have loved with the whole strength of her nature.

When she entered her room that night, Joan Lowrie was moved to some surprise by a scene which met her eyes. It was a simple thing, and under some circumstances would have meant little; but taken in connection with her remembrance of past events, it had a peculiar significance. Liz was sitting upon the hearth, with some odds and ends of bright-colored ribbon on her knee, and a little straw hat in her hand. She was trimming the hat, and using the scraps of ribbon for the purpose. When she heard Joan, she looked up and reddened somewhat, and then hung her head over her work again.

"I'm makin' up my hat agen," she said, almost deprecatingly. "It wur sich a faded thing."

"Are yo'?" said Joan.

She came and stood leaning against the fireplace, and looked down at Liz thoughtfully. The shallowness and simplicity of the girl baffled her continually. She herself, who was prompted in action by deep motive and strong feeling, found it hard to realize that there could be a surface with no depth below.

Her momentary embarrassment having died out, Liz had quite forgotten herself in the interest of her task. She was full of self-satisfaction and trivial pleasure. She looked really happy as she tried the effect of one bit of color after another, holding the hat up. Joan had never known her to show such interest in anything before. One would never have fancied, seeing the girl at this moment, that a blight lay upon her life, that she could only look back with shrinking and forward without hope. She was neither looking backward nor forward now,—all her simple energies were concentrated in her work. How was it? Joan asked herself. Had she forgotten—could she forget the past and be ready for petty vanities and follies? To Joan, Liz's history had been a tragedy—a tragedy which must be tragic to its end. There was something startlingly out of keeping in the present mood of this pretty seventeen-year-old girl sitting eager and delighted over her lapful of ribbons. Not that Joan begrudged her the slight happiness—she only wondered, and asked herself how it could be.

Possibly her silence attracted Liz's attention. Suddenly she looked up, and when she saw the gravity of Joan's face, her own changed.

"Yo're grudgin' me doin' it," she cried. "Yo' think I ha' no reet to care for sich things," and she dropped hat and ribbon on her knee with an angry gesture. "Happen I ha' na," she whimpered. "I ha' na getten no reet to no soart o' pleasure, I dare say."

"Nay," said Joan rousing herself from her revery. "Nay, yo' must na say that, Liz. If it pleases yo' it conna do no hurt; I'm glad to see yo' pleased."

"I'm tired o' doin' nowt but mope i' th' house," Liz fretted. "I want to go out a bit loike other foak. Theer's places i' Riggan as I could go to wi'out bein' slurred at—theer's other wenches as has done worse nor me. Ben Maxy towd Mary on'y yesterday as I was the prettiest lass i' th' place, fur aw their slurs."

"Ben Maxy!" Joan said slowly.

Liz twisted a bit of ribbon around her finger.

"It's not as I care fur what Ben Maxy says or what ony other mon says, fur th' matter o' that, but—but it shows as I need na be so mich ashamed o' mysen after aw, an' need na stay i' doors as if I dare na show my face."

Joan made no answer.

"An' yet," she said, smiling faintly at her own train of thought afterward, "I dunnot see what I'm complainin' on. Am I out o' patience because her pain is na deeper? Surely I am na wantin' her to mak' th' most o' her burden. I mun be a queer wench, tryin' to mak' her happy, an' then feelin' worrited at her forgettin' her trouble. It's well as she con let things slip so easy."

But there came times when she could not help being anxious, seeing Liz gradually drifting out into her old world again. She was so weak, and pretty, and frivolous, so ready to listen to rough flatteries. Riggan was more rigid in its criticism than in its morality, and criticism having died out, offence was forgotten through indifference rather than through charity. Those who had been

85

hardest upon Liz in her day of darkness were carelessly ready to take her up again when her fault was an old story overshadowed by some newer scandal.

Joan found herself left alone with the child oftener than she used to be, but in truth this was a relief rather than otherwise. She was accustomed to solitude, and the work of self-culture she had begun filled her spare hours with occupation.

Since his dismissal from the mines, she saw but little of her father. Sometimes she saw nothing of him for weeks. The night after he lost his place, he came into the house, and making up a small bundle of his personal effects, took a surly leave of the two women.

"I'm goin' on th' tramp a bit," he said. "If yo're axed, yo' con say I'm gone to look fur a job. My day has na coom yet, but it's on th' way."

Since then he had only returned once or twice, and his visits had always been brief and unexpected, and at night. The first time he had startled Joan by dropping in upon her at midnight, his small bundle on his knob-stick over his shoulder, his clothes bespattered with road-side mud. He said nothing of his motive in coming—merely asked for his supper and ate it without much remark.

"I ha' na had luck," he said. "Luck's not i my loine; I wur na born to it, loike some foak. Happen th' tide'll tak' a turn after a bit."

"Yore feyther wur axin me about th' engineer," Liz said to Joan the next morning. "He wanted to know if we seed him pass heer i' his road hoam. D'yo' think he's getten a spite agen th' engineer yet, Joan?"

"I'm afeard," Joan answered. "Feyther's loike to bear a grudge agen them as put him out, whether they're reet or wrong. Liz——" hesitating.

"What is it, Joan?"

"Dunnot yo' say no more nor yo' con help when he axes yo' about th' engineer. I'm worritin' mysen lest feyther should get hissen into trouble. He's hasty, yo' know."

In the evening she went out and left the child to its mother. She had business to look after, she told Liz, and it would keep her out late. Whatever the business was, it kept her out so late that Liz was tired of waiting, and went to bed worn out and a trifle fretted.

She did not know what hour it was when she awakened; voices and a light in the road roused her, and almost as soon as she was fully conscious, the door opened and Joan came in. Liz raised her head from the pillow to look at her. She was pale and seemed excited. She was even trembling a little, and her voice was unsteady as she asked,

"Has th' little un been quiet, Liz?"

86

"Quiet enow," said Liz. "What a toime yo' ha' been, Joan! It mun be near midneet. I got so worn out wi' waitin' fur yo' that I could na sit up no longer. Wheer ha' yo' been?"

"I went to Riggan," said Joan, "Theer wur summat as I wur obliged to see to, an' I wur kept beyond my toime by summat as happent. But it is na quoite midneet, though it's late enow."

"Was na theer a lantern wi' yo'?" asked Liz. "I thowt I seed th' leet fro' a lantern."

"Yes," Joan answered, "theer wur a lantern. As I wur turnin' into th' road, I met Mester Derrick comin' fro' th' Rectory an'—an' he walked alongside o' me."

CHAPTER XX

The New Gate-Keeper

Sammy Craddock made his appearance at Mr. Haviland's promptly, and being shown into the library, which was empty, took a seat and proceeded to regard the surroundings critically.

"Dunnot scald thy nose wi' thy own broth," Mrs. Craddock had said to him warningly, when he left her. "Keep a civil tongue i' thy head. Thy toime fur saucin' thy betters is past an' gone. Tha'lt ha' to tak' both fat an' lean together i' these days, or go wi'out mate."

Sammy remembered these sage remarks rather sorely, as he sat awaiting the master of the household. His independence had been very dear to him, and the idea that he must relinquish it was a grievous thorn in the flesh. He glanced round at the pictures and statuettes and shook his head dubiously.

"A mon wi' so many crinkum-crankums as he seems to ha' getten 'll be apt to be reyther set i' polytics. An' I'll warrant this is na th' best parlor neyther. Aw th' wall covered wi' books too, an' a ornymental step-lather to climb up to th' high shelves. Well, Sammy, owd lad, tha's not seen aw th' world yet, tha finds out. Theer's a bit o' summat outside Riggan. After aw, it does a mon no hurt to travel. I should na wonder if I mought see things as I nivver heerd on if I getten as fur as th' Contynent. Theer's France now—foak say as they dunnot speak Lancashire i' France, an' conna so much as understand it. Well, theer's ignorance aw o'er th' world."

The door opened at this juncture, and Mr. Haviland entered—fresh, florid and cordial. His temperament being an easy one, he rather dreaded collision with anybody, and would especially have disliked an uncomfortable interview with this old fellow. He would like to be able to preserve his affability of demeanor for his own sake as well as for Miss Barholm's.

"Ah!" he said, "Craddock, is it? Glad to see you, Craddock."

Sammy rose from his seat

"Aye," he answered. "Sam'll Craddock fro' Riggan. Same to you, Mester."

Mr. Haviland waved his hand good-naturedly.

"Take your seat again," he said. "Don't stand. You are the older man of the two, you know, and I dare say you are tired with your walk. You came about the lodge-keeper's place?"

"That little lass o' th' owd Parson's——" began Sammy.

"Miss Anice Barholm," interposed Mr. Haviland. "Yes, she

told me she would send you. I never had the pleasure of seeing her until she drove here yesterday to ask for the place for you. She was afraid to lose time in waiting for her father's return."

"Yo' nivver saw her afore?"

"No."

"Well," rubbing his hands excitedly over the knob of his stick, "hoo's a rarer un than I thowt fur, even. Hoo'll stond at nowt, wont that little wench," and he gave vent to his feelings in a delighted chuckle. "I'd loike to ax yo'," he added, "wheer's th' other lass, as ud ha' had the pluck to do as mich?"

"I don't think there is another woman in the country who would have done it," said Mr. Haviland smiling. "We shall agree in our opinion of Miss Barholm, I see, Craddock, if we quarrel about everything else."

Sammy took out his flowered bandanna and wiped his bald forehead. He was at once mollified and encouraged. He felt that he was being treated with a kind of respect and consideration. Here was one of the gentry who placed himself on a friendly footing with him. Perhaps upon the whole he should not find it so difficult to reconcile himself to his change of position after all. And being thus encouraged, a certain bold simplicity made him address himself to Mr. Haviland not as a servant in prospective to a prospective master, but as man to man.

"Th' fact is," he said, "as I am na mich o' a lass's mon mysen, and I wunnot say as I ha' mich opinion o' woman foak i' general—they're flighty yo' see—they're flighty; but I mun say as I wur tuk by that little wench o' th' Parson's—I wur tuk by her."

"She would be glad to hear it, I am sure," with an irony so suave that Sammy proceeded with fresh gravity.

"I mak' no doubt on't," dogmatically. "I mak' no doubt on't i' th' world, but I dunnot know as th' flattery ud do her good. Sugar sop is na o'er digestible to th' best o' 'em. They ha' to be held a bit i' check, yo' see. But hoo's a wonderfu' little lass—fur a lass, I mun admit. Seems a pity to ha' wasted so mich good lad metal on a slip o' a wench,—does na it?"

"You think so? Well, that is a matter of opinion, you know. However—concerning the lodge-keeper's place. You understand what your duties would be, I suppose?"

"Tendin' th' gates an' th' loike. Aye sir. Th' little lass towd me aw about it. Hoo is na one as misses owt."

"So I see," smiling again. "And you think you can perform them?"

"I wur thinkin' so. It did na stroike me as a mon need to be partic'lar muskylar to do th' reet thing by 'em. I think I could tackle 'em wi'out breakin' down."

After a brief discussion of the subject, it was agreed that Mr. Craddock should be installed as keeper of the lodge the week following.

"As to politics," said Mr. Haviland, when his visitor rose to depart, "I hear you are something of a politician, Craddock."

"Summat o' one, sir," answered Sammy, his evident satisfaction touched with a doubtful gravity. "Summat o' one. I ha' my opinions o' things i' gineral."

"So I have been told; and they have made you rather unpopular among our county people, per-haps?"

"I am na mich o' a favorite," with satisfaction.

"No, the fact is that until Miss Barholm came to me I had rather a bad idea of you, Craddock."

This looked somewhat serious, Craddock regarding it rather in the light of a challenge.

"I'd loike well enow to ha' yo' change it," he said, "but my coat is na o' th' turnin' web. I mun ha' my say about things—gentry or no gentry." And his wrinkled old visage expressed so crabbed a determination that Mr. Haviland laughed outright.

"Oh! don't misunderstand me," he said, "stick to your party, Craddock. We will try to agree, for Miss Barholm's sake. I will leave you to your opinion, and you will leave me to mine—even a Member of Parliament has a right to an opinion, you know, if he doesn't intrude it upon the public too much."

Craddock went home in a mollified frame of mind. He felt that he had gained his point and held his ground, and he respected himself accordingly. He felt too that his associates had additional right to respect him. It was their ground too, and he had held it for them as well as for himself. He stopped at The Crown for his midday glass of ale; and his self-satisfaction was so evident that his friends observed it, and remarked among themselves that "th' owd lad wur pickin' up his crumbs a bit."

"Yo're lookin' graidely to-day, Sammy," said one.

"I'm feelin' a trifle graidelier than I ha' done," he answered, oracularly. "Things is lookin' up."

"I'm main glad to hear it. Tell us as how."

"Well,"—with studied indifference,—"it's noan so great luck i' comparison, but it's summat to be thankfu' fur to a mon as is down i' th' world. I've getten the lodge-keeper's place at Mr. Haviland's."

"Tha' nivver says! Who'd a' thowt it? How ivver did that coom about?"

"Friends i' coort," with dignity. "Friends i' coort. Hond me

90

that jug o' ale, Tummy. Haviland's a mon o' discretion, if he is a Member o' Parlyment. We've had quoite a friendly chat this mornin' as we set i' th' loibery together. He is na so bad i' his pollytics after aw's said an' done. He'll do, upo' th' whole."

"Yo' stood up to him free enow, I warrant," said Tummy. "Th' gentle folk dunnot often hear sich free speakin' as yo' gi' 'em, Sammy."

"Well, I had to be a bit indypendent; it wur nat'ral. It would na ha' done to ha' turnt soft, if he wur th' mester an' me th' mon. But he's a mon o' sense, as I say, an' he wur civil enow, an' friendly enow. He's getten gumption to see as pollytics is pollytics. I'll tell yo' what, lads, I'm comin' to th' opinion as happen theer's more sense i' some o' th' gentry than we gi' em credit fur; they ha' not mich but book larnin i' their heads, it's true, but they're noan so bad—some on 'em—if yo're charytable wi' 'em."

"Who was thy friend i' coort, Sammy?" was asked next.

Sammy's fist went down upon the table with a force which made the mugs dance and rattle.

"Now tha'rt comin' to the meat i' th' egg." he said. "Who should tha think it wur 'at had th' good-will an' th' head to tak' th' business i' hond?"

"It ud be hard to say."

"Why, it wur that little lass o' th' owd Parsen's again. Dom'd if she wunnot run aw Riggan i' a twelvemonth. I dunnot know wkeer she getten her head-fillin' fro' unless she robbed th' owd Parson, an' left his nob standin' empty. Happen that's what's up wi' th' owd chap."

91

CHAPTER XXI

Derrick's Question

Derrick had had a great deal to think about of late. Affairs at the mines had been troublesome, as usual, and he had been often irritated by the stupidity of the men who were in authority over him. He began to feel, moreover, that an almost impalpable barrier had sprung up between himself and his nearest friend. When he came to face the matter, he was obliged to acknowledge to himself that there were things he had kept from Grace, though it had been without any positive intention of concealment And, perhaps, being the sensitive fellow he had called him, Grace had felt that there was something behind his occasional abstraction and silence, and had shrunk within himself, feeling a trifle hurt at Derrick's want of frankness and confidence.

Hardly a day passed in which he did not spend some short time in the society of his Pythias. He rarely passed his lodgings without dropping in, and, to-night, he turned in on his way from the office, and fell upon Grace hard at work over a volume of theology.

"Lay your book aside," he said to him. "I want to gossip this evening, old fellow."

Grace closed his book and came to his usual seat, smiling affectionately. There was a suggestion of feminine affectionateness in his bearing toward his friend.

"Gossip," he remarked. "The word gossip——

"Oh," put in Derrick, "it's a woman's word; but I am in a womanish sort of humor. I am going to be—I suppose, one might say—confidential."

The Reverend Paul reddened a little but as Derrick rather avoided looking at him he did not observe the fact.

"Grace," he said, after a silence, "I have a sort of confession to make. I am in a difficulty, and I rather blame myself for not having come to you before."

"Don't blame yourself," said the Curate, faintly. "You—you are not to blame."

Then Derrick glanced up at him quickly. This sounded so significant of some previous knowledge of his trouble, that he was taken aback. He could not quite account for it.

"What!" he exclaimed. "Is it possible that you have guessed it already?"

"I have thought so—sometimes I have thought so—though I feel as if I ought almost to ask your pardon for going so far."

Grace had but one thought as he spoke. His friend's trouble meant his friend's honor and regard for himself. It was for his sake that Derrick was hesitating on the brink of a happy love—unselfishly fearing for him. He knew the young man's impetuous generosity, and saw how under the circumstances, it might involve him. Loving Anice Barholm with the full strength of a strong nature, Derrick was generous enough still to shrink from his prospect of success with the woman his friend had failed to win.

Derrick flung himself back in his chair with a sigh. He was thinking, with secret irritation, that he must have felt even more than he had acknowledged to himself since he had in all unconsciousness, confessed so much.

"You have saved me the trouble of putting into words a feeling I have not words to explain," he said. "Perhaps that is the reason why I have not spoken openly before. Grace,"—abruptly,—"I have fancied there was a cloud between us."

"Between us!" said Grace, eagerly and warmly. "No, no! That was a poor fancy indeed; I could not bear that."

"Nor I," impetuously. "But I cannot be explicit even now, Grace—even my thoughts are not explicit. I have been bewildered and—yes, amazed—amazed at finding that I had gone so far without knowing it. Surely there never was a passion—if it is really a passion—that had so little to feed upon."

"So little!" echoed Grace.

Derrick got up and began to walk across the floor.

"I have nothing—nothing, and I am beset on every side."

There was something extraordinary in the blindness of a man with an absorbing passion. Absorbed by his passion for one woman, Grace was blind to the greatest of inconsistencies in his friend's speech and manner. Absorbed in his passion for another woman, Derrick forgot for the hour everything concerning his friend's love for Anice Barholm.

Suddenly he paused in his career across the room.

"Grace," he said, "I cannot trust myself; but I can trust you, I cannot be unselfish in this—you can. Tell me what I am to do—answer me this question, though God knows, it would be a hard one for any man to answer. Perhaps I ought not to ask it—perhaps I ought to have decision enough to answer it myself without troubling you. But how can I? And you who are so true to yourself and to me in other things, will be true in this I know. This feeling is stronger than all else—so strong that I have feared and failed to comprehend it. I had not even thought of it until it came upon me with fearful force, and I am conscious that it has not reached its height yet. It is not an ignoble passion, I know. How could a passion for such a creature be ignoble? And yet again, there have been times when I have felt that perhaps it was best to struggle against it. I am beset on every side, as I have said, and I appeal to you. Ought love to be stronger than all else? I used to tell myself so, before it came upon me—and now I can only wonder at myself and tremble to find that I have grown weak."

God knows it was a hard question he had asked of the man who loved him; but this man did not hesitate to answer it as freely as if he had had no thought that he was signing the death-warrant of all hopes for himself. Grace went to him and laid a hand upon his broad shoulder.

"Come, sit down and I will tell you," he said, with a pallid face.

Derrick obeyed his gentle touch with a faint smile.

"I am too fiery and tempestuous, and you want to cool me," he said. "You are as gentle as a woman, Grace."

The Curate standing up before him, a slight, not at all heroic figure in his well worn, almost threadbare garments, smiled in return.

"I want to answer your question," he said, "and my answer is this: When a man loves a woman wholly, truly, purely, and to her highest honor,—such a love is the highest and noblest thing in this world, and nothing should lead to its sacrifice,—no ambition, no hope, no friendship."

94

CHAPTER XXII

Master Landsell's Son

"I dunnot know what to mak' on her," Joan said to Anice, speaking of Liz. "Sometimes she is i' sich sperrits that she's fairly flighty, an' then agen, she's aw fretted an' crossed with ivvery-thing. Th' choild seems to worrit her to death."

"That lass o' Lowrie's has made a bad bargain, i' takin' up wi' that wench," said a townswoman to Grace. "She's noan one o' th' soart as 'll keep straight. She's as shallow as a brook i' midsummer. What's she doin' leavin' th' young un to Joan, and gaddin' about wi' ribbons i' her bonnet? Some lasses would na ha' th' heart to show theirsens."

The truth was that the poor weak child was struggling feebly in deep water again. She had not thought of danger. She had only been tired of the monotony of her existence, and had longed for a change. If she had seen the end she would have shrunk from it before she had taken her first step. She wanted no more trouble and shame, she only wanted variety and excitement.

She was going down a by-lane leading to the Maxy's cottage, and was hurrying through the twilight, when she brushed against a man who was lounging carelessly along the path, smoking a cigar, and evidently enjoying the balmy coolness of the summer evening. It was just light enough for her to see that this person was well-dressed, and young, and with a certain lazily graceful way of moving, and it was just light enough for the man to see that the half-frightened face she lifted was pretty and youthful. But, having seen this much, he must surely have recognized more, for he made a quick backward step. "Liz!" he said. "Why, Liz, my girl!" And Liz stood still. She stood still, because, for the moment, she lost the power of motion. Her heart gave a great wild leap, and, in a minute more, she was trembling all over with a strange, dreadful emotion. It seemed as if long, terrible months were blotted out, and she was looking into her cruel lover's face, as she had looked at it last. It was the man who had brought her to her greatest happiness and her deepest pain and misery. She could not speak at first; but soon she broke into a passion of tears. It evidently made the young man uncomfortable—perhaps it touched him a little. Ralph Landsell's nature was not unlike Liz's own. He was invariably swayed by the passing circumstance,—only, perhaps, he was a trifle more easily moved by an evil impulse than a good one. The beauty of the girl's tearful face, too, overbalanced his first feeling of irritation at seeing her and finding that he was in a difficult position. Then he did not want her to run away and per-haps betray him in her agitation, so he put out his hand and laid it on her shoulder.

"Hush," he said. "Don't cry. What a poor little goose you are. Somebody will hear you."

The girl made an effort to free herself from his detaining hand, but it was useless. Light as his grasp was, it held her.

"Let me a-be," she cried, sobbing petulantly. "Yo' ha' no reet to howd me. Yo' were ready enow to let me go when—when I wur i' trouble."

"Trouble!" he repeated after her. "Wasn't I in trouble, too? You don't mean to say you did not know what a mess I was in? I'll own it looked rather shabby, Liz, but I was obliged to bolt as I did. I hadn't time to stay and explain. The governor was down on us, and there'd have been an awful row. Don't be hard on a fellow, Lizzie. You're—you're too nice a little girl to be hard on a fellow."

But Liz would not listen.

"Yo' went away an' left me wi'out a word," she said; "yo' went away an' left me to tak' care o' mysen when I could na do it, an' had na strength to howd up agen th' world. I wur turned out o' house an' home, an' if it had na been fur th' hospytal, I might ha' deed i' th' street. Let me go. I dunnot want to ha' awt to do wi' yo'. I nivver wanted to see yore face agen. Leave me a-be. It's ower now, an' I dunnot want to get into trouble agen."

He drew his hand away, biting his lip and frowning boyishly. He had been as fond of Liz as such a man could be. But she had been a trouble to him in the end, and he had barely escaped, through his cowardly flight, from being openly disgraced and visited by his father's wrath.

"If you had not gone away in such a hurry, you would have found that I did not mean to treat you so badly after all," he said. "I wrote to you and sent you money, and told you why I was obliged to leave you for the time, but you were gone, and the letter was returned to me. I was not so much to blame."

"Th' blame did na fa' on yo'," said Liz. "I tell yo' I wur turnt out, but—it—it does na matter now," with a sob.

Now that she was out of his reach, he discovered that she had not lost all her old attractions for him. She was prettier than ever,—the shawl had slipped from her curly hair, the tears in her eyes made them look large and soft, and gave her face an expression of most pathetic helplessness,—and he really felt that he would like to defend, if not clear himself. So, when she made a movement as if to leave him, he was positively anxious to detain her.

"You are not going?" he said. "You won't leave a fellow in this way, Lizzie?"

The old tone, half caressing, half reproachful, was harder for the girl to withstand than a stronger will could comprehend. It brought back so much to her,—those first bright days, her poor, brief little reign, her childish pleasures, his professed love for her, all her lost delight. If she had been deliberately bad, she would have given way that instant, knowing that she was trifling on the brink of sin once more. But she was not bad, only emotional, weak and wavering. The tone held her one moment and then she burst into fresh tears.

"I wunnot listen to yo'," she cried. "I wunnot listen to yo'. I wunnot—I wunnot," and before he had time to utter another word, she had turned and fled down the lane back toward Joan's cottage, like some hunted creature fleeing for life.

Joan, sitting alone, rose in alarm, when she burst open the door and rushed in. She was quivering from head to foot, panting for breath, and the tears were wet upon her cheeks.

"What is it?" cried Joan. "Lizzie, my lass, what ails yo'?"

She threw herself down upon the floor and hid her face in the folds of Joan's dress.

"I—ha'—I ha' seed a ghost, or—summat," she panted and whimpered. "I—I met summat as feart me."

"Let me go and look what it wur," said Joan. "Was it i' th' lane? Tha art tremblin' aw o'er, Lizzie."

But Liz only clung to her more closely.

"Nay—nay," she protested. "Tha shall na go. I'm feart to be left—an'—an' I dunnot want yo' to go. Dunnot go, Joan, dunnot."

And Joan was fain to remain.

She did not go out into the village for several days after this, Joan observed. She stayed at home and did not even leave the cottage. She was not like herself, either. Up to that time she had seemed to be forgetting her trouble, and gradually slipping back into the enjoyments she had known before she had gone away. Now a cloud seemed to be upon her. She was restless and nervous, or listless and unhappy. She was easily startled, and now and then Joan fancied that she was expecting something unusual to happen. She lost color and appetite, and the child's presence troubled her more than usual. Once, when it set up a sudden cry, she started, and the next moment burst into tears.

"Why, Liz!" said Joan, almost tenderly. "Yo' mun be ailin', or yo' hannot getten o'er yo're fright yet. Yo're not yoresen at aw. What a simple little lass yo' are to be feart by a boggart i' that way."

97

"I dunnot know what's the matter wi' me," said Liz, "I dunnot feel reet, somehow. Happen I shall get o'er it i' toime."

But though she recovered herself somewhat, she was not the same girl again. And this change in her it was that made Joan open her heart to Anice. She saw that something was wrong, and noted a new influence at work even after the girl began to go out again and resume her visits to her acquaintances. Then, alternating with fretful listlessness, were tremulous high spirits and feverish fits of gayety.

There came a day, however, when Joan gained a clue to the meaning of this change, though never from her first recognition of it until the end did she comprehend it fully. Perhaps she was wholly unconscious of what narrower natures experience. Then, too, she had little opportunity for hearing gossip. She had no visitors, and she was kept much at home with the child, who was not healthy, and who, during the summer months, was constantly feeble and ailing.

Grace, hearing nothing more after the first hint of suspicion, was so far relieved that he thought it best to spare Joan the pain of being stung by it.

But there came a piece of news to Joan that troubled her.

"Theer's a young sprig o' one o' th' managers stayin' at th' 'Queen's Arms,'" remarked a pit woman one morning. "He's a foine young chap, too—dresses up loike a tailor's dummy, an' looks as if he'd stepped reet square out o' a bandbox. He's a son o' owd Landsell's."

Joan stopped a moment at her work.

"Are yo' sure o' that?" she asked, anxiously.

"Sure he's Mester Landsell's son? Aye, to be 'sure it's him. My mester towd me hissen."

This was Liz's trouble, then.

At noon Joan went home full of self-reproach because sometimes her patience had failed her. Liz looked up with traces of tears in her eyes, when Joan came in. Joan did not hesitate. She only thought of giving her comfort. She went and sat down in a chair near by—she drew the curly head down upon her lap, and laid her hand on it caressingly.

"Lizzie, lass," she said; "yo' need na ha' been afeard to tell me."

There was a quick little pant from Liz, and then stillness.

"I heard about it to-day," Joan went on, "an' I did na wonder as yo' wur full o' trouble. It brings it back, Liz, I dare say."

The pant became a sob—the sob broke into a low cry.

98

"Oh, Joan! Joan! dunnot blame me—dunnot. It wur na my fault as he coom, an'—an' I canna bear it."

Even then Joan had no suspicion. To her mind it was quite natural that such a cry of pain should be wrung from the weak heart. Her hand lost its steadiness as she touched the soft, tangled hair more tenderly than before.

"He wur th' ghost as yo' seed i' th' lane," she said. "Wur na he?"

"Aye," wept Liz, "he wur, an' I dare na tell yo'. It seemit loike it tuk away my breath, an' aw my heart owt o' me. Nivver yo' blame me, Joan—nivver yo' be hard on me—ivverything else is hard enow. I thowt I wur safe wi' yo'—I did fur sure."

"An' yo' are safe," Joan answered. "Dost tha' think I would turn agen thee? Nay, lass; tha'rt as safe as th' choild is, when I hold it i' my breast. I ha' a pain o' my own, Liz, as 'll nivver heal, an' I'd loike to know as I'd held out my hond to them as theer is healin' fur. I'd thank God fur th' chance—poor lass—poor lass—poor lass!" And she bent down and kissed her again and again.

CHAPTER XXIII

"Cannybles"

The night school gained ground steadily. The number of scholars was constantly on the increase, so much so, indeed, that Grace had his hands inconveniently full.

"They have dull natures, these people," said the Reverend Harold; "and in the rare cases where they are not dull, they are stubborn. Absolutely, I find it quite trying to face them at times, and it is not my fortune to find it difficult to reach people, as a rule. They seem to have made up their minds beforehand to resent what I am going to say. It is most unpleasant. Grace has been working among them so long that, I suppose, they are used to his methods; he has learned to place himself on a level with them, so to speak. I notice they listen to, and seem to understand him. The fact is, I have an idea that that sort of thing is Grace's forte. He is not a brilliant fellow, and will never make any particular mark, but he has an odd perseverance which carries him along with a certain class. Riggan suits him, I think. He has dropped into the right groove."

Jud Bates and "th' best tarrier i' Riggan" were among the most faithful attendants. The lad's fancy for Anice had extended to Grace. Grace's friendly toleration of Nib had done much for him. Nib always appeared with his master, and his manner was as composed and decorous as if rats were subjects foreign to his meditations. His part it was to lie at Jud's feet, his nose between his paws, his eyes twinkling sagaciously behind his shaggy eyebrows, while occasionally, as a token of approval, he wagged his tail. Once or twice, during a fitful slumber, he had been known to give vent to his feelings in a sharp bark, but he never failed to awaken immediately, with every appearance of the deepest abasement and confusion at the unconscious transgression.

During a visit to the Rectory one day, Jud's eyes fell upon a book which lay on Anice's table. It was full of pictures—illustrations depicting the adventures and vicissitudes of a fortunate unfortunate, whose desert island has been the paradise of thousands; whose goat-skin habiliments have been more worthy of envy than kingly purple; whose hairy cap has been more significant of monarchy than any crown. For the man who wore these savage garments has reigned supreme in realms of romance, known only in their first beauty to boyhood's ecstatic belief.

Jud put out his hand, and drawing the gold and crimson snare toward him, opened it. When Anice came into the room she found him poring over it. His ragged cap lay with Nib, at his feet, his face was in a glow, his hair was pushed straight up on his head, both elbows were resting on the table. He was spelling his way laboriously, but excitedly, through the story of the foot-print on the sand. Anice waited a moment, and then spoke:

"Jud," she said, "when you can read I will give you 'Robinson Crusoe.'"

In less than six months she was called upon to redeem her promise.

This occurred a few weeks after Craddock had been established at the lodge at the Haviland gates. The day Anice gave Jud his well-earned reward, she had a package to send to Mrs. Craddock, and when the boy came for the book, she employed him as a messenger to the park.

"If you will take these things to Mrs. Craddock, Jud, I shall be much obliged," she said; "and please tell her that I will drive out to see her to-morrow."

Jud accepted the mission readily. With Nib at his heels and "Robinson Crusoe" under his arm, three miles were a trivial matter. He trudged off, whistling with keen delight. As he went along he could fortify himself with an occasional glance at the hero and his man Friday. What would he not have sacrificed at the prospect of being cast with Nib upon a desert island?

"Owd Sammy" sat near the chimney-corner smoking his pipe, and making severe mental comments upon the conduct of Parliament, then in session, of whose erratic proceedings he was reading an account in a small but highly seasoned newspaper. Sammy shook his head ominously over the peppery reports, but feeling it as well to reserve his opinions for a select audience at The Crown, allowed Mrs. Craddock to perform her household tasks unmolested.

Hearing Jud at the door, he turned his head.

"It's yo', is it?" he said. "Tha con coom in. What's browten?"

"Summat fur th' missis fro' th' Rectory," Jud answered, producing his parcel; "Miss Anice sent me wi' it."

"Tak' it to th' owd lass, then," said Sammy. "Tak' it to her. Tha'lt find her in th' back kitchen."

Having done as he was bidden, Jud came back again to the front room. Mrs. Craddock had hospitably provided him with a huge sandwich of bread and cheese, and Nib followed him with expectant eyes.

"Sit thee down, lad," said Sammy, condescendingly. "Sit thee

101

down, tha'st getten a walk both afore and behind thee. What book 'st getten under thy arm?"

Jud regarded the volume with evident pride and exultation.

"It's Robyson Crusoe, that theer is," he answered.

Sammy shook his head dubiously.

"Dunnot know as I ivver heerd on him. He's noan scripter, is he?"

"No," said Jud, repelling the insinuation stoutly; "he is na."

"Hond him over, an' let's ha' a look at him."

Jud advanced.

"Theer's picters in it," he commented eagerly. "Theer's one at th' front. That theer un," pointing to the frontispiece, "that theer's him."

Sammy gave it a sharp glance, then another, and then held the book at arm's length, regarding Robinson's goat-skin habiliments over the rims of his spectacles.

"Well, I'm dom'd," he exclaimed. "I'm dom'd, if I would na loike to see that chap i' Riggan! What's th' felly getten on?"

"He's dressed i' goat-skins. He wur cast upon a desert island, an' had na owt else to wear."

"I thowt he must ha' been reduced i' circumstances, or he'd nivver ha' turnt out i' that rig less he thowt more o' comfort than appearances. What wur he doin' a-casting hissen on a desert island? Wur he reet i' th' upper story?"

"He wur shipwrecked," triumphantly. "Th' sea drifted him to th' shore, an' he built hissen a hut, an' gettin' goats an' birds, an'—an' aw sorts—an'—it's the graideliest book tha ivver seed. Miss Anice gave it me."

"Has she read it hersen?"

"Aye, it wur her as tellt me most on it."

Sammy turned the volume over, and looked at the back of it, at the edges of the leaves, at the gilt-lettered title.

"I would na be surprised," he observed with oracular amiability. "I would na be surprised—if that's th' case—as theer's summat in it."

"That as I've towd thee is nowt to th' rest on it," answered Jud in enthusiasm. "Theer's a mon ca'd Friday, an' a lot o' fellys as eats each other—cannybles they ca' 'em——"

"Look tha here," interposed Craddock, his curiosity and interest getting the better of him. "Sit thee down and read a bit. That's something as I nivver heard on—cannybles an' th' loike. Pick thee th' place, an' let's hear summat about th' cannybles if tha has na th' toime to do no more."

Jud needed no second invitation. Sharing the general opinion

102

that "Owd Sammy" was a man of mark, he could not help feeling that Crusoe was complimented by his attention. He picked out his place, as his hearer had advised him, and plunged into the details of the cannibal feast with pride and determination. Though his elocution may have been of a style peculiar to beginners and his pronunciation occasionally startling in its originality, still Sammy gathered the gist of the story. He puffed at his pipe so furiously that the foreign gentleman's turbaned head was emptied with amazing rapidity, and it was necessary to refill it two or three times; he rubbed his corduroy knees with both hands, occasionally he slapped one of them in the intensity of his interest, and when Jud stopped he could only express himself in his usual emphatic formula—

"Well, I am dom'd. An' tha says, as th' chap's name wur Robyson?"

"Aye, Robyson Crusoe."

"Well, I mun say, as I'd ha' loike to ha' knowed him. I did know a mon by th' name o' Robyson onct, but it could na ha' been him, fur he wur na mich o' a chap. If he'd a bin cast o' a desert island, he would na had th' gumption to do aw that theer—Jem Robyson could na. It could na ha' been him—an' besides, he could na ha' writ it out, as that theer felly's done."

There was a pause, in which Craddock held his pipe in his hand reflectively—shaking his head once more.

"Cannybles an' th' loike too," he said. "Theer's a soight o' things as a mon does na hear on. Why, I nivver heard o' cannybles mysen, an' I am na considert ignorant by th' most o' foak." Then, as Jud rose to go, "Art tha fur goin'?" he asked. "Weil, I mun say as I'd loike to hear summat more about Robyson; but, if tha mun go, tha mun, I suppose. Sithee here, could tha coom again an' bring him wi' thee?"

"I mowt; I dunna moind the walk."

"Then thee do it," getting up to accompany him to the gates. "An' I'll gi'e thee a copper now an' then to pay thee. Theer's summat i' a book o' that soart. Coom thee again as soon as tha con, an' we'll go on wi' the cannybles."

"What's th' lad been readin' to thee, Sammy?" asked Mrs. Craddock entering the room, after Jud had taken his departure.

"A bit o' litterytoor. I dunnot know as tha'd know what th' book wur, if I towd thee. Tha nivver wur mich o' a hand at litterytoor. He wur readin' Robyson Crusoe."

"Not a tract, sure-ly?"

"Nay, that it wur na! It wur th' dairy o' a mon who wur cast upo' a desert island 'i th' midst o' cannybles."

"The dairy?"

"Nay, lass, nay," testily, "not i' th' sense yo' mean. Th' dairy wur o' th' litterairy soart. He wur a litterairy mon."

"Cannybles an' th' loike," Sammy said to himself several times during the evening. "Cannybles an' th' loike. Theer's a power o' things i' th' universe."

He took his pipe after supper and went out for a stroll. Mental activity made him restless. The night was a bright one. A yellow harvest moon was rising slowly above the tree-tops, and casting a mellow light upon the road stretching out before him. He passed through the gates and down the road at a leisurely pace, and had walked a hundred yards or so, when he caught sight of two figures approaching him—a girl and a man, so absorbed that they evidently had not noticed him. The girl was of light and youthful figure, and the little old red shawl she wore over her head was pushed aside, and showed curly hair lying upon her brow. It was plain that she was uneasy or frightened, for, as soon as she was near enough, her voice reached him in a tone of frightened protest.

"Oh, dunnot!" she was saying, "I conna bear it I dunnot want to hear yo', an'—an' I will na. Yo' moight ha' let me be. I dunnot believe yo'. Let me go whoam. I'll nivver coom again," and then she broke out crying.

Craddock looked after them as they passed from sight.

"Theer's trouble there," he said, eagerly. "A working lass, an' a mon i' gentlemen's cloas. Dom sich loike chaps, say I. What would they think if workin' men ud coom meddlin' wi' theer lasses? I wish I'd had more toime to see th' wench's face."

104

CHAPTER XXIV

Dan Lowrie's Return

Not a pleasant road to travel at any time—the high road to Riggan, it was certainly at its worst to-night.

Between twelve and one o'clock, the rain which had been pouring down steadily with true English pertinacity for two days, was gradually passing into a drizzle still more unpleasant,—a drizzle that soaked into the already soaked clay, that made the mud more slippery, that penetrated a man's clothing and beat softly but irritatingly against his face, and dripped from his hair and hat down upon his neck, however well he might imagine himself protected by his outside wrappings. But, if he was a common traveller—a rough tramp or laborer, who was not protected from it at all, it could not fail to annoy him still more, and consequently to affect his temper.

At the hour I have named, such a traveller was making his way through the mire and drizzle toward Riggan,—a tramp in mud-splashed corduroy and with the regulation handkerchief bundle tied to the thick stick which he carried over his shoulder.

"Dom th' rain;—dom th' road," he said.

It was not alone the state of the weather that put him out of humor.

"Th' lass," he went on. "Dom her handsome face. Goin' agin a chap—workin' agin him, an' settin' hersen i' his road. Blast me," grinding his teeth—"Blast me if I dunnot ha' it out wi' her!"

So cursing, and alternating his curses with raging silence, he trudged on his way until four o'clock, when he was in sight of the cottage upon the Knoll Road—the cottage where Joan and Liz lay asleep upon their poor bed, with the child between them.

Joan had not been asleep long. The child had been unusually fretful, and had kept her awake. So she was the more easily awakened from her first light and uneasy slumber by a knock on the door. Hearing it, she started up and listened.

"Who is it?" she asked in a voice too low to disturb the sleepers, but distinct enough to reach Lowrie's hearing.

"Get thee up an' oppen th' door," was the answer. "I want thee."

She knew there was something wrong. She had not responded to his summons for so many years without learning what each tone meant. But she did not hesitate.

105

When she had hastily thrown on some clothing, she opened the door and stood before him.

"I did not expect to see yo' toneet," she said, quietly.

"Happen not," he replied. "Coom out here. I ha' summat to say to yo'."

"Yo' wunnot come in?" she asked.

"Nay. What I ha' to say mowt waken th' young un."

She stepped out without another word, and closed the door quietly behind her.

There was the faintest possible light in the sky, the first tint of dawn, and it showed even to his brutal eyes all the beauty of her face and figure as she stood motionless, the dripping rain falling upon her; there was so little suggestion of fear about her that he was roused to fresh anger.

"Dom yo'!" he broke forth. "Do yo' know as I've fun yo' out?"

She did not profess not to understand him, but she did not stir an inch.

"I did na know before," was her reply.

"Yo' thowt as I wur to be stopped, did yo'? Yo' thowt as yo' could keep quiet an' stond i' my way, an' houd me back till I'd forgetten? Yo're a brave wench! Nivver moind how I fun yo' out, an' seed how it wur—I've done it, that's enow fur yo'; an' now I've coom to ha' a few words wi' yo' and settle matters. I coom here toneet a purpose, an' this is what I've getten to say. Yo're stubborn enow, but yo' canna stop me. That's one thing I ha' to tell yo', an here's another. Yo're hard enow, an' yo're wise enow, but yo're noan so wise as yo' think fur, if yo' fancy as a hundred years ud mak' me forget what I ha' made up my moind to, an' yo're noan so wise as yo' think fur, if yo' put yoursen in my road. An' here's another yet," clinching his fist. "If it wur murder, as I wur goin' to do—not as I say it is—but if it wur murder itsen an' yo' wur i' my way, theer mowt be two blows struck i'stead o' one—theer mowt be two murders done— an' I wunnot say which ud coom first—fur I'll do what I've set my moind to, if I'm dom'd to hell fur it!"

She did not move nor speak. Perhaps because of her immobility he broke out again.

"What!" he cried. "Yo'' hangin' on to gentlemen, an' doggin' 'em, an' draggin' yoursen thro' th' dark an' mire to save 'em fro' havin' theer prutty faces hurt, an' getten theer dues! Yo'' creepin' behind a mon as cares no more fur yo' than he does for th' dirt at his feet, an' as laughs, ten to one, to know as yo're ready to be picked up or throwed down at his pleasure! Yo'' watchin' i' th' shade o' trees an' stoppin' a mon by neet as would na stop to speak to yo' by day.

106

Dom yo'! theer were na a mon i' Riggan as dare touch yo' wi' a yard-stick until this chap coom."

"I've listened to yo'," she said. "Will yo' listen to me?"

He replied with another oath, and she continued as if it had been an assent.

"Theer's a few o' them words as yo've spoken as is na true, but theer's others as is. It's true as I ha' set mysen to watch, an' it's true as I mean to do it again. If it's nowt but simple harm yo' mean, yo' shanna do it; if it's murder yo' mean—an' I dunnot trust yo' as it is na—if it's murder yo' mean, theer's yo' an' me for it before it's done; an' if theer's deathly blows struck, the first shall fa' on me. Theer!" and she struck herself upon her breast. "If I wur ivver afraid o' yo' i' my loife—if I ivver feared yo' as choild or woman, dunnot believe me now."

"Yo' mean that?" he said.

"Yo' know whether I mean it or not," she answered.

"Aye!" he said. "I'm dom'd if yo' dunnot, yo' she-devil, an' bein' as that's what's ailin' thee, I'm dom'd if I dunnot mean summat too," and he raised his hand and gave her a blow that felled her to the ground; then he turned away, cursing as he went.

She uttered no cry of appeal or dread, and Liz and the child slept on inside, as quietly as before. It was the light-falling rain and the cool morning air that roused her. She came to herself at last, feeling sick and dizzy, and conscious of a fierce pain in her bruised temple. She managed to rise to her feet and stand, leaning against the rough gate-post. She had borne such blows before, but she never felt her humiliation so bitterly as she did at this moment. She laid her brow upon her hand, which rested on the gate, and broke into heavy sobs.

"I shall bear th' mark for mony a day," she said. "I mun hide mysen away. I could na bear fur him to see it, even tho' I getten it fur his sake."

CHAPTER XXV

The Old Danger

It had been some time since Derrick on his nightly walks homeward had been conscious of the presence of the silent figure; but the very night after the occurrence narrated in the last chapter, he was startled at his first turning into the Knoll Road by recognizing Joan.

There was a pang to him in the discovery. Her silent presence seemed only to widen the distance Fate had placed between them. She was ready to shield him from danger, but she held herself apart from him even in doing so. She followed her own path as if she were a creature of a different world,—a world so separated from his own that nothing could ever bridge the gulf between them.

To-night, Derrick was seized with an intense longing to speak to the girl. He had forborne for her sake before, but to-night he was in one of those frames of mind in which a man is selfish, and is apt to let his course be regulated by his impulse. Why should he not speak, after all? If there was danger for him there was danger for her, and it was absurd that he should not show her that he was not afraid. Why should she interpose her single strength between himself and the vengeance of a man of whom he had had the best in their only encounter? As soon as they had reached the more unfrequented part of the road, he wheeled round suddenly, and spoke.

"Joan," he said.

He saw that she paused and hesitated, and he made up his mind more strongly. He took a few impetuous steps toward her, and seeing this, she addressed him hurriedly.

"Dunnot stop," she said. "If—if yo' want to speak to me, I'll go along wi' yo'."

"You think I'm in danger?"

He could not see her face, but her voice told him that her usual steady composure was shaken—it was almost like the voice of another woman.

"Yo' nivver wur i' more danger i' yo're loife."

"The old danger?"

"Th' old danger, as is worse to be feared now than ivver."

"And you!" he broke out. "You interpose yourself between that danger and me!"

His fire seemed to communicate itself to her.

108

"Th' harm as is meant to be done, is coward's harm," she said, "an' will be done i' coward's fashion—it is na a harm as will be done yo' wi' fair warnin', i' dayleet, an' face to face. If it wur, I should na fear—but th' way it is, I say it shanna be done—it shanna, if I dee fur it!" Then her manner altered again, and her voice returned to its first tremor. "It is na wi' me as it is wi' other women. Yo' munnot judge o' me as yo' judge o' other lasses. What mowtn't be reet fur other lasses to do, is reet enow fur me. It has na been left to me to be lass-loike, an' feart, an'—an' modest," and she drew her breath hard, as if she was forced to check herself.

"It has been left to you," he burst forth, "it has been left to you to stand higher in my eyes than any other woman God ever made."

He could not have controlled himself. And yet, when he had said this, his heart leaped for fear he might have wounded her or given her a false impression. But strange to say, it proved this time that he had no need for fear.

There was a moment's silence, and then she answered low.

"Thank yo'!"

They had gone some yards together, before he recovered himself sufficiently to remember what he had meant to say to her.

"I wanted to tell you," he said, "that I do not think any—enemy I have, can take me at any very great disadvantage. I am—I have prepared myself."

She shuddered.

"Yo' carry—summat?"

"Don't misunderstand me," he said quickly. "I shall not use any weapon rashly. It is to be employed more as a means of warning and alarm than anything else. Rigganites do not like firearms, and they are not used to them. I only tell you this, because I cannot bear that you should expose yourself unnecessarily."

There was that in his manner which moved her as his light touch had done that first night of their meeting, when he had bound up her wounded temple with his handkerchief. It was that her womanhood—her hardly used womanhood, of which she had herself thought with such pathetic scorn—was always before him, and was even a stronger power with him than her marvellous beauty.

She remembered the fresh bruise upon her brow, and felt its throb with less of shame, because she bore it for his sake.

"Promise me one thing," he went on. "And do not think me ungracious in asking it of you—promise me that you will not come out again through any fear of danger for me, unless it is a greater one than threatens me now and one I am unprepared to meet."

"I conna," she answered firmly. "I conna promise yo'. Yo' mun let me do as I ha' done fur th' sake o' my own peace."

109

She made no further explanation, and he could not persuade her to alter her determination. In fact, he was led to see at last, that there was more behind than she had the will or power to reveal to him; something in her reticence silenced him.

"Yo' dunnot know what I do," she said before they parted. "An' happen yo' would na quoite understand it if yo' did. I dunnot do things lightly,—I ha' no reason to,—an' I ha' set my moind on seein' that th' harm as has been brewin' fur long enow, shanna reach wheer it's aimed. I mun ha' my way. Dunnot ask me to gi'e it up. Let me do as I ha' been doin' fur th' sake o' mysen, if fur no one else."

The truth which he could not reach, and would not have reached if he had talked to her till doomsday, was that she was right in saying that she could not give it up. This woman had made no inconsequent boast when she told her father that if deadly blows fell, they must fall first upon herself. She was used to blows, she could bear them, she was fearless before them,—but she could not have borne to sit at home, under any possibility of wrong being done to this man. God knows what heavy sadness had worn her soul, through the months in which she had never for a moment flinched from the knowledge that a whole world lay between herself and him. God knows how she had struggled against the unconquerable tide of feeling as it crept slowly upon her, refusing to be stemmed and threatening to overwhelm her in its remorseless waves. She was only left endurance—yet even in this there was a gladness which she had in nothing else. She could never meet him as a happier woman might, but she could do for him what other women could not do—she could brave darkness and danger, she could watch over him, if need be; if the worst came to the worst, she could interpose herself between him and violence, or death itself.

But of all this, Fergus Derrick suspected nothing. He only knew that while she had not misinterpreted his appeal, some reason of her own held her firm.

CHAPTER XXVI

The Package Returned

As Joan turned the corner of a lane leading to the high road, she found herself awkwardly trying to pass a man who confronted her—a young fellow far too elegant and well-dressed to be a Rigganite.

"Beg pardon!" he said abruptly, as if he were not in the best of humors. And then she recognized him.

"It's Mester Ralph Landsell," she said to herself as she went on. "What is he doin' here?"

But before she had finished speaking, she started at the sight of a figure hurrying on before her,—Liz herself, who had evidently just parted from her lover, and was walking rapidly homeward.

It was a shock to Joan, though she did not suspect the whole truth. She had trusted the girl completely; she had never interfered with her outgoing or incoming; she had been generously lenient toward her on every point, and her pang at finding herself deceived was keen. Her sudden discovery of the subterfuge filled her with alarm.

What was the meaning of it? Surely it could not mean that this man was digging fresh pitfalls for the poor straying feet. She could not believe this,—she could only shudder as the ominous thought suggested itself. And Liz—nay, even Liz could not be weak enough to trifle with danger again.

But it was Liz who was hurrying on before her, and who was walking so fast that both were breathless when Joan reached her side and laid a detaining hand upon her shoulder.

"Liz," she said, "are yo' afeard o' me?"

Liz turned her face around, colorless and frightened. There was a tone in the voice she had never heard before, a reproach in Joan's eyes before which she faltered.

"I—did na know it wur yo'," she said, almost peevishly. "What fur should I be afeard o' yo'?"

Joan's hand dropped.

"Yo' know best," she answered. "I did na say yo' wur."

Liz pulled her shawl closer about her shoulders, as if in nervous protest.

"I dunnot see why I should be, though to be sure it's enow to fear one to be followed i' this way. Canna I go out fur a minnit wi'out—wi'out—"

111

"Nay, lass," Joan interrupted, "that's wild talk."

Liz began to whimper.

"Th' choild wur asleep," she said, "an' it wur so lonesome i' th' house. Theer wur no harm i' comin' out."

"I hope to God theer wur na," exclaimed Joan. "I'd rayther see thy dead face lyin' by th' little un's on th' pillow than think as theer wur. Yo' know what I mean, Liz. Yo' know I could na ha' caught up wi' yo' wi'out passin' thot mon theer,—th' mon as yo' ha' been meetin' on th' sly,—God knows why, lass, fur I canna see, unless yo' want to fa' back to shame an' ruin."

They were at home by this time, and she opened the door to let the girl walk in before her.

"Get thee inside, Liz," she said. "I mun hear what tha has to say, fur I conna rest i' fear for thee. I am na angered, fur I pity thee too much. Tha art naught but a choild at th' best, an' th' world is fu' o' traps an' snares."

Liz took off her hat and shawl and sat down. She covered her face with her hands, and sobbed appealingly.

"I ha' na done no harm," she protested. "I nivver meant none. It wur his fault. He wunnot let me a-be, an'—an' he said he wanted to hear summat about th' choild, an' gi'e me summat to help me along. He said as he wur ashamed o' hissen to ha' left me wi'out money, but he wur hard run at the toime, an' now he wanted to gi' me some."

"Money!" said Joan. "Did he offer yo' money?"

"Aye, he said——"

"Wait!" said Joan. "Did yo' tak' it?"

"What would yo' ha' me do?" restlessly. "Theer wur no harm"

"Ha' yo' getten it on yo'?" interrupting her again.

"Aye," stopping to look up questioningly.

Joan held out her hand.

"Gi'e it to me," she said, steadily.

Mr. Ralph Landsell, who was sitting in his comfortable private parlor at the principal hotel of the little town, was disturbed in the enjoyment of his nightly cigar by the abrupt announcement of a visitor,—a young woman, who surprised him by walking into the room and straight up to the table near which he sat.

She was such a very handsome young woman, with her large eyes and finely cut face, and heavy nut-brown hair, and, despite her common dress, so very imposing a young woman, that the young man was quite startled,—especially when she laid upon the table-cloth a little package, which he knew had only left his hands half an hour before.

"I ha' browt it back to yo';" she said, calmly.

He glanced down at the package and then up at her, irritated and embarrassed.

"You have brought it back to me?" he said. "May I ask what it is?"

"I dunnot think yo' need ask; but sin' yo' do so, I con answer. It's th' money, Mester Landsell,—th' money yo' give to poor Lizzie."

"And may I ask again, what the money I gave to poor Lizzie has to do with you?"

"Yo' may ask again, an' I con answer. I am th' poor lass's friend,—happen th' only friend she has i' th' world,—an' I tell yo' as I will na see yo' play her false again."

"The devil!" he broke forth, angrily. "You speak as—as if you thought I meant her harm."

He colored and faltered, even as he spoke. Joan faced him with bright and scornful eyes.

"If yo' dunnot mean her harm, dunnot lead her to underhand ways o' deceivin' them as means her well. If yo' dunnot mean her harm, tak' yore belongings and leave Riggan to-morrow morning."

He answered her by a short, uneasy laugh.

"By Jove!" he said. "You are a cool hand, young woman—but you can set your mind at rest. I shall not leave Riggan to-morrow morning, as you modestly demand—not only because I have further business to transact, but because I choose to remain. I shall not make any absurd promises about not seeing Lizzie, which, it seems to me, is more my business than yours, under the circumstances—and I shall not take the money back."

"Yo' willna?"

"No, I will not."

"Very well. I ha' no more to say," and she went out of the room, leaving the package lying upon the table.

When she reached home, Liz was still sitting as she had left her, and she looked up tearful and impatient.

"Well?" she said.

"He has th' money," was Joan's answer, "an' he ha' shown me as he is a villain."

She came and stood near the girl, a strong emotion in her half pitying, half appealing look.

"Lizzie, lass!" she said. "Tha mun listen to me,—tha mun. Tha mun mak' me a promise before tha tak's thy choild upo' thy breast toneet."

"I dunnot care," protested Liz, weeping fretfully. "I dunnot care what I do. It's aw as bad as ivver now. I dunnot care for nowt. Ivvery-body's at me—noan on yo' will let me a-be. What wi' first one an' then another I'm a'most drove wild."

"God help thee!" said Joan with a heavy sigh. "I dunnot mean to be hard, lass, but yo' mun promise me. It is na mich, Lizzie, if—if things is na worse wi' yo' than I would ivver believe. Yo're safe so far: promise me as yo' will na run i' danger—promise me as yo' will na see that man again, that yo'll keep out o' his way till he leaves Riggan."

"I'll promise owt," cried Liz. "I dunnot care, I tell yo'. I'll promise owt yo'll ax, if yo'll let me a-be," and she hid her face upon her arms and wept aloud.

CHAPTER XXVII

Sammy Craddock's "Manny-ensis."

At least twice a week Jud Bates made a pilgrimage to Haviland Park. Having been enlightened to the extent of two or three chapters of "Robinson Crusoe," Sammy Craddock was athirst for more. He regarded the adventures of the hero as valuable information from foreign shores, as information that might be used in political debates, and brought forth on state occasions to floor a presumptuous antagonist. Accordingly, he held out inducements to Jud such as the boy was not likely to think lightly of. A penny a night, and a good supper for himself and Nib, held solid attractions for Jud, and at this salary he found himself engaged in the character of what "Owd Sammy" called "a manny-ensis."

"What's that theer?" inquired Mrs. Craddock on first hearing this imposing title. "A manny—what?"

"A manny-ensis, owd lass," said Sammy, chuckling. "Did tha ivver hear o' a private gentleman as had na a manny-ensis?"

"Nay. I know nowt about thy manny-ensisses, an' I'll warrant tha does na know what such loike is thysen."

"It means a power o' things," answered Sammy; "a power o' things. It's a word as is comprehensive, as they ca' it, an' it's one as will do as well as any fur th' lad. A manny-ensis!" and manny-ensis it remained.

Surely the adventures of the island-solitary had never given such satisfaction as they gave in the cheery house room of the lodge. Sammy listened to them over numerous pipes, with a respect for literature such as had never before been engendered in his mind by the most imposing display of bindings.

"I've allus thowt as th' newspaper wur enow fur a mon to tackle," he would say, reflectively; "but theer's summat outside o' th' newspapers. I nivver seed a paper as had owt in it about desert islands, let alone cannybles."

"Cannybles, indeed!" replied Mrs. Craddock, who was occasionally one of the audience. "I conna mak' no sense out o' thee an' thy cannybles. I wonder they are na' shamt o' theirsens, goin' about wi'out so mich as a hat on, an' eatin' each other, as if there wur na a bit o' good victual i' th' place. I wonder th' Queen dunnot put a stop to it hersen if th' parlyment ha' not getten the sense to do it. It's noan respectable, let alone Christian."

"Eh!" said Sammy; "but tha'rt i' a muddle. Th'dst allus be i' a muddle if I'd let thee mak' things out thysen an' noan explain 'em to thee. Does tha think aw this here happent i' England? It wur i' furrin lands, owd wench, i' a desert island i' th' midst o' th' sea."

"Well, I wur hopin' it wur na i' Lancashire, I mun say!"

"Lancashire! Why, it happent further off nor Lunnon, i' a place as it's loike th' Queen has nivver seed nor heerd tell on."

The old woman looked dubious, if not disapproving. A place that was not in Lancashire, and that the Queen had nothing to do with, was, to her, a place quite "off color."

"Well! well!" she resumed, with the manner of an unbeliever, "thee go on thy way readin' if tha con tak' comfort i' it. But I mun say again as it does na sound Christian to me. That's the least I con say on't."

"Tha'rt slow i' understanding owd lass," was her husband's tolerant comment. "Tha' does na know enow o' litterytoor to appreciate. Th' female intylect is na strong at th' best, an' tha nivver wur more than ordinary. Get into it, Manny-ensis. It's getten late, and I'm fain to hear more about th' mon Friday, an' how th' poor' chap managed."

Both reader and audience were so full of interest that Jud's story was prolonged beyond the usual hour. But to the boy, this was a matter of small consequence. He had tramped the woods too often with Nib for a companion to feel fear at any time. He had slept under a hedge many a night from choice, and had enjoyed his slumber like a young vagabond, as he was.

He set out on this occasion in high good humor. There were no clouds to hide the stars; he had had an excellent supper, and he had enjoyed his evening. He trudged along cheerily, his enjoyment as yet unabated. The trees and hedges, half stripped of their leaves, were so suggestive of birds' nests, that now and then he stepped aside to examine them more closely. The nests might be there yet, though the birds had flown. Where throstles had built this year, it was just possible others might build again, and, at any rate, it was as well to know where their haunts had been. So, having objects enough to attract his attention, the boy did not find the way long. He was close upon the mine before he had time to feel fatigue possible, and, nearing the mine, he was drawn from his path again by a sudden remembrance brought up by the sight of a hedge surrounding a field near it.

"Theer wur a bird as built i' that hedge i' th' spring," he said. "She wur a new kind. I'd forgotten her. I meant to ha' watched her. I wonder if any other felly fun her. I'll go an' see if th' nest is theer."

He crossed the road to the place where he fancied he had seen this treasure; but not being quite certain as to the exact spot, he found his search lengthened by this uncertainty.

"It wur here," he said to himself; "at least I thowt it wur. Some chap mun ha' fun it an' tuk it."

At this moment he paused, as if listening.

"What's that theer?" he said. "Theer's some one on th' other side o' th' hedge."

He had been attracted by the sound of voices—men's voices—the voices of men who were evidently crouching under the shadow of the hedge on the other side, and whose tones in a moment more reached him distinctly and were recognized.

The first was Dan Lowrie's, and before he had heard him utter a dozen words, Jud dropped upon his knees and laid his hand warningly upon Nib's neck. The dog pricked his pointed ears and looked up at him restlessly. All the self-control of his nature could scarcely help him to suppress a whine.

"Them as is feared to stand by Dan Lowrie," said the voice, with an oath, "let 'em say so."

"Theer's not a mon here as is feart," was the gruff answer.

"Then theer's no need to gab no more," returned Lowrie. "Yo' know what yo' ha' getten to do. Yo' ha' th' vitriol an' th' sticks. Wait yo' fur him at th' second corner an' I'll wait at th' first. If he does na tak' one turn into th' road he'll tak' th' other, an' so which turn he tak's we'll be ready fur him. Blast him! he'll be done wi' engineerin' fur a while if he fa's into my hands, an' he'll mak' no more rows about th' Davvies."

Impatient for the word of command, Nib stirred uneasily among the dead leaves, and the men heard him. Not a moment's space was given to the two listeners, or they would have saved themselves. There was a smothered exclamation from three voices at once, a burst of profanity, and Dan Lowrie had leaped the low hedge and caught Jud by the collar. The man was ghastly with rage. He shook the lad until even he himself was breathless.

"Yo' young devil!" he cried, hoarsely, "yo've been listenin', ha' yo'? Nay, theer's no use o' yo' tryin' to brave it out. Yo've done for yorsen, by God!"

"Let me a-be," said Jud, but he was as pale as his captor. "I wur na doin' thee no harm. I on'y coom to look fur a bird's nest."

"Yo' listened," said Lowrie; "y o' heerd what we said."

"Let me a-be," was Jud's sullen reply.

At this moment a man's face rose above the whitethorn hedge.

"Who is it?" asked the fellow, in a low voice.

"A dom'd young rascal as has been eaves-droppin'. Yo' may as

117

well coom out, lads. We've getten to settle wi' him, or we'n fun ourselves in th' worst box yet."

The man scrambled over the hedge without further comment and his companion followed him; and seeing who they were, Jud felt that his position was even more dangerous than he fancied at first. The three plotters who grouped themselves about him were three of the most desperate fellows in the district—brutal, revengeful, vicious, combining all the characteristics of a bad class. The two last looked at him with evident discomfort and bewilderment.

"Here's a pretty go," said one.

"Aye, by th' Lord Harry!" added the other. "How long's he bin here?"

"How long'st bin here?" demanded Lowrie, with another shake.

"Long enow to look fur a bird's nest an' not find it," said Jud, trying to speak stoutly.

The three exchanged glances and oaths.

"He's heerd ivvery word," said Lowrie, in a savage answer.

There was a moment's silence, and then Lowrie broke out again.

"Theer's on'y one road to stop his gab," he said. "Pitch him into th' mine, an' be dom'd to him. He shall na spoil th' job, if I ha' to swing fur it."

Nib gave a low whine, and Jud's heart leaped within him. Every lad in Riggan knew Dan Lowrie and feared him. There was not a soul within hearing, and people were not fond of visiting the mine at night, so if they chose to dispose of him in any way, they would have time and opportunity to do it without risk of being interfered with. But it happened that upon the present occasion Lowrie's friends were not as heated as himself. It was not a strictly personal grudge they were going to settle, and consequently some remnant of humanity got the better of them.

"Nay," said the youngest, "one's enow."

"Nay," Lowrie put in; "one's not enow fur me, if theer's another as is goin' to meddle. Summat's getten to be done, an' done quick."

"Mak' him promise to keep his mouth shut," suggested No. 3. "He'll do it sooner nor get hissen into trouble."

"Wilt ta?" demanded the young one.

Jud looked up at him. He had the stubborn North country blood in him, and the North country courage. Having heard what he had, he was sharp enough to comprehend all. There was only one engineer whom Lowrie could have a grudge against, and that one was Derrick. They were going to work some harm against "Mester Derrick," who was his friend and Miss Anice's.

"Wilt ta?" repeated his questioner, feeling quite sure of him. The youth of Riggan were generally ready enough for mischief, and troubled by no scruples of conscience, so the answer he received took him by surprise.

"Nay," said Jud, "I will na."

"Tha will na?"

"Nay."

The fellow fell back a step or two to stare at him.

"Well, tha'rt a plucky one at ony rate," he growled, discomfited.

Jud stood his ground.

"Mester Derrick's bin good to me," he said, "an' he's bin good to Nib. Th' rest o' yo' ha' a kick for Nib whenivver he gits i' yo're way; but he nivver so much as spoke rough to him. He's gin me a penny more nor onct to buy him summat to eat. Chuck me down the shaft, if yo' want to."

Though he scarcely believed they would take him at his word, since the two were somewhat in his favor, it was a courageous thing to say. If his fate had rested in Lowrie's hands alone, heaven knows what the result might have been; but having the others to contend with, he was safe so far. But there was not much time to lose, and even the less interested parties to the transgression had a stolid determination to stand by their comrade. There was a hurried consultation held in undertones, and then the youngest man bent suddenly, and, with a short laugh, caught Nib in his arms. He was vicious enough to take a pleasure in playing tormentor, if in his cooler moods he held back from committing actual crime.

"Tha'rt a plucky young devil," he said; "but tha's getten to swear to howd thy tongue between thy teeth, an' if tha wunnot do it fur thy own sake, happen tha will fur th' dog's."

"What art tha goin' to do wi' him?" cried Jud, trembling. "He has na done yo' no hurt."

"We're goin' to howd him over th' shaft a minnit till tha mak's up thy mind. Bring th' young chap along, lads."

He had not struggled before, but he began to struggle now with all his strength. He grew hot and cold by turns. It might not be safe to kill him; but it would be safe enough to kill Nib.

"Let me a-be," he cried. "Let that theer dog loose. Nib, Nib,— seize him, lad!"

"Put thy hond over his mouth," said the young man.

And so Jud was half dragged, half carried to the shaft. It was as useless for him to struggle as it was for Nib. Both were powerless.

But Jud's efforts to free himself were so frantic that the men laughed,—Lowrie grimly, the other two with a kind of malicious enjoyment of the grotesqueness of the situation.

"Set him down, but keep him quiet," was the command given when they reached the pit's side.

The next instant a dreadful cry was smothered in the boy's grappled throat. They were leaning against the rail and holding Nib over the black abyss.

"Wilt ta promise?" he was asked. "Tha may let him speak, Lowrie; he canna mak' foak hear."

Nib looked down into the blackness, and broke into a terrific whine, turning his head toward his master.

"I—I—conna promise," said Jud; but he burst into tears.

"Let th' dog go," said Lowrie.

"Try him again. Wilt ta promise, or mun we let th' dog go, lad? We're noan goin' to do th' chap ony great harm; we're on'y goin' to play him a trick to pay him back fur his cheek."

Jud looked at Nib.

"Lowrie said you had vitriol and knob-sticks," he faltered. "Yo' dunnat play tricks wi' them."

"Yo' see how much he's heerd," said Lowrie. "He'll noan promise."

The one who held the dog was evidently losing patience.

"Say yes or no, yo' young devil," he said, and he made a threatening gesture. "We conna stand here aw neet. Promise ta will na tell mon, woman, nor choild, what tha heerd us say. When I say 'three,' I'll drop th' dog. One—two—"

The look of almost human terror in Nib's eyes was too much for his master. Desperation filled him. He could not sacrifice Nib— he could not sacrifice the man who had been Nib's friend; but he might make a sort of sacrifice of himself to both.

"Stop!" he cried. "I'll promise yo'"

He had saved Nib, but there was some parleying before he was set free, notwithstanding his promise to be silent. But for the fact that he was under the control of the others for the time being, Lowrie would have resorted to harsher precautions; but possibly influenced by a touch of admiration for the lad, the youngest man held out against his companions. They wrangled together for a few minutes, and then Nib was handed over.

"Here, cut an' run, tha young beggar," said the fellow who had stood by him, "an' dunnot let's hear ony more on thee. If we do, it'll be worse fur thee an' th' dog too. So look out."

Jud did not wait for a second command. The instant he felt Nib in his arms, he scudded over the bare space of ground before him at his best speed. They should not have time to repent their decision. If the men had seen his face, they might not have felt so safe. But the truth was, they were reckoning upon Jud Bates as they would have reckoned upon any other young Riggan rascal of his age. After all, it was not so much his promise they relied on as his wholesome fear of the consequences of its being broken. It was not a matter of honor but of dread.

CHAPTER XXVIII

Warned

It was even later than usual this evening when Fergus Derrick left the Rectory. When Mr. Barholm was in his talkative mood, it was not easy for him to break away. So Derrick was fain to listen and linger, and then supper was brought in and he was detained again, and at eleven o'clock Mr. Barholm suddenly hit upon a new topic.

"By the by," he said, "where is that fellow, Lowrie? I thought he had left Riggan."

"He did leave Riggan," answered Derrick.

"So I heard," returned the Rector, "and I suppose I was mistaken in fancying I caught sight of him to-day. I don't know the man very well and I might easily be deceived. But where is he?"

"I think," said Derrick, quietly, "that he is in Riggan. I am not of the opinion that you were mistaken at all. I am sure he is here, but for reasons of his own he is keeping himself quiet. I know him too well to be deceived by any fancied resemblance."

"But what are his reasons?" was the next question. "That looks bad, you know. He belongs to a bad crew."

"Bad enough," said Derrick.

"Is it a grudge? He is just the rascal to bear a grudge."

"Yes," said Derrick. "It is a grudge against me."

He looked up then across the table at Anice and smiled reassuringly.

"You did not tell us that you had seen him," she said.

"No. You think I ought to be afraid of him, and I am too vain to like to admit the possibility that it would be better to fear any man, even a Riggan collier."

"But such a man!" put in Mrs. Barholm. "It seems to me he is a man to be feared."

"I can thrash him," said Derrick. He could not help feeling some enjoyment in this certainty. "I did thrash him upon one occasion, you know, and a single combat with a fellow of that kind is oftener than not decisive."

"Yes," said the Rector, "that is the principal cause of his grudge, I think. He might forgive you for getting him into trouble, but he will never forgive you for thrashing him."

They were still sitting at the table discussing the matter, when

122

Anice, who sat opposite a window, rose from her seat, and crossing the room to it, drew aside the curtain and looked out.

"There was somebody there," she said, in answer to the questioning in the faces of her companions. "There was a face pressed close against the glass for a minute, and I am sure it was Jud Bates."

Derrick sprang from his chair. To his mind, it did not appear at all unlikely that Jud Bates had mischief in hand. There were apples enough in the Rectory garden to be a sore trial to youthful virtue.

He opened the door and stepped into the night, and in a short time a sharp familiar yelp fell upon the ears of the listeners. Almost immediately after, Derrick returned, holding the trespasser by the arm.

It was Jud Bates, but he did not look exactly like a convicted culprit, though his appearance was disordered enough. He was pale and out of breath, he had no cap on, and he was holding Nib, panting and excited, in his arms.

"Jud," exclaimed Anice, "what have you been doing? Why did you come to the window?"

Jud drew Nib closer, and turned, if possible, a trifle paler.

"I coom," he said, tremulously, "to look in."

Nobody smiled.

"To look in?" said Anice. "Why, whom did you want to see?"

Jud jerked his elbow at Derrick.

"It was him" he answered. "I wanted to see if he had gone home yet."

"But why?" she asked again.

He shuffled his feet uneasily and his eyes fell. He looked down at Nib's head and faltered.

"I—" he said. "I wanted to stop him. I—I dunnot know——" And then the rest came in a burst. "He munnot go," he cried, trembling afresh. "He mun keep away fro' th' Knoll Road."

The party exchanged glances.

"There is mischief in hand," said Mr. Barholm; "that is plain enough."

"He munnot go," persisted Jud; "he mun keep away fro' th' Knoll Road. I'm gettin' myself i' trouble," he added, the indifference of despair in his pale face. "If I'm fun out they'll mill me."

Derrick stepped aside into the hall and returned with his hat in his hand. He looked roused and determined.

"There are two or three stout colliers in Riggan who are my friends, I think," he said, "and I am going to ask them to face the Knoll Road with me. I should like to settle this matter to-night. If I give these fellows the chance to attack me, they will be the more easily disposed of. A few years in jail might have a salutary effect upon Lowrie."

In his momentary heat, he forgot all but the strife into which he was forced. He did not question Jud closely. He knew Riggan and the mining districts too well not to have a clear enough idea of what means of vengeance would be employed.

But when he got out into the night he had not gone many yards before a new thought flashed upon him, and quickened his pulse. It was not a pleasant thought because it checked him, and he was in a mood to feel impatient of a check. But he could not throw it off. There arose within his mind a picture of a silent room in a cottage,—of a girl sitting by the hearth. He seemed to see quite clearly the bent head, the handsome face, the sad eyes. He had a fancy that Liz was not with her to-night, that the silence of the room was only broken by the soft breathing of the child upon Joan's knee.

He stopped with an impatient gesture.

"What was I thinking of?" he demanded of himself, "to have forgotten her, and what my madness would bring upon her? I am a selfish fool! Let it go. I will give it up. I will stay in Riggan for the future—it will not be long, and she need torture herself no more. I will give it up. Let them think I am afraid to face him. I am afraid—afraid to wound the woman I—yes—the woman I love."

CHAPTER XXIX

Lying in Wait

Liz crept close to the window and looked down the road. At this time of the year it was not often that the sun set in as fair a sky. In October, Riggan generally shut its doors against damps and mist, and turned toward its fire when it had one. And yet Liz had hardly seen that the sun had shone at all to-day. Still, seeing her face a passer-by would not have fancied that she was chilled. There was a flush upon her cheeks, and her eyes were more than usually bright. She was watching for Joan with a restless eagerness.

"She's late," she said. "I mought ha' knowed she'd be late. I wisht she'd coom—I do. An' yet—an' yet I'm feart. I wisht it wur over;" and she twisted her fingers together nervously.

She had laid the child down upon the bed, and presently it roused her with a cry. She went to it, took it up into her arms, and, carrying it to the fire, sat down.

"Why couldn't tha stay asleep?" she said. "I nivver seed a choild loike thee."

But the next minute, the little creature whimpering, she bent down in impatient repentance and kissed it, whimpering too.

"Dunnot," she said. "I conna bear to hear thee. Hush, thee! tha goes on as if tha knew. Eh! but I mun be a bad lass. Ay, I'm bad through an' through, an' I conna be no worse nor I am."

She did not kiss the child again, but held it in her listless way even after it fell asleep. She rested an elbow on her knee and her chin upon her hand while her tearful eyes searched the fire, and thus Joan found her when she came in at dusk.

"Tha'rt late again, Joan," she said.

"Ay," Joan answered, "I'm late."

She laid her things aside and came to the firelight. The little one always won her first attention when she came from her day's labor.

"Has she been frettin'?" she asked.

"Ay," said Liz, "she's done nowt else but fret lately. I dunnot know what ails her."

She was in Joan's arms by this time, and Joan stood looking at the puny face.

"She is na well," she said in a low voice. "She has pain as we know nowt on, poor little lass. We conna help her, or bear it fur her. We would if we could, little un,"—as if she forgot Liz's presence.

125

"Joan," Liz faltered, "what if yo' were to lose her?"

"I hope I shanna. I hope I shanna."

"Yo' could na bear it?"

"Theer is na mich as we conna bear."

"That's true enow," said Liz. "I wish foak could dee o' trouble."

"Theer's more nor yo' has wished th' same," Joan answered.

She thought afterward of the girl's words and remembered how she looked when she uttered them,—her piteous eyes resting on the embers, her weak little mouth quivering, her small hands at work,—but when she heard them, she only recognized in them a new touch of the old petulance to which she had become used.

Joan went about her usual tasks, holding the baby in her arms. She prepared the evening meal with Liz's assistance and they sat down to eat it together. But Liz had little appetite. Indeed neither of them ate much and both were more than usually silent. A shadow of reserve had lately fallen between them.

After the meal was ended they drew their seats to the hearth again, and Liz went back to her brooding over the fire. Joan, lulling the child, sat and watched her. All Liz's beauty had returned to her. Her soft, rough hair was twisted into a curly knot upon her small head, her pretty, babyish face was at its best of bloom and expression—that absent, subdued look was becoming to her.

"Theer's honest men as mought ha' loved her," said Joan, inwardly. "Theer's honest men as would ha' made her life happy."

It was just as she was thinking this that Liz turned round to her.

"If she lived to be a woman," with a gesture toward the child; "if she lived to be a woman, do yo' think as sh'd remember me if—if owt should happen to me now?"

"I conna tell," Joan answered, "but I'd try to mak' her."

"Would yo'?" and then she dropped her face upon her hands. "It ud be best if she'd forget me," she said. "It ud be best if she'd forget me."

"Nay, Liz," said Joan. "Tha'rt out o' soarts."

"Ay, I am," said the girl, "an' I need be. Eh, Joan! tha'rt a good wench. I wish I wur loike thee."

"Tha need na, lass."

"But I do. Tha'd nivver go wrong i' th' world. Nowt could mak' thee go wrong. Tha'rt so strong like. An' tha'rt patient, too, Joan, an' noan loike the rest o' women. I dunnot think—if owt wur to happen me now—as tha'd ha' hard thowts o' me. Wouldst tha?" wistfully.

"Nay, lass. I've been fond o' thee, an' sorry fur thee, and if tha wur to dee tha mayst mak' sure I'd noan be hard on thee. But tha art na goin' to dee, I hope."

126

To her surprise the girl caught her hand, and, pulling it down upon her knee, laid her cheek against it and burst into tears.

"I dunnot know; I mought, or—or—summat. But nivver tha turn agen me, Joan,—nivver tha hate me. I am na loike thee,—I wur na made loike thee. I conna stand up agen things, but I dunnot think as I'm so bad as foaks say!"

When this impassioned mood passed away, she was silent again for a long time. The baby fell asleep upon Joan's breast, but she did not move it,—she liked to feel it resting there; its close presence always seemed to bring her peace. At length, however, Liz spoke once more.

"Wheer wur thy feyther goin' wi' Spring an' Braddy?" she asked.

Joan turned a pale face toward her.

"Wheer did yo' see him wi' Spring an' Braddy?"

"Here," was Liz's reply. "He wur here this afternoon wi' em. They did na coom in, though,—they waited i' th' road, while he went i' th' back room theer fur summat. I think it wur a bottle. It wur that he coom fur, I know, fur I heerd Braddy say to him, 'Hast getten it?' an' thy feyther said, 'Ay,' an' th' other two laughed as if they wur on a spree o' some soart."

Joan rose from her chair, white and shaking.

"Tak' th' choild," she said, hoarsely. "I'm goin' out."

"Out!" cried Liz. "Nay, dunnot go out. What ails thee, Joan?"

"I ha' summat to do," said Joan. "Stay tha here with th' choild." And almost before she finished speaking she was gone, and the door had closed behind her.

There would be three of them against one man. She walked faster as she thought of it, and her breath was drawn heavily.

Lowrie bent down in his hiding-place, smiling grimly. He knelt upon the grass behind a hedge at the road-side. He had reached the place a quarter of an hour before, and he had chosen his position as coolly as if he had been sitting down to take his tramp dinner in the shade. There was a gap in the hedge and he must not be too near to it or too far from it. It would be easier to rush through this gap than to leap the hedge; but he must not risk being seen. The corner where the other men lay concealed was not far above him. It was only a matter of a few yards, but if he stood to wait at one turn and the engineer took the other, the game would escape.

So he had placed his comrades at the second, and he had taken the first.

"I'd loike to ha' th' first yammer at him," he had said, savagely. "Yo' can coom when yo' hear me."

127

As he waited by the hedge, he put his hand out stealthily toward his "knob-stick" and drew it nearer, saying to himself:

"When I ha' done settlin' wi' him fur mysen, I shall ha' a bit o' an account to settle fur her. If it's his good looks as she's takken wi', she'll be noan so fond on him when she sees him next, I'll warrant."

He had hit upon the greater villainy of stopping short of murder,—if he could contain himself when the time came.

At this instant a sound reached his ears which caused him to start. He bent forward slightly toward the gap to listen. There were footsteps upon the road above him—footsteps that sounded familiar. Clouds had drifted across the sky and darkened it, but he had heard that tread too often to mistake it now when every nerve was strung to its highest tension. A cold sweat broke out upon him in the impotence of his wrath.

"It's th' lass hersen," he said. "She's heerd summat, an' she's as good as her word!"—with an oath.

He got up and stood a second trembling with rage. He drew his sleeve across his forehead and wiped away the sweat, and then turned round sharply.

"I'll creep up th' road an' meet her afore she reaches th' first place," he panted. "If she sees th' lads, it's aw up wi' us. I'll teach her summat as she'll noan forget."

He was out into the Knoll Road in a minute more.

"I'll teach her to go agen me," he muttered.

"I'll teach her, by ———" But the sentence was never ended. There was a murmur he did not understand, a rush, a heavy rain of blows, a dash of something in his face that scorched like liquid fire, and with a shriek, he fell writhing.

128

CHAPTER XXX

The Slip of Paper

A minute after there rushed past Joan, in the darkness, two men,—stumbling and cursing as they went, out of breath, horror-stricken and running at the top of their speed.

"It wur Lowrie hissen, by ———!" she heard one say, as he dashed by.

"Feyther! Feyther, wheer are yo'? Feyther, are yo' nigh me?" she cried, for she heard both the blows and the shriek.

But there came no answer to her ear. The rapid feet beating upon the road, their echo dying in the distance, made the only sound that broke the stillness. There was not even a groan. Yet a few paces from her, lay a battered, bleeding form. There was no starlight now, she could see only the vague outline of the figure, which might be that of either one man or the other. For an instant, the similarity in stature which had deceived his blundering companions, deceived her also; but when she knelt down and touched the shoulder, she knew it was not the master who lay before her.

"It's feyther hissen," she said, and then she drew away her hand, shuddering. "It's wet wi' blood," she said. "It's wet wi' blood!"

He did not hear her when she spoke; he was not conscious that she tried to raise him; his head hung forward when she lifted him; he lay heavily, and without motion, upon her arms.

"They ha' killed him!" she said. "How is it, as it is na him?"

There was neither light nor help nearer than "The Crown" itself, and when her brain became clearer, she remembered this. Without light and assistance, she could do nothing; she could not even see what hurt he had sustained. Dead or dying, he must lie here until she had time to get help.

She took off her shawl, and folding it, laid his head gently upon it. Then she put her lips to his ear.

"Feyther," she said, "I'm goin' to bring help to thee. If tha con hear me, stir thy hond."

He did not stir it, so she disengaged her arm as gently as possible, and, rising to her feet, went on her way.

There were half a dozen men in the bar-room when she pushed the door inward and stood upon the threshold. They looked up in amazement.

"Those on yo' as want to help a deeing mon," she said, "come wi' me. My feyther's lyin' in the Knoll Road, done to death."

129

All were astir in a moment. Lanterns and other necessaries were provided, and bearing one of these lanterns herself, Joan led the way.

As she stepped out onto the pavement a man was passing, and, attracted by the confusion, turned to the crowd:

"What is the matter?" he asked.

"There's a mon been killed up on th' Knoll Road," answered one of the colliers. "It's this lass's feyther, Dan Lowrie."

The man strode into the light and showed an agitated face.

"Killed!" he said, "Dan Lowrie!"

It was Fergus Derrick.

He recognized Joan immediately, and went to her.

"For pity's sake," he exclaimed, "don't go with them. If what they say is true, this is no place for you. Let me take you home. You ought not——"

"It wur me," interrupted Joan, in a steady voice, "as found him."

He could not persuade her to remain behind, so he walked on by her side. He asked her no questions. He knew enough to understand that his enemy had reaped the whirlwind he had himself sown.

It was he who knelt first by the side of the prostrate man, holding the lantern above the almost unrecognizable face. Then he would have raised the lifeless hand, but Joan, who had bent down near him, stopped him with a quick move.

"Dunnot do that," she faltered, and when he looked up in surprise, he comprehended her meaning, even before she added, in a passionate undertone, the miserable words:

"Ther's blood on it, as might ha' bin yo're own."

"Theer's a bottle here," some one cried out suddenly. "A bottle as I just set my foot on. Chaps, theer's been vitriol throwed."

"Ay," cried another, "so theer has; chaps, look yo' here. Th' villains has vitriolled him."

They laid him upon the shutter they had brought, and carried him homeward. Joan and Derrick were nearest to him as they walked.

They were not far from the cottage, and it was not long before the light glimmered through the window upon them. Seeing it, Joan turned to Derrick suddenly.

"I mun hurry on before," she said. "I mun go and say a word to Liz. Comin' aw at onct th' soight ud fear her."

Reaching the house, she pushed the door open and went in. Everything was so quiet that she fancied the girl must have gone to bed.

"Liz," she said aloud. "Liz!"

Her voice fell with an echoing sound upon the silent room. She looked at the bed and saw the child lying there asleep. Liz was not with it. She passed quickly into the room adjoining and glanced around. It was empty. Moved by some impulse she went back to the bed, and in bending over the child, saw a slip of paper pinned upon its breast, and upon this paper Joan read, in the sprawling, uncertain hand she knew so well:

"Dunnot be hard on me, Joan, dunnot—Good-bye!"

When Derrick entered the door, he found Joan standing alone in the centre of the room, holding the scrap of paper in her hand.

CHAPTER XXXI

The Last Blow

"He won't live," the doctor said to Derrick. "He's not the man to get over such injuries, powerful as he looks. He has been a reckless, drunken brute, and what with the shock and reaction nothing will save him. The clumsy rascals who attacked him meant to do him harm enough, but they have done him more than they intended, or at least the man's antecedents will help them to a result they may not have aimed at. We may as well tell the girl, I suppose—fine creature, that girl, by the way. She won't have any sentimental regrets. It's a good riddance for her, to judge from what I know of them."

"I will tell her," said Derrick.

She listened to him with no greater show of emotion than an increased pallor. She remembered the wounded man only as a bad husband and a bad father. Her life would have been less hard to bear if he had died years ago, but now that death stood near him, a miserable sense of desolateness fell upon her, inconsistent as such a feeling might seem.

The village was full of excitement during this week. Everybody was ready with suggestions and conjectures, everybody wanted to account for the assault. At first there seemed no accounting for it at all, but at length some one recollected that Lowrie had been last seen with Spring and Braddy. They had "getten up a row betwixt theirsens, and t'others had punsed him."

The greatest mystery was the use of vitriol. It could only be decided that it had not been an ordinary case of neighborly "punsing," and that there must have been a "grudge" in the matter. Spring and Braddy had disappeared, and all efforts to discover their whereabouts were unavailing.

On the subject of Liz's flight Joan was silent, but it did not remain a secret many hours. A collier's wife had seen her standing, crying, and holding a little bundle on her arm at the corner of a lane, and having been curious enough to watch, had also seen Landsell join her a few minutes later.

"She wur whimperin' afore he coom," said the woman, "but she cried i' good earnest when he spoke to her, an' talked to him an' hung back as if she could na mak' up her moind whether to go or no. She wur a soft thing, that wench, it wur allus whichivver way th' wind blowed wi' her. I could nivver see what that lass o' Lowrie's wanted wi' her. Now she's getten th' choild on her honds."

The double shock had numbed Joan. She went about the place and waited upon her father in a dull, mechanical way. She said but little to the curious crowd, who, on pretence of being neighborly, flocked to the house. She had even had very little to say to Anice. Perhaps after all, her affection for poor Liz had been a stronger one than she had thought.

"I think," Grace said gently to Anice, "that she does not exactly need us yet."

He made the remark in the Rector's presence and the Reverend Harold did not agree with him.

"I am convinced that you are mistaken, Grace," he said. "You are a little too—well, too delicately metaphysical for these people. You have sensitive fancies about them, and they are not a sensitive class. What they want is good strong doctrine, and a certain degree of wholesome frankness. They need teaching. That young woman, now—it seems to me that this is the time to rouse her to a sense of her—her moral condition. She ought to be roused, and so ought the man. It is a great pity that he is unconscious."

Of Joan's strange confession of faith, Anice had told him something, but he had been rather inclined to pronounce it "emotional," and somehow or other could not quite divest himself of the idea that she needed the special guidance of a well-balanced and experienced mind. The well-balanced and experienced mind in view was his own, though of course he was not aware of the fact that he would not have been satisfied with that of any other individual. He was all the more disinclined to believe in Joan's conversion because his interviews with her continued to be as unsatisfactory as ever. Her manner had altered; she had toned down somewhat, but she still caused him to feel ill at ease. If she did not defy him any longer or set his teachings at naught, her grave eyes, resting on him silently, had sometimes the effect of making his words fail him; which was a novel experience with the Rector.

In a few days Lowrie began to sink visibly. As the doctor predicted, the reaction was powerful, and remedies were of no avail. He lay upon the bed, at times unconscious, at times tossing to and fro in delirium. During her watching at the bedside, Joan learned the truth. Sometimes he fancied himself tramping the Knoll Road homeward through the rain, and then he muttered sullenly of the "day" that was coming to him, and the vengeance he was returning to take; sometimes he went through the scene with Joan herself, and again, he waited behind the hedge for his enemy, one moment exultant, the next striving to struggle to his feet with curses upon his lips and rage in his heart, as he caught the sound of the advancing steps he knew so well. As he went over these scenes again and again, it was plain enough to the listener that his vengeance had fallen upon his own head.

The day after he received his hurts a collier dropped into "The Crown" with a heavy stick in his hand.

"I fun this knob-stick nigh a gap i' th' hedge on th' Knoll Road," he said. "It wur na fur fro' wheer they fun Lowrie. Happen them chaps laid i' wait fur him an' it belongs to one o' 'em."

"Let's ha' a look at it," said a young miner, and on its being handed to him he inspected it closely.

"Why!" he exclaimed. "It's Lowrie's own. I seed him wi' it th' day afore he wur hurt. I know th' shape o' th' knob. How could it ha' coom theer?"

But nobody could guess. It was taken to Joan and she listened to the story without comment. There was no reason why they should be told what she had already discovered.

When Lowrie died, Anice and Grace were in the room with Joan. After the first two days the visitors had dropped off. They had satisfied their curiosity. Lowrie was not a favorite, and Joan had always seemed to stand apart from her fellows, so they were left to themselves.

Joan was standing near the bed when there came to him his first and last gleam of consciousness. The sun was setting, and its farewell glow streaming through the window fell upon his disfigured face and sightless eyes. He roused himself, moving uneasily.

"What's up wi' me?" he muttered. "I conna see—I conna—"

Joan stepped forward.

"Feyther," she said.

Then memory seemed to return to him. An angry light shot across his face. He flung out his hands and groaned:

"What!" he cried, "tha art theer, art tha?" and helpless and broken as he was, he wore that moment a look Joan had long ago learned to understand.

"Ay, feyther," she answered.

It appeared as if, during the few moments in which he lay gasping, a full recognition of the fact that he had been baffled and beaten after all—that his plotting had been of no avail—forced itself upon him. He made an effort to speak once or twice and failed, but at last the words came.

"Tha went agen me, did tha?" he panted. "Dom thee!" and with a struggle to summon all his strength, he raised himself, groping, struck at her with his clenched hand, and failing to reach her, fell forward with his face upon the bed.

It was all over when they raised him and laid him back again. Joan stood upright, trembling a little, but otherwise calm.

134

CHAPTER XXXII

"Turned Methody!"

It had been generally expected that when all was over the cottage upon the Knoll Road would be closed and deserted, but some secret fancy held Joan to the spot. Perhaps the isolation suited her mood; perhaps the mere sense of familiarity gave her comfort.

"I should na be less lonely any wheer else," she said to Anice Barholm. "Theer's more here as I feel near to than i' any other place. I ha' no friends, yo' know. As to th' choild, I con carry it to Thwaite's wife i' th' mornin' when I go to th' pit, an' she'll look after it till neet, for a trifle. She's getten childern o' her own, and knows their ways."

So she went backward and forward night and morning with her little burden in her arms. The child was a frail, tiny creature, never strong, and often suffering, and its very frailty drew Joan nearer to it. It was sadly like Liz, pretty and infantine. Many a rough but experienced mother, seeing it, prophesied that its battle with life would be brief. With the pretty face, it had inherited also the helpless, irresolute, appealing look. Joan saw this in the baby's eyes sometimes and was startled at its familiarity; even the low, fretted cry had in it something that was painfully like its girl-mother's voice. More than once a sense of fear had come upon Joan when she heard and recognized it. But her love only seemed to strengthen with her dread.

Day by day those who worked with her felt more strongly the change developing so subtly in the girl. The massive beauty which had almost seemed to scorn itself was beginning to wear a different aspect; the defiant bitterness of look and tone was almost a thing of the past; the rough, contemptuous speech was less scathing and more merciful when at rare intervals it broke forth.

"Summat has coom over her," they said among themselves. "Happen it wur trouble. She wur different, somehow."

They were somewhat uneasy under this alteration; but, on the whole, the general feeling was by no means unfriendly. Time had been when they had known Joan Lowrie only as a "lass" who held herself aloof, and yet in a manner overruled them; but in these days more than one stunted, overworked girl or woman found her hard task rendered easier by Joan's strength and swiftness.

It was true that his quiet and unremitted efforts had smoothed Grace's path to some extent. There were ill-used women whom he had helped and comforted; there were neglected children

135

whose lives he had contrived to brighten; there were unbelievers whose scoffing his gentle simplicity and long-suffering had checked a little. He could be regarded no longer with contempt in Riggan; he even had his friends there.

Among those who still mildly jeered at the little Parson stood foremost, far more through vanity than malice, "Owd Sammy Craddock." A couple of months after Lowrie's death, "Owd Sammy" had sauntered down to the mine one day, and was entertaining a group of admirers when Grace went by.

It chanced that, for some reason best known to himself, Sammy was by no means in a good humor. Something had gone wrong at home or abroad, and his grievance had rankled and rendered him unusually contumacious.

Nearing the group, Grace looked up with a faint but kindly smile.

"Good-morning!" he said; "a pleasant day, friends!"

"Owd Sammy" glanced down at him with condescending tolerance. He had been talking himself, and the greeting had broken in upon his eloquence.

"Which on us," he asked dryly; "which on us said it wur na?"

A few paces from the group of idlers Joan Lowrie stood at work. Some of the men had noted her presence when they lounged by, but in the enjoyment of their gossip, they had forgotten her again. She had seen Grace too; she had heard his greeting and the almost brutal laugh that followed it; and, added to this, she had caught a passing glimpse of the Curate's face. She dropped her work, and, before the laugh had died out, stood up confronting the loungers.

"If theer is a mon among yo' as he has harmed," she said; "if theer's one among yo' as he's ivver done a wrong to, let that mon speak up."

It was "Owd Sammy" who was the first to recover himself. Probably he remembered the power he prided himself upon wielding over the weaker sex. He laid aside his pipe for a moment and tried sarcasm,—an adaptation of the same sarcasm he had tried upon the Curate.

"Which on us said theer wur?" he asked.

Joan turned her face, pale with repressed emotion, toward him.

"There be men here as I would scarce ha' believed could ha' had much agen him. I see one mon here as has a wife as lay nigh death a month or so ago, an' it were the Parson as went to see her day after day, an' tuk her help and comfort. Theer's another mon here as had a little un to dee, an' when it deed, it wur th' Parson as

136

knelt by its bed an' held its hond an' talkt to it when it were feart. Theer's other men here as had help fro' him as they did na know of, an' it wur help from a mon as wur na far fro' a-bein' as poor an' hard worked i' his way as they are i' theirs. Happen th' mon I speak on dunnot know much about th' sick wife, an' deein choild, an' what wur done for 'em, an' if they dunnot, it's th' Parson's fault."

"Why!" broke in "Owd Sammy." "Blame me, if tha art na turned Methody! Blame me," in amazement, "if tha art na!"

"Nay," her face softening; "it is na Methody so much. Happen I'm turnin' woman, fur I conna abide to see a hurt gi'en to them as has na earned it. That wur why I spoke. I ha' towd yo' th' truth o' th' little chap yo' jeered at an' throw'd his words back to."

Thus it became among her companions a commonly accepted belief that Joan Lowrie had turned "Methody." They could find no other solution to her championship of the Parson.

"Is it true as tha's j'ined th' Methodys?" Thwaite's wife asked Joan, somewhat nervously.

She had learned to be fond of the girl, and did not like the idea of believing in her defection.

"No," she answered, "it is na."

The woman heaved a sigh of relief.

"I thowt it wur na," she said. "I towd th' Maxys as I did na believe it when they browt th' tale to me. They're powerful fond o' talebearing that Maxy lot."

Joan stopped in her play with the child.

"They dunnot understand," she said, "that's aw. I ha' learned to think different, an' believe i' things as I did na use to believe in. Happen that's what they mean by talkin' o' th' Methodys."

People learned no more of the matter than this. They felt that in some way Joan had separated herself from their ranks, but they found it troublesome to work their way to any more definite conclusion.

"Hast heard about that lass o' Lowrie's?" they said to one another; "hoo's takken a new turn sin' Lowrie deed; hoo allus wur a queer-loike, high-handed wench."

After Lowrie's death, Anice Barholm and Joan were oftener together than ever. What had at first been friendship had gradually become affection.

"I think," Anice said to Grace, "that Joan must go away from here and find a new life."

"That is the only way," he answered. "In this old one there has been nothing but misery for her, and bitterness and pain."

Fergus Derrick was sitting at a table turning over a book of engravings. He looked up sharply.

"Where can you find a new life for her?" he asked. "And how can you help her to it? One dare not offer her even a semblance of assistance."

They had not spoken to him, but he had heard, as he always heard, everything connected with Joan Lowrie. He was always restless and eager where she was concerned. All intercourse between them seemed to be at an end. Without appearing to make an effort to do so, she kept out of his path. Try as he might, he could not reach her. At last it had come to this: he was no longer dallying upon the brink of a great and dangerous passion,—it had overwhelmed him.

"One cannot even approach her," he said again.

Anice regarded him with a shade of pity in her face.

"The time is coming when it will not be so," she said.

The night before Joan Lowrie had spent an hour with her. She had come in on her way from her work, before going to Thwaite's, and had knelt down upon the hearth-rug to warm herself. There had been no light in the room but that of the fire, and its glow, falling upon her face, had revealed to Anice something like haggardness.

"Joan," she said, "are you ill?"

Joan stirred a little uneasily, but did not look at her as she answered:

"Nay, I am na ill; I nivver wur ill i' my loife."

"Then," said Anice, "what—what is it that I see in your face?"

There was a momentary tremor of the finely moulded, obstinate chin.

"I'm tired out," Joan answered. "That's all," and her hand fell upon her lap.

Anice turned to the fire.

"What is it?" she asked, almost in a whisper.

Joan looked up at her,—not defiant, not bitter, not dogged,—simply in appeal against her own despair.

"Is na theer a woman's place fur me i' th' world? Is it allus to be this way wi' me? Con I nivver reach no higher, strive as I will, pray as I will,—fur I have prayed? Is na theer a woman's place fur me i' th' world?"

"Yes," said Anice, "I am sure there is."

"I've thowt as theer mun be somewheer. Sometimes I've felt sure as theer mun be, an' then agen I've been beset so sore that I ha' almost gi'en it up. If there is such a place fur me I mun find it—I mun!"

"You will find it," said Anice. "Some day, surely."

Anice thought of all this again when she glanced at Derrick. Derrick was more than usually disturbed to-day. He had for some

138

time been working his way to an important decision, fraught with some annoyance and anxiety to himself. There was to be a meeting of the owners in a few weeks, and at this meeting he had determined to take a firm stand.

"The longer I remain in my present position, the more fully I am convinced of the danger constantly threatening us," he said to Anice. "I am convinced that the present system of furnaces is the cause of more explosions than are generally attributed to it. The mine here is a 'fiery' one, as they call it, and yet day after day goes by and no precautions are taken. There are poor fellows working under me whose existence means bread to helpless women and children. I hold their lives in trust, and if I am not allowed to place one frail barrier between them and sudden death, I will lead them into peril no longer,—I will resign my position. At least I can do that."

The men under him worked with a dull, heavy daring, born of long use and a knowledge of their own helplessness against their fate. There was not one among them who did not know that in going down the shaft to his labor, he might be leaving the light of day behind him forever. But seeing the blue sky vanish from sight thus during six days of fifty-two weeks in the year, engendered a kind of hard indifference. Explosions had occurred, and might occur again; dead men had been carried up to be stretched on the green earth,— men crushed out of all semblance to humanity; some of themselves bore the marks of terrible maiming; but it was an old story, and they had learned to face the same hazard recklessly.

With Fergus Derrick, however, it was a different matter. It was he who must lead these men into new fields of danger.

139

CHAPTER XXXIII

Fate

The time came, before many days, when the last tie that bound Joan to her present life was broken. The little one, who from the first had clung to existence with a frail hold, at last loosened its weak grasp. It had been ill for several days,—so ill that Joan had remained at home to nurse it,—and one night, sitting with it upon her knee in her accustomed place, she saw a change upon the small face.

It had been moaning continuously, and suddenly the plaintive sound ceased. Joan bent over it. She had been holding the tiny hand as she always did, and at this moment the soft fingers closed upon one of her own quietly. She was quite alone, and for an instant there was a deep silence. After her first glance at the tiny creature, she broke this silence herself.

"Little lass," she said in a whisper, "what ails thee? Is thy pain o'er?"

As she looked again at the baby face upturned as if in silent answer, the truth broke in upon her.

Folding her arms around the little form, she laid her head upon its breast and wept aloud,—wept as she had never wept before. Then she laid the child upon a pillow and covered its face. Liz's last words returned to her with a double force. It had not lived to forget or blame her. Where was Liz to-night,—at this hour, when her child was so safe?

The next morning, on her way downstairs to the breakfast-room, Anice Barholm was met by a servant.

"The young woman from the mines would like to see you, Miss," said the girl.

Anice found Joan awaiting her below.

"I ha' come to tell yo'," she said, "that th' little un deed at midneet. Theer wur no one I could ca' in. I sat alone wi' it i' th' room aw th' neet, an' then I left it to come here."

Anice and Thwaite's wife returned home with her. What little there was to be done, they re-mained to do. But this was scarcely more than to watch with her until the pretty baby face was hidden away from human sight.

When all was over, Joan became restless. The presence of the child had saved her from utter desolation, and now that it was gone, the emptiness of the house chilled her. At the last, when her companions were about to leave her, she broke down.

"I conna bear it," she said. "I will go wi' yo'."

Thwaite's wife had proposed before that she should make her home with them; and now, when Mrs. Thwaite returned to Riggan, Joan accompanied her, and the cottage was locked up.

This alteration changed greatly the routine of her life. There were children in the Thwaite household—half a dozen of them—who, having overcome their first awe of her, had learned before the baby died to be fond of Joan. Her handsome face attracted them when they ceased to fear its novelty; and the hard-worked mother said to her neighbors:

"She's getten a way wi' childer, somehow,—that lass o' Lowrie's. Yo'd wonder if yo' could see her wi' 'em. She's mony a bit o' help to me."

But as time progressed, Anice Barholm noted the constant presence of that worn look upon her face. Instead of diminishing, it grew and deepened. Even Derrick, who met her so rarely, saw it when he passed her in the street.

"She is not ill, is she?" he asked Anice once, abruptly.

Anice shook her head.

"No, she is not ill."

"Then she has some trouble that nobody knows about," he said. "What a splendid creature she is!" impetuously—"and how incomprehensible!"

His eyes chanced to meet Anice's, and a dark flush swept over his face. He got up almost immediately after and began to pace the room, as was his habit.

"Next week the crisis will come at the mines," he said. "I wonder how it will end for me."

"You are still determined?" said Anice.

"Yes, I am still determined. I wish it were over. Perhaps there will be a Fate in it"—his voice lowering itself as he added this last sentence.

"A Fate?" said Anice.

"I am growing superstitious and full of fancies," he said. "I do not trust to myself, as I once did. I should like Fate to bear the responsibility of my leaving Riggan or remaining in it."

"And if you leave it?" asked Anice.

For an instant he paused in his walk, with an uncertain air. But he shook this uncertainty off with a visible effort, the next moment.

"If I leave it, I do not think I shall return, and Fate will have settled a long unsettled question for me."

"Don't leave it to Fate," said Anice in a low tone. "Settle it for yourself. It does not—it is not—it looks——"

"It looks cowardly," he interrupted her. "So it does, and so it is. God knows I never felt myself so great a coward before!"

He had paused again. This time he stood before her. The girl's grave, delicate face turned to meet his glance and seeing it, a thought seemed to strike him.

"Anice," he said, the dark flush rising afresh. "I promised you that if the time should ever come when I needed help that it was possible you might give, I should not be afraid to ask you for it. I am coming to you for help. Not now—some day not far distant. That is why I remind you of the compact."

"I did not need reminding," she said to him.

"I might have known that," he answered,—"I think I did know it But let us make the compact over again."

She held out her hand to him, and he took it eagerly.

142

CHAPTER XXXIV

The Decision

The owners of the Riggan collieries held their meeting. That a person in their employ should differ from them boldly, and condemn their course openly, was an extraordinary event; that a young man in the outset of his career should dare so much was unprecedented. It would be a ruinous thing, they said among themselves, for so young a man to lose so important a position on the very threshold of his professional life, and they were convinced that his knowledge of this would restrain him. But they were astounded to find that it did not.

He brought his plans with him, and laid them before them. They were plans for the abolition of old and dangerous arrangements, for the amelioration of the condition of the men who labored at the hourly risk of their lives, and for rendering this labor easier. Especially, there were plans for a newer system of ventilation—proposing the substitution of fans for the long-used furnace. One or two of the younger men leaned toward their adoption. But the men with the greatest influence were older, and less prone to the encouragement of novelty.

"It's all nonsense," said one. "Furnaces have been used ever since the mines were opened, and as to the rest—it arises, I suppose, from the complaints of the men. They always will complain—they always did."

"So far they have had reason for complaint," remarked Derrick. "As you say, there have been furnaces ever since there have been mines, and there have also been explosions which may in many cases be attributed to them. There was an explosion at Browton a month ago which was to some extent a mystery, but there were old miners who understood it well enough. The return air, loaded with gas, had ignited at the furnace, and the result was that forty dead and wounded men were carried up the shaft, to be recognized, when they were recognizable, by mothers, and wives, and children, who depended upon them for their scant food."

Derrick argued his cause well and with spirit, keeping a tight rein upon himself; but when, having exhausted his arguments, he found that he had not advanced his cause, and that it was a settled matter that he should not, he took fire.

"Then, gentlemen," he said, "I have but one resource. I will

143

hold no human life lightly in my hands. I have the honor to tender you my resignation."

There was a dead silence for a moment or so. They had certainly not expected such a result as this. A well-disposed young man, who sat near to Derrick, spoke to him in a rapid undertone.

"My dear fellow," he said, "it will be the ruin of you. For my part, I admire your enthusiasm, but do not be rash."

"A man with a will and a pair of clean hands is not easily ruined," returned Derrick a trifle hotly. "As to being rash or enthusiastic, I am neither the one nor the other. It is not enthusiasm which moves me, it is a familiarity with stern realities."

When he left the room his fate had been decided. At the end of the week he would have no further occupation in Riggan. He had only two more days' work before him and he had gained the unenviable reputation of being a fire-and-tow young fellow, who was flighty enough to make a martyr of himself.

Under the first street-lamp he met Grace, who was evidently making his way home.

"I will go with you," he said, taking his arm.

Once within the walls of the pleasant little room, he found it easy to unbosom himself. He described his interview with his employers, and its termination.

"A few months ago, I flattered myself that my prospects were improving," he said; "but now it seems that I must begin again, which is not an easy matter, by the way."

By the time he ended he found his temporary excitement abating somewhat, but still his mood was by no means undisturbed.

It was after they had finished tea and the armchairs had been drawn to the fire that Grace himself made a revelation.

"When you met me to-night, I was returning from a visit I had paid to Joan Lowrie."

"At Thwaite's?" said Derrick.

"At Thwaite's. She—the fact is I went on business—she has determined to change her plan of life."

"In what manner?"

"She is to work no more at the mines. I am happy to say that I have been able to find her other employment."

There was an interval of silence, at length broken by Derrick.

"Grace," he said, "can you tell me why she decided upon such a course?"

Grace looked at him with questioning surprise.

"I can tell you what she said to me on the subject," he replied. "She said it was no woman's work, and she was tired of it."

144

"She is not the woman to do anything without a motive," mused Derrick.

"No," returned the Curate.

A moment later, as if by one impulse, their eyes met. Grace started as if he had been stung. Derrick simply flushed.

"What is it?" he asked.

"I—I do not think I understand," Grace faltered. "Surely I am blundering."

"No," said Derrick, gloomily. "You cannot blunder since you know the truth. You did not fancy that my feeling was so trivial that I could have conquered it so soon? Joan Lowrie——"

"Joan Lowrie!"

Grace's voice had broken in upon him with a startled sound.

The two men regarded each other in bewilderment. Then again Derrick was the first to speak.

"Grace," he said, "you have misunderstood me."

Grace answered him with a visible tremor.

"If," he said, "it was to your love for Joan Lowrie you referred when you spoke to me of your trouble some months ago, I have misunderstood you. If the obstacles you meant were the obstacles you would find in the path of such a love, I have misunderstood you. If you did not mean that your heart had been stirred by a feeling your generous friendship caused you to regard as unjust to me, I have misunderstood you miserably."

"My dear fellow!" Derrick exclaimed, with some emotion. "My dear fellow, do you mean to tell me that you imagined I referred to Miss Barholm?"

"I was sure of it," was Grace's agitated reply. "As I said before, I have misunderstood you miserably."

"And yet you had no word of blame for me?"

"I had no right to blame you. I had not lost what I believed you had won. It had never been mine. It was a mistake," he added, endeavoring to steady himself. "But don't mind me, Derrick. Let us try to set it right; only I am afraid you will have to begin again."

Derrick drew a heavy breath. He took up a paper-knife from the table, and began to bend it in his hands.

"Yes," he said, "we shall have to begin again. And it is told in a few words," he said, with a deliberateness painful in its suggestion of an intense effort at self-control. "Grace, what would you think of a man who found himself setting reason at defiance, and in spite of all obstacles confronting the possibility of loving and marrying—if she can be won—such a woman as Joan Lowrie?"

"You are putting me in a difficult position," Paul answered. "If

145

he would dare so much, he would be the man to dare to decide for himself."

Derrick tossed the paper-knife aside.

"And you know that I am the person in question. I have so defied the world, in spite of myself at first, I must confess. I have confronted the possibility of loving Joan Lowrie until I do love her. So there the case stands."

Gradually there dawned upon the Curate's mind certain remembrances connected with Joan. Now and then she had puzzled and startled him, but here, possibly, might be a solution of the mystery.

"And Joan Lowrie herself?" he asked, questioningly.

"Joan Lowrie herself," said Derrick, "is no nearer to me to-day than she was a year ago."

"Are you,"—hesitatingly,—"are you quite sure of that?"

The words had escaped his lips in spite of himself.

Derrick started and turned toward him with a sudden movement

"Grace!" he said.

"I asked if you were sure of that," answered Grace, coloring. "I am not."

146

CHAPTER XXXV

In the Pit

The next morning Derrick went down to the mine as usual. There were several things he wished to do in these last two days. He had heard that the managers had entered into negotiations with a new engineer, and he wished the man to find no half-done work. The day was bright and frosty, and the sharp, bracing air seemed to clear his brain. He felt more hopeful, and less inclined to view matters darkly.

He remembered afterward that, as he stepped into the cage, he turned to look at the unpicturesque little town, brightened by the winter's sun; and that, as he went down, he glanced up at the sky and marked how intense appeared the bit of blue, which was framed in by the mouth of the shaft.

Even in the few hours that had elapsed since the meeting the rumor of what he had said and done had been bruited about. Some collier had heard it and had told it to his comrades, and so it had gone from one to the other. It had been talked over at the evening and morning meal in divers cottages, and many an anxious woman had warmed into praise of the man who had "had a thowt for th' men."

In the first gallery he entered he found a deputation of men awaiting him,—a group of burly miners with picks and shovels over their shoulders,—and the head of this deputation, a spokesman burlier and generally gruffer than the rest, stopped him.

"Mester," he said, "we chaps 'ud loike to ha' a word wi' yo'."

"All right," was Derrick's reply, "I am ready to listen."

The rest crowded nearer as if anxious to participate as much as possible, and give their spokesman the support of their presence.

"It is na mich as we ha' getten to say," said the man, "but we're fain to say it. Are na we, mates?"

"Ay, we are, lad," in chorus.

"It's about summat as we'n heerd. Theer wur a chap as towd some on us last neet, as yo'd getten th' sack fro' th' managers—or leastways as yo'd turned th' tables on 'em an' gi'en them th' sack yo'rsen. An' we'n heerd as it begun wi' yo're standin' up fur us chaps—axin fur things as wur wanted i' th' pit to save us fro' runnin' more risk than we need. An' we heerd as yo' spoke up bold, an' argied fur us an' stood to what yo' thowt war th' reet thing, an' we set our moinds on tellin' yo' as we'd heerd it an' talked it over, an'

147

we'd loike to say a word o' thanks i' common fur th' pluck yo' showed. Is na that it, mates?"

"Ay, that it is, lad!" responded the chorus.

Suddenly one of the group stepped out and threw down his pick.

"An' I'm dom'd, mates," he said, "if here is na a chap as 'ud loike to shake hands wi' him."

It was the signal for the rest to follow his example. They crowded about their champion, thrusting grimy paws into his hand, grasping it almost enthusiastically.

"Good luck to yo', lad!" said one. "We'n noan smooth soart o' chaps, but we'n stand by what's fair an' plucky. We shall ha' a good word fur thee when tha hast made thy flittin'."

"I'm glad of that lads," responded Derrick, heartily, by no means unmoved by the rough-and-ready spirit of the scene. "I only wish I had had better luck, that's all."

A few hours later the whole of the little town was shaken to its very foundations, by something like an earthquake, accompanied by an ominous, booming sound which brought people flocking out of their houses, with white faces. Some of them had heard it before—all knew what it meant. From the colliers' cottages poured forth women, shrieking and wailing,—women who bore children in their arms and had older ones dragging at their skirts, and who made their desperate way to the pit with one accord. From houses and workshops there rushed men, who, coming out in twos and threes joined each other, and, forming a breathless crowd, ran through the streets scarcely daring to speak a word—and all ran toward the pit.

There were scores at its mouth in five minutes; in ten minutes there were hundreds, and above all the clamor rose the cry of women:

"My Mester's down!"

"An' mine!"

"An' mine!"

"Four lads o' mine is down!"

"Three o' mine!"

"My little un's theer—th' youngest—nobbut ten year owd—nobbut ten year owd, poor little chap! an' on'y been at work a week!"

"Ay, wenches, God ha' mercy on us aw'—God ha' mercy!" And then more shrieks and wails in which the terror-stricken children joined.

It was a fearful sight. How many lay dead and dying in the noisome darkness below, God only knew! How many lay mangled and crushed, waiting for their death, Heaven only could tell!

In five minutes after the explosion occurred, a slight figure in

148

clerical garb made its way through the crowd with an air of excited determination.

"The Parson's feart," was the general comment.

"My men," he said, raising his voice so that all could hear, "can any of you tell me who last saw Fergus Derrick?"

There was a brief pause, and then came a reply from a collier who stood near.

"I coom up out o' th' pit an hour ago," he said, "I wur th' last as coom up, an' it wur on'y chance as browt me. Derrick wur wi' his men i' th' new part o' th' mine. I seed him as I passed through."

Grace's face became a shade or so paler, but he made no more inquiries.

His friend either lay dead below, or was waiting for his doom at that very moment. He stepped a little farther forward.

"Unfortunately for myself, at present," he said, "I have no practical knowledge of the nature of these accidents. Will some of you tell me how long it will be before we can make our first effort to rescue the men who are below?"

Did he mean to volunteer—this young whipper-snapper of a parson? And if he did, could he know what he was doing?

"I ask you," he said, "because I wish to offer myself as a volunteer at once; I think I am stronger than you imagine and at least my heart will be in the work. I have a friend below,—myself," his voice altering its tone and losing its firmness,—"a friend who is worthy the sacrifice of ten such lives as mine if such a sacrifice could save him."

One or two of the older and more experienced spoke up. Under an hour it would be impossible to make the attempt—it might even be a longer time, but in an hour they might, at least, make their first effort.

If such was the case, the Parson said, the intervening period must be turned to the best account. In that time much could be thought of and done which would assist themselves and benefit the sufferers. He called upon the strongest and most experienced, and almost without their recognizing the prominence of his position, led them on in the work. He even rallied the weeping women and gave them something to do. One was sent for this necessary article and another for that. A couple of boys were despatched to the next village for extra medical assistance, so that there need be no lack of attention when it was required. He took off his broadcloth and worked with the rest of them until all the necessary preparations were made and it was considered possible to descend into the mine.

When all was ready, he went to the mouth of the shaft and took his place quietly.

It was a hazardous task they had before them. Death would stare them in the face all through its performance. There was choking after-damp below, noxious vapors, to breathe which was to die; there was the chance of crushing masses falling from the shaken galleries—and yet these men left their companions one by one and ranged themselves, without saying a word, at the Curate's side.

"My friends," said Grace, baring his head, and raising a feminine hand. "My friends, we will say a short prayer."

It was only a few words. Then the Curate spoke again.

"Ready!" he said.

But just at that moment there stepped out from the anguished crowd a girl, whose face was set and deathly, though there was no touch of fear upon it.

"I ax yo'," she said, "to let me go wi' yo' and do what I con. Lasses, some on yo' speak a word fur Joan Lowrie!"

There was a breathless start. The women even stopped their outcry to look at her as she stood apart from them,—a desperate appeal in the very quiet of her gesture as she turned to look about her for some one to speak.

"Lasses," she said again. "Some on yo' speak a word fur Joan Lowrie!"

There rose a murmur among them then, and the next instant this murmur was a cry.

"Ay," they answered, "we con aw speak fur yo'. Let her go, lads! She's worth two o' th' best on yo'. Nowt fears her. Ay, she mun go, if she will, mun Joan Lowrie! Go, Joan, lass, and we'n not forget thee!"

But the men demurred. The finer instinct of some of them shrank from giving a woman a place in such a perilous undertaking—the coarser element in others rebelled against it.

"We'n ha' no wenches," these said, surlily.

Grace stepped forward. He went to Joan Lowrie and touched her gently on the shoulder.

"We cannot think of it," he said. "It is very brave and generous, and—God bless you!—but it cannot be. I could not think of allowing it myself, if the rest would."

"Parson," said Joan coolly, but not roughly, "tha'd ha' hard work to help thysen, if so be as th' lads wur willin'."

"But," he protested, "it may be death. I could not bear the thought of it. You are a woman. We cannot let you risk your life."

She turned to the volunteers.

"Lads," she cried, passionately, "yo' munnot turn me back. I—

150

sin I mun tell yo'——" and she faced them like a queen,—"theer's a mon down theer as I'd gi' my heart's blood to save."

They did not know whom she meant, but they demurred no longer.

"Tak' thy place, wench," said the oldest of them. "If tha mun, tha mun."

She took her seat in the cage by Grace, and when she took it she half turned her face away. But when those above began to lower them, and they found themselves swinging downward into what might be to them a pit of death, she spoke to him.

"Theer's a prayer I'd loike yo' to pray," she said. "Pray that if we mun dee, we may na dee until we ha' done our work."

It was a dreadful work indeed that the rescuers had to do in those black galleries. And Joan was the bravest, quickest, most persistent of all. Paul Grace, following in her wake, found himself obeying her slightest word or gesture. He worked constantly at her side, for he, at least, had guessed the truth. He knew that they were both engaged in the same quest. When at last they had worked their way—lifting, helping, comforting—to the end of the passage where the collier had said he last saw the master then, for one moment, she paused, and her companion, with a thrill of pity, touched her to attract her attention.

"Let me go first," he said.

"Nay," she answered, "we'n go together."

The gallery was a long and low one, and had been terribly shaken. In some places the props had been torn away, in others they were borne down by the loosened blocks of coal. The dim light of the "Davy" Joan held up showed such a wreck that Grace spoke to her again.

"You must let me go first," he said, with gentle firmness. "If one of these blocks should fall——"

Joan interrupted him,—

"If one on 'em should fall I'm th' one as it had better fall on. There is na mony foak as ud miss Joan Lowrie. Yo' ha' work o' yo're own to do."

She stepped into the gallery before he could protest, and he could only follow her. She went before, holding the Davy high, so that its light might be thrown as far forward as possible. Now and then she was forced to stoop to make her way around a bending prop; sometimes there was a fallen mass to be surmounted, but she was at the front still when they reached the other end without finding the object of their search.

"It—he is na there," she said. "Let us try th' next passage," and she turned into it.

151

It was she who first came upon what they were looking for; but they did not find it in the next passage, or the next, or even the next. It was farther away from the scene of the explosion than they had dared to hope. As they entered a narrow side gallery, Grace heard her utter a low sound, and the next minute she was down upon her knees.

"Theer's a mon here," she said, "It's him as we're lookin' fur."

She held the dim little lantern close to the face,—a still face with closed eyes, and blood upon it Grace knelt down too, his heart aching with dread.

"Is he——" he began, but could not finish.

Joan Lowrie laid her hand upon the apparently motionless breast and waited almost a minute, and then she lifted her own face, white as the wounded man's—white and solemn, and wet with a sudden rain of tears.

"He is na dead," she said. "We ha' saved him."

She sat down upon the floor of the gallery and lifting his head laid it upon her bosom, holding it close as a mother might hold the head of her child.

"Mester," she said, "gi' me th' brandy flask, and tak' thou thy Davy an' go fur some o' th' men to help us get him to th' leet o' day. I'm gone weak at last. I conna do no more. I'll go wi' him to th' top."

When the cage ascended to the mouth again with its last load of sufferers, Joan Lowrie came with it, blinded and dazzled by the golden winter's sunlight as it fell upon her haggard face.

She was holding the head of what seemed to be a dead man upon her knee. A great shout of welcome rose up from the bystanders.

She helped them to lay her charge upon a pile of coats and blankets prepared for him, and then she turned to the doctor who had hurried to the spot to see what could be done.

"He is na dead," she said. "Lay yo're hond on his heart. It beats yet, Mester,—on'y a little, but it beats."

"No," said the doctor, "he is not dead—yet," with a breath's pause between the two last words. "If some of you will help me to put him on a stretcher, he may be carried home, and I will go with him. There is just a chance for him, poor fellow, and he must have immediate attention. Where does he live?"

"He must go with me," said Grace. "He is my friend."

So they took him up, and Joan stood a little apart and watched them carry him away,—watched the bearers until they were out of sight, and then turned again and joined the women in their work among the sufferers.

CHAPTER XXXVI

Alive Yet

In the bedroom above the small parlor a fire was burning at midnight, and by this fire Grace was watching. The lamp was turned low and the room was very quiet; a dropping cinder made quite a startling sound. When a moan or a movement of the patient broke the stillness—which was only at rare intervals—the Curate rose and went to the bedside. But it was only to look at the sufferer lying upon it, bandaged and unconscious. There was very little he could do. He could follow the instructions given by the medical man before he went away, but these had been few and hurried, and he could only watch with grief in his heart. There was but a chance that his friend's life might be saved. Close attention and unremitting care might rescue him, and to the best of his ability the Curate meant to give him both. But he could not help feeling a deep anxiety. His faith in his own skill was not very great, and there were no professional nurses in Riggan.

"It is the care women give that he needs," he said once, standing near the pillow and speaking to himself. "Men cannot do these things well. A mother or sister might save him."

He went to the window and drew back the curtain to look out upon the night. As he did so, he saw the figure of a woman nearing the house. As she approached, she began to walk more slowly, and when she reached the gates she hesitated, stopped and looked up. In a moment it became evident that she saw him, and was conscious that he saw her. The dim light in the chamber threw his form into strong relief. She raised her hand and made a gesture. He turned away from the window, left the room quietly, and went down-stairs. She had not moved, but stood at the gate awaiting him. She spoke to him in a low tone, and he distinguished in its sound a degree of physical exhaustion.

"Yo' saw me," she said. "I thowt yo' did though I did na think o' yo' bein' at th' winder when I stopped—to—to see th' leet."

"I am glad I saw you," said Grace. "You have been at work among the men who were hurt?"

"Ay," pulling at a bush of evergreen nervously, and scattering the leaves as she spoke. "Theer's scarce a house o' th' common soart i' Riggan as has na trouble in it."

"God help them all!" exclaimed Grace, fervently.

"Have you seen Miss Barholm?" he asked next.

153

"She wur on th' ground i' ten minnits after th' explosion. She wur in th' village when it happent, an' she drove to th' pit. She's been workin' as hard as ony woman i' Riggan. She saw us go down th' mine, but she did not see us come up. She wur away then wi' a woman as had a lad to be carried home dead. She would ha' come to him but she knowed yo' were wi' him, an' theer wur them as needed her. When th' cages coom up theer wur women as screamed an' held to her, an' throwed theirsens on their knees an' hid their faces i' her dress, an' i' her honds, as if they thowt she could keep th' truth fro' 'em."

Grace trembled in his excitement.

"God bless her! God bless her!" he said, again and again.

"Where is she now?" he asked at length.

"Theer wur a little chap as come up i' the last cageful—he wur hurt bad, an' he wur sich a little chap as it went hard wi' him. When th' doctor touched him he screamed an' begged to be let alone, an' she heerd an' went to him, an' knelt down an' quieted him a bit. Th' poor little lad would na let go o' her dress; he held to it fur dear life, an' sobbed an' shivered and begged her to go wi' him an' howd his head on her lap while th' doctor did what mun be done. An' so she went, an' she's wi' him now. He will na live till day-leet, an' he keeps crying out for th' lady to stay wi' him."

There was another silence, and then Joan spoke:

"Canna yo' guess what I coom to say?"

He thought he could, and perhaps his glance told her so.

"If I wur a lady," she said, her lips, her hands trembling, "I could na ax yo' what I've made up my moind to; but I'm noan a lady, an' it does na matter. If yo' need some one to help yo' wi' him, will yo' let me ha' th' place? I dunnot ax nowt else but—but to be let do th' hard work."

She ended with a sob. Suddenly she covered her face with her hands, weeping wildly.

"Don't do that," he said, gently. "Come with me. It is you he needs."

He led the way into the house and up the stairs, Joan following him. When they entered the room they went to the bedside.

The injured man lay motionless.

"Is theer loife i' him yet?" asked Joan. "He looks as if theer might na be."

"There is life in him," Grace answered; "and he has been a strong man, so I think we may feel some hope."

CHAPTER XXXVII

Watching and Waiting

The next morning the pony-carriage stopped before the door of the Curate's lodgings. When Grace went downstairs to the parlor, Anice Barholm turned from the window to greet him. The appearance of physical exhaustion he had observed the night before in Joan Lowrie, he saw again in her, but he had never before seen the face which Anice turned toward him.

"I was on the ground yesterday, and saw you go down into the mine," she said. "I had never thought of such courage before."

That was all, but in a second he comprehended that this morning they stood nearer together than they had ever stood before.

"How is the child you were with?" he asked.

"He died an hour ago."

When they went upstairs, Joan was standing by the sick man.

"He's worse than he wur last neet," she said. "An' he'll be worse still. I ha' nursed hurts like these afore. It'll be mony a day afore he'll be better—if th' toime ivver comes."

The Rector and Mrs. Barholm, hearing of the accident, and leaving Browton hurriedly to return home, were met by half a dozen different versions on their way to Riggan, and each one was so enthusiastically related that Mr. Barholm's rather dampened interest in his daughter's protégé was fanned again into a brisk flame.

"There must be something in the girl, after all," he said, "if one could only get at it. Something ought to be done for her, really."

Hearing of Grace's share in the transaction, he was simply amazed.

"I think there must be some mistake," he said to his wife. "Grace is not the man—not the man physically" straightening his broad shoulders, "to be equal to such a thing."

But the truth of the report forced itself upon him after hearing the story repeated several times before they reached Riggan, and arriving at home they heard the whole story from Anice.

While Anice was talking, Mr. Barholm began to pace the floor of the room restlessly.

"I wish I had been there," he said. "I would have gone down myself."

(It is true: he would have done so.)

"You are a braver man than I took you for," he said to his

155

Curate, when he saw him,—and he felt sure that he was saying exactly the right thing. "I should scarcely have expected such dashing heroism from you, Grace."

"I hardly regarded it in that light," said the little gentleman, coloring sensitively. "If I had, I should scarcely have expected it of myself."

The fact that Joan Lowrie had engaged herself as nurse to the injured engineer made some gossip among her acquaintances at first, but this soon died out. Thwaite's wife had a practical enough explanation of the case.

"Th' lass wur tired o' pit-work; an' no wonder. She's made up her moind to ha' done wi' it; an' she's a first-rate one to nurse,—strong i' the arms, an' noan sleepy-headed. Happen she'll tak' up wi' it fur a trade. As to it bein' him as she meant when she said theer wur a mon as she meant to save, it wur no such thing. Joan Lowrie's noan th' kind o' wench to be runnin' after gentlefolk,—yo' know that yoresens. It's noan o' our business who the mon wur. Happen he's dead; an' whether he's dead or alive, you'd better leave him a-be, an' her too."

In the sick man's room the time passed monotonously. There were days and nights of heavy slumber or unconsciousness,—restless mutterings and weary tossings to and fro. The face upon the pillow was sometimes white, sometimes flushed with fever; but whatever change came to pass, Death never seemed far away.

Grace lost appetite, and grew thin with protracted anxiety and watching. He would not give up his place even to Anice or Mrs. Barholm, who spent much of their time in the house. He would barely consent to snatch a few minutes' rest in the day-time; in truth, he could not have slept if he would. Joan held to her post unflinchingly. She took even less respite than Grace. Having almost forced her to leave the room one morning, Anice went downstairs to find her lying upon the sofa,—her hands clasped under her head, her eyes wide open.

"I conna sleep yet a while," she said. "Dunnot let it trouble yo'. I'm used to it."

Sometimes during the long night Joan felt his hollow eyes following her as she moved about the room, and fixed hungrily upon her when she stood near him.

"Who are you?" he would say. "I have seen you before, and I know your face; but—but I have lost your name. Who are you?"

One night, as she stood upon the hearth, alone in the room,—Grace having gone downstairs for something,—she was startled by the sound of Derrick's voice falling with a singular distinctness upon the silence.

156

"Who is it that is standing there?" he said.

"Do I know you? Yes—it is——-" but before he could finish, the momentary gleam of recognition had passed away, and he had wandered off again into low, disjointed murmurings.

It was always of the mine, or one other anxiety, that he spoke. There was something he must do or say,—some decision he must reach. Must he give up? Could he give up? Perhaps he had better go away,—far away. Yes; he had better go. No,—he could not,—he must wait and think again. He was tired of thinking,—tired of reasoning and arguing with himself. Let it go for a few minutes. Give him just an hour of rest. He was full of pain; he was losing himself, somehow. And then, after a brief silence, he would begin again and go the weary round once more.

"He has had a great deal of mental anxiety of late,—too much responsibility," said the medical man; "and it is going rather against him."

157

CHAPTER XXXVIII
Recognition

The turning-point was reached at last. One evening, at the close of his usual visit, the doctor said to Grace:

"To-morrow, I think, you will see a marked alteration. I should not be surprised to find on my next visit that his mind had become permanently cleared. The intervals of half consciousness have become lengthened. Unless some entirely unlooked-for change occurs, I feel sure that the worst is over. Give him close attention to-night. Don't let the young woman leave the room."

That night Anice watched with Joan. It was a strange experience through which these two passed together. If Anice had not known the truth before, she would have learned it then. Again and again Derrick went the endless round of his miseries. How must it end? How could it end? What must he do? How black and narrow the passages were! There she was, coming toward him from the other end,—and if the props gave way———! They were giving way!—Good God! the light was out, and he was held fast by the mass which had fallen upon him. What must he do about her whom he loved, and who was separated from him by this horrible wall? He was dying, and she would never know what he wanted to tell her. What was it that he wanted to say,—That he loved her,—loved her,—loved her! Could she hear him? He must make her hear him before he died,—"Joan! Joan!"

Thus he raved hour after hour; and the two sat and listened, often in dead silence; but at last there rose in Joan Lowrie's face a look of such intense and hopeless pain, that Anice spoke.

"Joan! my poor Joan!" she said.

Joan's head sank down upon her hands.

"I mun go away fro' Riggan," she whispered. "I mun go away afore he knows. Theer's no help fur me."

"No help?" repeated Anice after her.

She did not understand.

"Theer's none," said Joan. "Dunnot yo' see as ony place wheer he is con be no place fur me? I thowt—I thowt the trouble wur aw on my side, but it is na. Do yo' think I'd stay an' let him do hissen a wrong?"

Anice wrung her hands together.

"A wrong?" she cried. "Not a wrong, Joan—I cannot let you call it that."

"It would na be nowt else. Am I fit wife fur a gentlemon? Nay, my work's done when the danger's ower. If he wakes to know th' leet o' day to-morrow morning, it's done then."

"You do not mean," said Anice, "that you will leave us?"

"I conna stay i' Riggan; I mun go away."

Toward morning Derrick became quieter. He muttered less and less until his voice died away altogether, and he sank into a profound slumber. Grace, coming in and finding him sleeping, turned to Joan with a look of intense relief.

"The worst is over," he said; "now we may hope for the best."

"Ay," Joan answered, quietly, "th' worst is ower—fur him."

At last darkness gave way to a faint gray light, and then the gray sky showed long slender streaks of wintry red, gradually widening and deepening until all the east seemed flushed.

"It's mornin'," said Joan, turning from the window to the bed. "I mun gi' him th' drops again."

She was standing near the pillow when the first flood of the sunlight poured in at the window. At this moment Derrick awoke from his sleep to a full recognition of all around him. But the strength of his delirium had died out; his prostration was so utter, that for the moment he had no power to speak and could only look up at the pale face hopelessly. It seemed as if the golden glow of the morning light transfigured it.

"He's awake," Joan said, moving away and speaking to those on the other side of the room. "Will one on yo' pour out th' medicine? My hand's noan steady."

Grace went to the bedside hurriedly.

"Derrick," he said, bending down, "do you know me?"

"Yes," Derrick answered in a faltering whisper, and as he said it the bedroom door closed. Both of them heard it. A shadow fell upon the sick man's face. His eyes met his friend's with a question in them, and the next instant the question put itself into words:

"Who—went out?"

Grace bent lower.

"It was Joan Lowrie."

He closed his eyes and waited a little as if to gain fresh strength. There rose a faint flush upon his hollow cheeks and his mouth trembled.

"How"—he said next—"how—long?"

"You mean to ask me," said Grace, "how long she has been here?"

A motion of assent.

"She has been here from the first."

He asked no further questions. His eyes closed once more and he lay silent.

159

CHAPTER XXXIX

A Testimonial

Joan went back to her lodgings at the Thwaites' and left Mrs. Barholm and Anice to fill her place.

Too prostrate to question his nurses, Derrick could only lie with closed eyes helpless and weary. He could not even keep himself awake long enough to work his way to any very clear memories of what had happened. He had so many half recollections to tantalize him. He could remember his last definite sensation,—a terrible shock flinging him to the ground, a second of pain and horror, and then utter oblivion. Had he awakened one night and seen Joan Lowrie by the dim fire-light and called out to her, and then lost himself? Had he awakened for a second or so again and seen her standing close to his pillow, looking down at him with an agony of dread in her face?

In answer to his question, Grace had told him that she had been with him from the first. How had it happened? This he asked himself again and again, until he grew feverish over it.

"Above all things," he heard the doctor say, "don't let him talk and don't talk to him."

But Grace comprehended something of his mental condition.

"I see by your look that you wish to question me," he said to him. "Have patience for a few days and then I will answer every question you may ask. Try to rest upon that assurance."

There was one question, however, which would not wait. Grace saw it lying in the eager eyes and answered it.

"Joan Lowrie," he said, "has gone home."

Joan's welcome at the Thwaites' house was tumultuous. The children crowded about her, neighbors dropped in, both men and women wanting to have a word with her. There were few of them who had not met with some loss by the explosion, and there were those among them who had cause to remember the girl's daring.

"How's th' engineer?" they asked. "What do th' doctors say o' him?"

"He'll get better," she answered. "They say as he's out o' danger."

"Wur na it him as had his head on yo're knee when yo' come up i' th' cage?" asked one woman.

Mrs. Thwaite answered for her with some sharpness. They should not gossip about Joan, if she could help it.

160

"I dunnot suppose as she knowd th' difference betwixt one mon an' another," she said. "It wur na loikely as she'd pick and choose. Let th' lass ha' a bit o' quoiet, wenches. Yo' moither her wi' yo're talk."

"It's an ill wind as blows nobody good," said Thwaite himself. "Th' explosion has done one thing—it's made th' mesters change their minds. They're i' th' humor to do what th' engineer axed fur, now."

"Ay," said a tired-looking woman, whose poor attempt at mourning told its own story; "but that wunnot bring my mester back."

"Nay," said another, "nor my two lads."

There had been a great deal of muttered discontent among the colliers before the accident, and since its occurrence there had been signs of open rebellion. Then, too, results had proved that the seasonable adoption of Derrick's plan would have saved some lives at least, and, in fact, some future expenditure. Most of the owners, perhaps, felt somewhat remorseful; a few, it is not impossible, experienced nothing more serious than annoyance and embarrassment, but it is certain that there were one or two who were crushed by a sense of personal responsibility for what had occurred.

It was one of these who made the proposition that Derrick's plan be accepted unreservedly, and that the engineer himself should be requested to resume his position and undertake the management of the work. There was some slight demurring at first, but the catastrophe was so recent that its effect had not had time to wear away, and finally the agreement was made.

But at that time Derrick was lying senseless in the bedroom over the parlor, and the deputation from the company could only wait upon Grace, and make an effort at expressing their sympathy.

After Joan's return to her lodgings, she, too, was visited. There was some curiosity felt concerning her. A young and handsome woman, who had taken so remarkable a part in the tragedy, was necessarily an object of interest.

Mr. Barholm was so fluently decided in his opinion that something really ought to be done, that a visit to the heroine of the day was the immediate result. There was only one form the appreciation of a higher for a lower social grade could take, and it was Mr. Barholm who had been, naturally, selected as spokesman. He explained to Joan the nature of the visit. His friends of the Company had heard the story of her remarkable heroism, and had felt that something was due to her—some token of the admiration her conduct had inspired in them. They had agreed that something

161

ought to be done, and they had called this evening to present her with a little testimonial.

The bundle of crisp bank-notes burned the hand of the man who held them, as Joan Lowrie listened to this speech. She stood upright before them, resting one hand upon the back of a chair, but when the bearer of the testimonial in question rose, she made a step forward. There was more of her old self in her gesture than she had shown for months. Her eyes flashed, her face hardened, a sudden red flew to her cheek.

"Put it up," she said. "I wunnot tak' it."

The man who had the money laid it upon the table, as if he were anxious to be rid of it He was in a glow of anger and shame at the false step they had made.

"I beg your pardon," he said. "I see we have made a mistake."

"Ay," she said, "yo' ha' made a mistake. If yo' choose to tak' that an' gi'e it to th' women an' childer as is left to want bread, yo' may do it an' welcome."

CHAPTER XL

Going South

The first day Fergus Derrick was allowed to spend an hour in an easy-chair by the fire, he heard the story of his rescue from the lips of his friend, listening to it as he rested against the propping cushions.

"Don't be afraid of exciting me," he had said to Grace. "I have conjectured until I am tired of it. Tell me the whole story. Let me hear the end now."

Derrick's breath came quick and short as he listened, and his haggard face flushed. It was not only to his friend he owed his life, but to Joan Lowrie.

"I should like to see her," he said when Grace had finished. "As for you, Grace—well—words are poor things."

"They are very poor things between friends," was Grace's answer; "so let us have none of them. You are on this side of the grave, dear fellow—that is enough."

During the rest of the day Derrick was silent and abstracted, but plainly full of active thought.

By nightfall a feverish spot burned upon his cheek, and his pulse had quickened dangerously.

"I must wait," he said to Grace, "and it is hard work."

Just at that time Anice was sitting in her room at the Rectory, thinking of Joan also, when there came to her the sound of footsteps in the passage and then a summons to the door.

"You may come in," she said.

But it was not a servant, as she had supposed; it was Joan, with a bundle upon her arm.

"You are going away, Joan?" she said. "Tonight?"

"Ay," Joan answered, as she came and stood upon the hearth. "I'm goin' away toneet."

"You have quite made up your mind?"

"Ay," said Joan. "I mun break loose. I want to get as far fro' th' owd life as I con. I'd loike to forget th' most on it. I'm goin' toneet, because I dunnot want to be axed questions. If I passed thro' th' town by day-leet, theer's them as ud fret me wi' their talk."

"Have you seen Mr. Grace?" Anice asked.

"No. I shanna ha' th' chance to say good-by to him. I coom partly to ax yo' to say it fur me."

163

"Yes, I will say it I wish there were no need that I should, though. I wish I could keep you."

There was a brief silence. Joan knelt on one knee by the fender.

"I ha' bin thinkin' o' Liz," she said. "I thowt I'd ax yo'—if it wur to happen so as she'd drift back here agen while I wur away—as yo'd say a kind word to her, an' tell her about th' choild, an' how as I nivver thowt hard on her, an' as th' day nivver wur as I did na pity her fro' th' bottom o' my soul. I'm goin' toward th' south," she said again after a while. "They say as th' south is as different fro' th' north as th' day is fro' the neet. I ha' money enow to help me on, an' when I stop I shall look fur work."

Anice's face lighted up suddenly.

"To the south!" she said. "Why did I not think of that before? If you go toward the south, there is Ashley-Wold and grandmamma, Mrs. Galloway. I will write to her now, if you will let me," rising to her feet.

"If yo'll gi' me th' letter, I'll tak' it an' thank yo'," said Joan. "If she could help me to work or th' loike, I should be glad enow."

Anice's mother's mother had always been her safest resource in the past, and yet, curiously enough, she had not thought of turning toward her in this case until Joan's words had suggested such a course.

Joan took the letter and put it in the bosom of her dress.

"Theer's no more danger fur him?" she said. "Thwaite towd me he wur better."

She spoke questioningly, and Anice answered her—

"Yes, he is out of danger. Joan, what am I to say to him?"

"To say to him!"

She started slightly, but ended with a strained quietness of manner.

"Theer's nowt to say," she added, rising, and preparing to go.

Anice rose also. She held out both her hands, and Joan took them.

"I will go downstairs with you," said Anice; and they went out together.

When they reached the front door, they kissed each other, and Anice stood in the lighted hall and watched the girl's departure.

"Good-by!" she said; "and God bless you!"

Early in the morning, Derrick called his friend to his bedside.

"I have had a bad night," he said to him.

"Yes," Grace answered. "It is easy enough to see that."

There was an unnatural sparkle in the hollow eyes, and the flush upon the cheek had not faded away.

164

Derrick tried to laugh, and moved restlessly upon his pillow.

"So I should imagine," said he. "The fact is—well you see I have been thinking."

"About—"

"Yes—yes—Grace, I cannot wait—I must hear something. A hundred things might happen. I must at least be sure she is not far away. I shall never regain strength as long as I have not the rest that knowledge will bring me. Will you go to her and take her a few words of gratitude from me?"

"Yes, readily."

"Will you go now?"

"Yes."

Grace would have left the room, but Derrick stretched out his hand and touched him.

"Stay—" he said.

Grace turned to him again.

"You know"—in the old resolute way—"you know what I mean the end to be, if it may be?"

"I think I do."

Grace appeared at the Rectory very soon afterward, and asked for Miss Barholm. Anice came down into the parlor to meet him at once. She could not help guessing that for some reason or other he had come to speak of Joan, and his first words confirmed her impression.

"I have just left the Thwaites'," he said. "I went there to see Joan Lowrie, and find that she is not there. Mrs. Thwaite told me that she had left Riggan. Is that true?"

"Yes. She went away last night She came here to bid me good-by, and leave a farewell message for you."

Grace was both troubled and embarrassed.

"I——" he faltered. "Do you understand it?"

"Yes," Anice answered.

Their eyes met, and she went on:

"You know we have said that it was best that she should break away entirely from the past. She has gone to try if it is possible to do it. She wants another life altogether."

"I do not know what I must do," said Grace. "You say she has gone away, and I—I came to her from Derrick."

"From Mr. Derrick!" Anice exclaimed; and then both relapsed into silence.

It was Anice who spoke first

"Mamma was going to send some things to Mr. Derrick this morning," she said. "I will have the basket packed and take it myself. If you will let me, I will go with you as soon as I can have the things prepared."

CHAPTER XLI

"A Soart o' Pollygy"

The interview between Anice and Derrick was a long one. At the end Derrick said:

"I shall go to Ashley-Wold."

Grace had been called out almost immediately after his return to the house; but on his way home he met Anice, and having something to say about the school, he turned toward the Rectory with her.

They had not gone far, however, before they were joined by a third party,—Mr. Sammy Craddock, who was wending his way Crownward. Seeing them, Mr. Craddock hesitated for a moment, as if feeling somewhat doubtful; but as they approached him, he pulled off his hat. "I dunnot know," he said, "after aw, if it would not be as well to ha' a witness. Hope yo're nicely, Miss," affably; "an' th' same to yo', Parson. Would yo'" clearing his throat, "would yo' moind shakin' honds wi' a chap?"

Grace gave him his hand.

"Thank yo', Parson," said "Owd Sammy." "It's th' first toime, yo' know, but it shanna be th' last, if yo' dnnnot see owt agen it. Th' truth is, as it's summat as has been on my moind for some toime,—ivver sin' th' accident, i' fact. Pluck's pluck, yo' see, whether yo're for a mon or agen him. Yo're not mich to look at. Yo' mowt be handsomer, an' yo' mowt be likelier,—yo' mowt easily ha' more muscle, an' yo' dnnnot look as if yo' wnr like to be mich i' argyment; but yo're getten a backbone o' yo're own,—I'm danged if yo' ha' na."

"I'm much obliged to you, I am sure," said Grace.

"Yo' need na be," answered Sammy, encouragingly. "Yo' need na be. If yo'd getten owt to be obleeged to me fur, I should na ha' so mich to say. Yo' see I'm makin' a soart o' pollygy,—a soart o' pollygy," with evident enjoyment of the word. "An' that's why I said as it mowt be as well to ha' a witness. I wur allus one as set more store by th' State than th' Church, an' parsons wur na i' my line, an' happen I ha' ben a bit hard on yo', an' ha' said things as carried weight agen yo' wi' them as valleyed my opinion o' things i' general. An' sin' th' blow-up, I ha' made up my moind as I would na moind tellin' yo' as I wur agoin' to w'draw my oppysition, sin' it seemit as if I'd made a bit o' a mistake. Yo're neyther knave nor foo', if yo' are a parson. Theer now! Good-mornin' to yo'!"

"Noan on 'em con say as I wur na fair," Owd Sammy said to

himself, as he went on his way shaking his head, "I could na ha' done no fairer. He desarved a bit o' commendation, an' I let him ha' it. Be fair wi a mon, say I, parson or no. An' he is na th' wrong sort, after aw."

He was so well pleased with himself, that he even carried his virtue into The Crown, and diffused it abroad over his pint of sixpenny. He found it not actually unpleasant to display himself as a magnate, who, having made a most natural mistake, had been too independent and straightforward to let the matter rest, and consequently had gone to the magnificent length of apologetic explanation.

"I ha' bin havin' a word or so wi' th' little Parson," he said. "I ha' ben tellin' him what I thowt o' what he did th' day o' th' blow-up. I changed my moind about th' little chap that day, an' I ha' ben tellin' him so."

"Yo' ha'?" in an amazed chorus. "Well, now, that theer wur a turn, Sammy."

"Ay, it wur. I'm noan afeard to speak my moind one way or t'other, yo' see. When a mon shows as he's med o' th' reet cloth, I am na afeard to tell him I loike th' web."

167

CHAPTER XLII

Ashley-Wold

Two weeks after Joan left Riggan, she entered the village of Ashley-Wold on foot. With the exception of a few miles here and there, when a friendly wagoner had offered her a lift, she had made all her journey in this manner. She had met with discouragement and disappointment. She had not fancied that it would be an easy matter to find work, though she had expressed no doubt to Anice, but it was even a more difficult matter than she had imagined. At some places work was not to be had, in others the fact that she was an utter stranger went against her.

It was evening when she came to Ashley-Wold; the rain was falling soft and slowly, and the air was chill. She was cold, and faint with hunger. The firelight that shone through the cottage windows brought to her an acute sense of her bodily weariness through its suggestion of rest and cheerfulness. The few passers-by—principally men and women returning from their daily labor—glanced at her curiously.

She had held to the letter as a last resource. When she could not help herself she would ask for assistance, but not until then. Still she had always turned her face toward Ashley-Wold, Now she meant to go to Mrs. Galloway and deliver the letter.

Upon entering the village she had stopped and asked a farmer for directions. He had stared at her at first, hardly comprehending her northern dialect, but had finally understood and pointed out the house, whose gables could be seen from the road-side.

So Joan made her way toward it through the evening rain and mist. It was a pretty place, with a quaint picturesqueness. A hedge, which was a marvel of trimness, surrounded the garden, ivy clung to the walls and gables, and fancifully clipped box and other evergreens made a modest greenery about it, winter though it was. At her first glance at this garden Joan felt something familiar in it. Perhaps Anice herself had planned some portion of it. Joan paused a moment and stood looking over the hedge.

Mrs. Galloway, sitting at her work-table near the window, had found her attention attracted a few moments before by a tall young woman coming down the road which passed on one side of the hedge.

"There is something a little remarkable about her," she said. "She certainly does not belong to Ashley-Wold."

Then Joan stopped by the hedge and she saw her face and uttered a low exclamation of surprise at its beauty. She drew nearer to the window and looked out at her.

"She must be very cold," said Mrs. Galloway. "She looks as if she had made a long journey. I will send Hollis to her."

A few minutes later there tripped down the garden-walk a trimly attired young housemaid.

The mistress had seen her from the window and thought she looked cold and tired. Would she come into the house to rest?

Joan answered with a tinge of color on her cheek. She felt a little like a beggar.

"Thank yo'; I'll come," she said. "If th' mistress is Mrs. Galloway, I ha' a letter fur her fro' Lancashire."

Mrs. Galloway met them on the threshold.

"The young woman, ma'am," said the servant, "has a letter from Lancashire."

"From Lancashire!" said Mrs. Galloway.

"Fro' Riggan, mistress," said Joan. "Fro' Miss Anice. I'm Joan Lowrie."

That Joan Lowrie was a name familiar to her was evident by the change in Mrs. Galloway's face. A faint flush of pleasure warmed it, and she spoke quickly.

"Joan Lowrie!" she said. "My dear child's friend! Then I know you very well. Come into the room, my dear."

She led her into the room and closed the door.

"You are very cold and your shawl is wet," laying a kind hand upon it. "Give it to me, and take a seat by the fire. You must warm yourself thoroughly and have a cup of tea," she said, "and then I will begin to ask questions."

There was a wide, low-seated, low-armed, soft-cushioned chair at one side of the fire, and in this chair she had made Joan seat herself. The sudden change from the chill dampness of the winter day to the exquisite relief and rest, almost overcame the girl. She was deadly pale when Mrs. Galloway ceased, and her lips trembled; she tried to speak, and for a moment could not; tears rushed to her eyes and stood in them. But she managed to answer at last.

"I beg yo're pardon," she said. "Yo' ha' no need to moind me. Th' warmth has made me a bit faint, that's aw. I've noan been used to it lately."

Mrs. Galloway came and stood near her.

"I am sorry to hear that, my dear," she said.

"Yo're very kind, ma'am," Joan answered.

She drew the letter from her dress and handed it to her.

169

"I getten that fro' Miss Anice the neet I left Riggan," she said.

When the tea was brought in and Joan had sat down, the old lady read the letter.

"Keep her with you if you can. Give her the help she needs most. She has had a hard life, and wants to forget it"

"Now, I wonder," said Mrs. Galloway to herself, "what the help is that she needs most?"

The rare beauty of the face impressed her as it invariably impressed strangers, but she looked beneath the surface and saw something more in it than its beauty. She saw its sadness, its resolution.

When Joan rose from the table, the old lady was still standing with the letter in her hand. She folded it and spoke to her.

"If you are sufficiently rested, I should like you to sit down and talk to me a little. I want to speak to you about your plans."

"Then," said Joan, "happen I'd better tell yo' at th' start as I ha' none."

Mrs. Galloway put her hand upon her shoulder.

"Then," she returned, "that is all the better for me, for I have in my mind one of my own. You would like to find work to help you——"

"I mun find work," Joan interrupted, "or starve."

"Of any kind?" questioningly.

"I ha' worked at th' pit's mouth aw my life," said Joan. "I need na be dainty, yo' see."

Mrs. Galloway smoothed the back of the small, withered hand upon her knee with the palm of the other.

"Then, perhaps," she said slowly, "you will not refuse to accept my offer and stay here—with me?"

"Wi' yo'?" Joan exclaimed. "I am an old woman, you see," Mrs. Galloway answered. "I have lived in Ashley-Wold all my life, and have, as it were, accumulated duties, and now as the years go by, I do not find it so easy to perform them as I used to. I need a companion who is young and strong, and quick to understand the wants of those who suffer. Will you stay here and help me?"

"Wi' yo'?" said Joan again. "Nay," she cried; "nay—that is not fur me. I am na fit."

On her way to her chamber some hours later Mrs. Galloway stopped at the room which had been Anice's, and looked in upon her guest. But Joan was not asleep, as she had hoped to find her. She stood at the fireside, looking into the blaze.

"Will you come here a minnit?" she said.

She looked haggard and wearied, but the eyes she raised to her hostess were resolute.

170

"Theer's summat as I ha' held back fro' sayin' to yo'," she said, "an' th' more I think on it, th' more I see as I mun tell yo' if I mean to begin fair an' clear. I ha' a trouble as I'm fain to hide; it's a trouble as I ha' fowt wi' an' ha' na helped mysen agen. It's na a shame," straightening herself; "it's a trouble such as ony woman might bear an' be honest. I coom away fro' Riggan to be out o' th' way on it—not to forget it, for I conna—but so as I should na be so near to—to th' hurt on it."

"I do not need another word," Mrs. Galloway answered. "If you had chosen to keep it a secret, it would have been your own secret as long as you chose that it should be so. There is nothing more you need? Very well Good-night, my dear!"

CHAPTER XLIII

Liz Comes Back

"Miss," said Mrs. Thwaite, "it wur last neet, an' you mowt ha' knocked me down wi' a feather, fur I seed her as plain as I see yo'."

"Then," said Anice, "she must be in Riggan now."

"Ay," the woman answered, "that she mun, though wheer, God knows, I dunnot. It wur pretty late, yo' see, an' I wur gettin' th' mester's supper ready, an' as I turns mysen fro' th' oven, wheer I had been stoopin' down to look at th' bit o' bacon, I seed her face agen th' winder, starin' in at me wild loike. Ay, it wur her sure enow, poor wench! She wur loike death itsen—main different fro' th' bit o' a soft, pretty, leet-headed lass she used to be."

"I will go and speak to Mr. Grace," Anice said.

The habit of referring to Grace was growing stronger every day. She met him not many yards away, and before she spoke to him saw that he was not ignorant of what she had to say.

"I think you know what I am going to tell you," she said.

"I think I do," was his reply.

The rumor had come to him from an acquaintance of the Maxys, and he had made up his mind to go to them at once.

"Ay," said the mother, regarding them with rather resentful curiosity, "she wur here this mornin'—Liz wur. She wur in a bad way enow—said she'd been out on th' tramp fur nigh a week—seemit a bit out o' her head. Th' mon had left her again, as she mowt ha' knowed he would. Ay, lasses is foo's. She'd ben i' th' Union, too, bad o' th' fever. I towd her she'd better ha' stayed theer. She wanted to know wheer Joan Lowrie wur, an' kept axin fur her till I wur tired o' hearin' her, and towd her so."

"Did she ask about her little child?" said Anice.

"Ay, I think she did, if I remember reet. She said summat about wantin' to know wheer we'd put it, an' if Joan wur dead, too. But it did na seem to be th' choild she cared about so much as Joan Lowrie."

"Did you tell her where we buried it?" Grace asked.

"Ay."

"Thank you. I will go to the church-yard," he said to Anice. "I may find her there."

"Will you let me go too?" Anice asked.

He paused a moment

"I am afraid that it would be best that I should go alone."

172

"Let me go," she pleaded. "Don't be afraid for me. I could not stay away. Let me go—for Joan's sake."

So he gave way, and they passed out together. But they did not find her in the church-yard. The gate had been pushed open and hung swinging on its hinges. There were fresh footprints upon the damp clay of the path that led to the corner where the child lay, and when they approached the little mound they saw that something had been dropped upon the grass near it. It was a thin, once gay-colored, little red shawl. Anice bent down and picked it up. "She has been here," she said.

It was Anice who, after this, first thought of going to the old cottage upon the Knoll Road. The afternoon was waning when they left the church-yard; when they came within sight of the cottage the sun had sunk behind the hills. In the red, wintry light, the place looked terribly desolate. Weeds had sprung up about the house, and their rank growth covered the very threshold, the shutters hung loose and broken, and a damp greenness had crept upon the stone step.

A chill fell upon her when they stood before the gate and saw what was within. Something besides the clinging greenness had crept upon the step,—something human,—a homeless creature, who might have staggered there and fallen, or who might have laid herself there to die. It was Liz, lying with her face downward and with her dead hand against the closed door.

CHAPTER XLIV

Not Yet

Mrs. Galloway arose and advanced to meet her visitor with a slightly puzzled air.

"Mr. ———" she began.

"Fergus Derrick," ended the young man. "From Riggan, madam."

She held out her hand cordially.

"Joan is in the garden," she said, after a few moments of earnest conversation. "Go to her."

It was a day very different from the one upon which Joan Lowrie had come to Ashley-Wold. Spring had set her light foot fairly upon the green Kentish soil. Farther north she had only begun to show her face timidly, but here the atmosphere was fresh and balmy, the hedges were budding bravely, and there was a low twitter of birds in the air. The garden Anice had so often tended was flushing into bloom in sunny corners, and the breath of early violets was sweet in it. Derrick was conscious of their springtime odor as he walked down the path, in the direction Mrs. Galloway had pointed out. It was a retired nook where evergreens were growing, and where the violet fragrance was more powerful than anywhere else, for the rich, moist earth of one bed was blue with them. Joan was standing near these violets,—he saw her as he turned into the walk,—a motionless figure in heavy brown drapery.

She heard him and started from her revery. With another half-dozen steps he was at her side.

"Don't look as if I had alarmed you," he said. "It seems such a poor beginning to what I have come to say."

Her hand trembled so that one or two of the loose violets she held fell at his feet. She had a cluster of their fragrant bloom fastened in the full knot of her hair. The dropping of the flowers seemed to help her to recover herself. She drew back a little, a shade of pride in her gesture, though the color dyed her cheeks and her eyes were downcast.

"I cannot—I cannot listen," she said.

The slight change which he noted in her speech touched him unutterably. It was not a very great change; she spoke slowly and uncertainly, and the quaint northern burr still held its own, and here and there a word betrayed her effort.

"No, no," he said, "you will listen. You gave me back my life.

You will not make it worthless. If you cannot love me," his voice shaking, "it would have been less cruel to have left me where you found me—a dead man,—for whom all pain was over."

He stopped. The woman trembled from head to foot. She raised her eyes from the ground and looked at him catching her breath.

"Yo' are askin' me to be yo're wife!" she said. "Me!"

"I love you," he answered. "You, and no other woman!"

She waited a moment and then turned suddenly away from him, and leaned against the tree under which they were standing, resting her face upon her arm. Her hand clung among the ivy leaves and crushed them. Her old speech came back in the quick hushed cry she uttered.

"I conna turn yo' fro' me," she said. "Oh! I conna!"

"Thank God! Thank God!" he cried.

He would have caught her to his breast, but she held up her hand to restrain him.

"Not yet," she said, "not yet. I conna turn you fro' me, but theer's summat I must ask. Give me th' time to make myself worthy—give me th' time to work an' strive; be patient with me until th' day comes when I can come to yo' an' know I need not shame yo'. They say I am na slow at learnin'—wait and see how I can work for th' mon—for th' mon I love."

www.ingramcontent.com/pod-product-compliance
Lightning Source LLC
Chambersburg PA
CBHW011505170626
46812CB00008B/2981

9 781647 997571